Crooked Cruise

Carrie Rachelle Johnson

Copyright © 2024 Carrie Rachelle Johnson
All rights reserved.
ISBN: 9798874124397

DEDICATION

I dedicate this novel to
the fans who keep on wanting more

CONTENTS

Acknowledgments
Prologue: Aggressive Asphalt — 1
Chapter 1: Boarding Blues — 4
Chapter 2: Coarse Company — 17
Chapter 3: Detailed Dinner — 29
Chapter 4: Enraged Effects — 43
Chapter 5: Fishy Findings — 60
Chapter 6: Gifted Guise — 73
Chapter 7: Hopeful Hunt — 82
Chapter 8: Illusive Idol — 92
Chapter 9: Jumbled Judgment — 105
Chapter 10: Keen Keepsake — 121
Chapter 11: Loaded Labors — 133
Chapter 12: Mixed Matter — 149
Chapter 13: Needy Nonsense — 158
Chapter 14: Obscure Opinions — 172
Chapter 15: Panicky Pleas — 185
Chapter 16: Quotable Quirks — 197
Chapter 17: Rampant Reveal — 214
Chapter 18: Savvy Solutions — 223
Epilogue: Tactful Tourist — 236
About the Author — 237
Other Books — 238
Sneak Peek — 239

ACKNOWLEDGMENTS

This book would not be possible without the help of several people. First and foremost, I thank God for being my eternal Inspiration who has given me a great imagination and guided me every step of the way. I also thank my mother who encourages me to write and follow my dreams. To my aunt, Pam, I give my thanks for her endless support and editing ideas to help me make my books the best they can be. My writing would be different without you all.

Finally, I thank my family, friends, and readers who have experienced my written works and shared their opinions of them. I deeply appreciate all your continued support and encouragement

PROLOGUE

AGGRESSIVE ASPHALT

"Ten-year-old Frankie 'Lemon Lime' Lemmons is the youngest WNBA champion ever. She has been waiting for this moment her whole life. If she makes this shot, she will win it all. She shoots and…Shoot!"

Frankie growled at how the basketball missed the hoop. She shook her head. Her mind raced for a way to get another chance. "I think that deserves a redo."

Silence. Frankie turned toward her best friend. She narrowed her eyes at how he was not even watching her. "What's wrong, Dill Pickle?"

Dillon stared at the other end of the basketball court. He muttered, "I think we should go."

Frankie spun around to look in the direction he was staring. Nothing looked out of the ordinary.

A group of African American guys sat on the short bleachers cussing, smoking, and laughing. They belonged to a neighborhood gang called the Black Skulls. Though they were bad news, the gang had never bothered the kids in the past. Why would Dillon be upset today?

Dillon repeated, "We should go."

Frankie wrinkled her nose at the suggestion. Why would she want to go home? Her mother was entertaining her lady friends today. Frankie would be forced to put on a dress and act ladylike with them. She would rather hang out with Dillon and play basketball.

Frankie said, "Let's stay a little longer. They're not bothering us…Come on, Dill Pickle. It's your turn."

Dillon bounced the basketball. He said, "Get ready to be humiliated, Lemon Lime."

Frankie rolled her eyes. She crossed her arms. "Just shoot it, Hot Shot."

The basketball flew from Dillon's fingers. It circled the rim then fell into the hoop.

Dillon whooped and hollered. He wiggled his body in his silly victory dance. "Beat that."

Frankie smirked at the dance. She stepped forward grabbing the bouncing basketball. "My turn, Show-Off."

"Good luck," Dillon teased.

Frankie held the ball above her head. She froze at the sudden silence on the court. Turning back toward the Black Skulls, she lowered the ball to hold it against her stomach.

A Hispanic gang strutted across the court. It was their rival gang, The Flames. There had been bad blood between the two gangs since before Frankie was born.

The Flames stopped and faced the other gang.

The men's angry faces caused Frankie to back up. She could not hear their words, but it was obvious a fight was about to happen. *Maybe we should get out of here.*

One of the Black Skulls stood on the bleachers. Frankie recognized him as Jontray Scott. Her grandpa had told stories about the troublemaker. He had arrested him a few times for assault and drug possession.

Jontray Scott pulled a gun out of his waistband and pointed it at the leader of the Flames. A loud pop filled the park.

Frankie screamed seeing the dead man lying on the ground. She could not believe she had witnessed a murder.

Jontray turned toward her. He raised his gun pointing it at her.

Dillon shrieked, "Run!"

Frankie dropped the basketball and turned in the opposite direction. She ran like the wind praying she would get out of range fast enough. Her heart pounded as more gunshots rang out in her direction. She expected to feel bullets hit her. Yet, no pain came.

Refusing to look back, Frankie focused on her nearing driveway. She halted on the curb outside her house. Giggling, she turned to celebrate their survival with Dillon, only to find him nowhere in sight. Where was he? Could he have fallen behind?

Panting, Frankie scanned the neighborhood street. She counted in her head to ten expecting him to come around the corner at any moment. No doubt he would joke about how he couldn't even outrun a scared girl. She would have a good retort for him.

Frankie took a step forward. *Where are you, Dill Pickle?*

Nothing. Frankie shook her head. It should not take Dillon this long to reach their street. "Dillon!"

Running, Frankie's sneakers slapped the concrete as she hurried back the way she had come. She heard the screen door of her house creak behind her.

"Frankie!"

"Francesca!"

Ignoring her grandpa and mother, Frankie focused on returning to the park. Her eyes darted around searching for her best friend. "Dillon!"

Reaching the edge of the basketball court, Frankie froze when she saw two bodies on the ground.

Dillon lay on his stomach motionless. Blood covered his back.

Hands jerked Frankie around from the view of her dead best friend. She stared into her grandpa's face.

"Frankie, are you shot?"

Frankie shook her head. Her throat choked making it hard to speak. She wrapped her arms around her grandpa's neck. Tears streamed down her face.

Grandpa returned the hug clinging to her tightly. He placed a gentle kiss on the side of her head. "Don't worry, honey. I'll find out who did this."

Frankie whispered, "Jontray Scott."

"What? Are you sure?"

Closing her eyes, Frankie said, "Yes. Jontray Scott killed them." *And Grandpa will make him pay.*

CHAPTER 1

BOARDING BLUES

Sitting at a corner booth in Alice's Diner, Frankie Lemmons picked up her Pie Burger. Her stomach growled impatiently. She turned her head to look at D'Angelo through the opening to the kitchen. When would he have a break? They needed to talk about her plan.

Frankie glanced at her cell phone screen. She nodded at the time. If everything had gone as planned, then Leo and the others would be boarding the Wanderer of the Sea cruise ship in the next hour. She liked the idea of her police detective partner being out of town. Leo would not like what she had planned for Jontray Scott. He liked to follow the rules too much.

"Sour Face Lemmons."

Frankie jerked up her head.

A tall woman with curly black hair and mocha skin towered over her with a smirk on her face.

"London Bridges Falling Down," Frankie said.

London Bridges was a police officer they had to deal with at the Heavenly Hideaways Resort. She had annoyed Frankie at first. However, by the end of the case, the two women had become friends. They had even enjoyed pestering Leo together.

Frankie motioned to the other side of the booth. "What are you doing here?"

London slid into the seat. She shrugged, "I live here now."

"You're kidding. Why did you come here?"

Picking up a menu, London replied, "I got tired of the peaceful country life. It's so boring. I became a cop to make a difference. I thought I might be more useful in the big city."

Frankie could see how the country could be boring. Luckily, they had had a murder to solve while they were there, or she would have been driven into madness by the peaceful life herself.

"Actually, I'm working as a detective in your precinct," London added.

Frankie stared at her. She could not believe London would be working in the same precinct. Could Leo handle the chaos the two women would throw at him?

Smiling, Frankie made a mental note to contact Leo about the work change. She could imagine how he would whine at the news. Nodding, she said, "Okay. How did you find me?"

"Captain Beasley said you were out for lunch so I should check here. Come here often?"

Frankie shrugged, "Almost every day."

London opened the plastic menu. She studied it with a frown. "I guess I'll eat something before we get to work."

Frankie's cop senses activated at the words. "Get to work?"

"I'm your temporary partner while the Handsome Knight is out of town. You're supposed to show me the ropes."

"What's the punchline?" Frankie muttered.

London lowered the menu. "What?"

Crossing her arms, Frankie leaned back against the booth leather. "There's no way Beasley chose me to be your tour guide."

Averting her gaze, London examined the diner atmosphere. She bit her lip.

Frankie waited for her to share the truth. She could name at least a dozen other detectives who would be better than her at getting London familiar with police protocol and procedures. Captain Beasley had practically begged Leo to postpone the cruise or take Frankie with him so he would not have to deal with her on his own.

"Well, I suggested you. He said we could try it. I don't think he liked the idea," London said.

Frankie said, "That's sounds more likely."

A shadow fell over the table. Frankie glanced up with a smile.

D'Angelo pulled a stool to the table and sat down. Looking at London, he grunted, "Sorry. I didn't mean to intrude."

"No intrusion. This is London Bridges. We met her at Heavenly Hideaways. Remember?" Frankie said.

D'Angelo nodded. He opened his mouth to speak. "Nice to see…"

"Is there someone who can take my order?" interrupted London staring at the menu.

Frankie wrinkled her nose at her rudeness. She glanced over at D'Angelo. Shrugging, she picked up her Pie Burger and took a big bite. She knew all too well that D'Angelo could take care of himself.

D'Angelo pulled out his notepad and pencil. "I can. What do you want?"

"I'll have a spinach salad with diced apples not sliced, goat cheese not feta, and almonds instead of walnuts…Oh, and no red onion."

D'Angelo jotted her order on his notepad. He asked, "Any dressing?"

"Balsamic vinaigrette, but not too much. Just a drizzle…Actually, I'll have the dressing in a container on the side. Then I can pour what I want."

Shaking his head, D'Angelo stood. He flashed an exasperated look at Frankie.

Ignoring him, Frankie took a sip of her soda. Her mouth curved into a teasing smirk.

D'Angelo returned his stool to the counter. He headed toward the kitchen.

Focusing on London, Frankie snorted, "Picky, are we?"

"I look after my health."

London stared at Frankie's plate. She wrinkled her nose at the Pie Burger. "Maybe you should try it."

Frankie lifted the burger to her mouth again. She took another big bite. Chewing, she cherished the look of disgust on the other woman's face. Maybe she would enjoy getting on her nerves like Leo's. Swallowing, she said, "Yummy."

Magnolia Ruby climbed out of the taxi. She placed a hand up to shield the sun from her eyes. The massive cruise ship towered over her. She could not believe it would serve as her home for the next nine days.

Dropping a hand, Magnolia pulled out her camera. Aiming it, she took a picture of the Wanderer of the Sea. She glanced over at Gloria smiling warmly at her daughter.

Gloria's face beamed at the ship. Her eyes danced with excitement as she took in the overwhelming view of the cruise liner.

Seeking out the others, Magnolia scanned the loading area. Leo's father, Ellison, stood near the front of the check-in line with Lydia. He held his special needs daughter's hand to keep her from wandering off. Weldon waited behind them. He glanced back with a scowl on his face.

Following his gaze, Magnolia smiled warmly at Leo and Charlie standing in line kissing. She assumed Weldon wanted to talk to the younger woman.

Weldon had recently announced he was Charlie's biological father. Though things had been strained, the father and daughter had agreed to spend time on the cruise together. Yet, Leo and Charlie were sticking closer together as newlyweds should.

Magnolia blinked away her joyful tears. After all the havoc Rose Woods had caused, it was almost hard to believe the couple had finally been able to get married. *Thank You, Lord, for this miracle. May they be as happy as Edward and me.*

Wincing at the reminder of her husband, Magnolia marveled at how much his death still affected her. She longed for the happiness they had shared for all those years. Would she ever feel safe and loved again?

Shaking away the dismal thoughts, Magnolia grabbed her bags. She would not let anything spoil the happy mood of this vacation. After all her family and friends had been through, the break was both well-deserved and earned. Enjoyment was on the agenda.

Magnolia placed her luggage on a cart for the porters to deliver to their cabins. She showed her room information to one of the porters then thanked him.

Following the group, Magnolia approached the lengthy line at the check-in area. She hummed softly. *We will just have to be patient.*

"Is there any way around this line?"

Magnolia bit her lip. She could not believe they were going to spend another vacation with Gloria's difficult-to-handle, wealthy aunt, Lucretia Cushings. Lucretia had been a rival for Gloria's attention as well as her future for the past few years. She had invited herself on the cruise when she heard they were traveling to the Bahamas. Buying her own ticket and making her own arrangements, no one could stop her from joining the group.

Taking a deep breath, Magnolia said, "I don't think so. We'll have to be patient." *Lord, please distract her so I don't lose my temper with her.*

Magnolia glanced over at Gloria entertaining Lydia while Ellison waited to get them checked in. Her daughter was distracting the other girl by talking about the ship and its various areas.

"There has to be someone I can bribe to pass up this line," Lucretia grumbled.

Magnolia did not understand why Lucretia always had to have her way. Would she have to endure her at every step of the journey? *I won't let her control everything on this vacation. She didn't pay our way. She can't boss us around.*

Lucretia whined, "Why is the sun so bright?"

Magnolia pursed her lips. She prayed for the wisdom to deal with Lucretia and any other surprises on the trip.

"The wind is ruining my hair," Lucretia added.

Magnolia stared straight ahead. Her temper began to flare in annoyance. She took a deep breath. *This cruise may not be as restful as I thought.*

Charlotte Knight thanked the check-in attendant who wished them a pleasant cruise. She held Leo's hand relieved to be checked in. Walking toward the ramp leading to the ship, she spotted a porter waiting to show them their cabin.

Charlotte glanced down at her left hand. She stared at her engagement ring and wedding band resting on her ring finger. Now that they were finally married, she loved the thought of spending nine days on a cruise to the Bahamas with her new husband. *It's like a dream come true.*

"May I get your picture?"

Charlotte smiled at the photographer. Releasing Leo's hand, she moved closer to him placing her arm around his waist.

Leo put his arm around her shoulder. He tilted his head toward her.

The photographer clicked twice. She pulled out a card, jotted down a number, then handed it to Leo. "Here's where you can get a digital print."

Thanking her, Leo pulled out his wallet to place the card into it. Returning it to his back pocket, he asked, "Are you ready to go to the cabin?"

Charlotte scanned the loading area to see where the rest of the group were in the process.

Mags stood in the check-in line staring straight ahead with her nose wrinkled. She appeared to be barely enduring her misery of waiting in line with Lucretia.

Ellison talked with Lydia and Gloria while waiting on the others.

Weldon stood off to the side by himself. His eyes darted from place to place like a caged animal.

Charlotte said, "I think we should wait for the rest of the group, Leo."

"Works for me."

The couple walked over to join the group.

Charlotte set her carry-on bag on the ground by her feet. "Are you okay, Pop?"

Her father smiled at her with a nod. "I'm fine. Just a bit nervous. I've never been on a ship this size before."

"Pop, it's like a floating amusement park. It's going to be so much fun."

Weldon turned to look out at the ocean.

Charlotte pursed her lips. What could the father and daughter do before getting on the ship? She spotted the photographer waiting near the ramp to photograph more people.

Charlotte grabbed her father's hand. "Come take a picture with me."

Weldon squeezed her hand. He followed her with a smile growing on his face.

Gaining the photographer's attention, Charlotte posed for a picture with her father.

Weldon put his arm around her shoulder.

"Wait!"

Charlotte jerked her head at the shout. Her fear faded in the next instant.

Lydia jumped into the picture. "You can't take a picture without me, silly sister."

Laughing, Charlotte wrapped an arm around her drawing her closer.

The photographer took the picture. She held out a card.

Weldon took it from her. His smile widened at how he could get a digital print of their photo.

Charlotte beamed back at him. *This is going to be the greatest vacation ever.*

Tapping her foot, Magnolia Ruby fumed at each negative comment from behind her. She had tried to be patient, but Lucretia's complaints grated on her nerves. Leaning to the side, she could see three people in line in front of her. What was taking the first person so long?

An older woman with gray hair pulled into a bun took an offered paper. She wore a purple and green floral shirt and khaki pants. Finishing her business, she turned around.

Magnolia's mouth fell open. *It can't be.*

Genevieve Sterling spotted her then averted her gaze. Clutching a straw bag, she marched over to where Weldon stood with Charlie.

Magnolia bit her lip at the added surprise. It would be hard for her to enjoy a vacation with the awful woman on board. Would Genevieve be joining them for all the activities? Maybe she would hide in her cabin until the end of the cruise.

Magnolia's cell phone buzzed. She pulled it out of her pocket and checked the screen seeing Charlie's name. Glancing over at her friend, she answered the call. "Hi, Charlie."

"Mags, I forgot to tell you at the hotel. Aunt Genevieve decided she wanted to come since she helped Pop pay for it…I'm sorry, Mags."

Magnolia pasted a smile on her face. She did not want to upset Charlie on her honeymoon. It was supposed to be a joyous trip for her. "Oh, well. The more the merrier."

Glancing behind her, Magnolia spotted Lucretia busy on her phone. She whispered, "She can't be any worse than Lucretia."

Charlie giggled, "Thanks for understanding."

Ending the call, Magnolia turned back to the check-in table. Seeing it was almost her turn, she pulled out her boarding documents and her passport.

"Magnolia."

Tensing, Magnolia turned toward the speaker. She gritted her teeth. "Hello, Genevieve."

Genevieve scowled at her. She wrung her hands in front of her. "I'm sorry to disturb you, but there's been a mistake."

Magnolia tilted her head. She waited for the woman to explain.

"My fool nephew has messed up already."

"Oh?"

"Yes. He decided to include me in your cabin accommodations when he made the reservations. He said he had forgotten we have…issues. Typical Weldon…Anyway…"

Magnolia gritted her teeth at the incoming request. She waited in silence. Maybe another option would come up first.

Genevieve lowered her head. "I know I haven't been kind to you. In fact, I have been a real beast…I…"

"Genevieve, you are welcome in our cabin."

"Are you sure?"

"Yes. The girls and I would love to have you join us."

Genevieve raised her head. She looked at her. "Thank you."

Walking away, Genevieve halted. She spun back with a sneer. "This doesn't change anything. I still haven't forgiven you for what you did to my brother. He's dead because of your interference."

Magnolia shook her head.

"It's your turn, Magnolia. Let's not prolong this any longer," Lucretia said.

Turning back to the check-in area, Magnolia pursed her lips. *Great. Nine days with two of the worst women in the world. Lucky me.*

Frankie Lemmons stared at D'Angelo as he returned to the table with London's food. She wanted to give him a signal to keep the Jontray Scott business private. Though London was her temporary partner, she did not trust her enough to share her unauthorized investigation.

D'Angelo set the plate in front of London. He glanced over at Frankie. "Need anything, Lemmons."

"Nope. I'm good. We'll talk later."

Taking the hint, D'Angelo headed back to the kitchen.

Frankie returned her attention to London. She narrowed her eyes. What was she staring at?

London smirked toward the kitchen. "They do grow them big in the city."

"What?"

"That big boy is cute. Please tell me he isn't married."

Frankie bristled at London's interest in D'Angelo. She liked him more than a friend. However, she hadn't admitted that to anyone, especially D'Angelo. "No. He's not married."

London rubbed her hands. "Good. I might like the big city after all."

Forcing her face to stay neutral, Frankie turned her head toward the window. She did not know if London was going to survive until Leo returned. *He better not extend his honeymoon.*

Leo Knight slid the keycard into the cabin lock. He could not wait to see the balcony cabin the couple had booked for the cruise. He opened the door then turned back to Charlie holding up a hand.

"What?" asked Charlie.

"It's customary to carry the bride over the threshold."

"You carried me over the threshold on our wedding night and last night at the hotel. How long are you planning to do this?"

"For as long as I wish, Mrs. Knight. Stop complaining."

Charlie laughed.

Scooping her up, Leo carried her into the cabin. He used his foot to close the door. Walking over to the king-sized bed with a red velvet headboard, he placed her on the red and gold comforter. "So, what do you think?"

"You must be pretty strong to carry me."

Leo rolled his eyes. "Not what I meant. The room?"

Charlie sat up. She looked around the extravagant room. Besides the bed, the cabin had a sitting area with a red velvet sofa, a matching armchair, and a large flat screen television.

Charlie said, "It's perfect."

Rolling off the bed, Charlie headed toward the bathroom. She peered inside. "Wow."

Leo joined her. He looked into the bathroom at a huge tub. "We could both fit in that thing."

Charlie stepped out of the bathroom. Her cheeks blushed. She averted her gaze.

Realizing how his harmless statement had been interpreted, Leo stuttered, "I didn't mean that."

His embarrassment faded at the idea of a romantic moment with his wife. Leo said, "But we could you know."

Leo leaned forward for a kiss.

Charlie dodged him. She walked to the other side of the cabin. "Let's see the balcony."

Leo followed her to the sliding glass doors. He pulled them open then gestured for her to go first. The balcony contained a white table set between two red lounge chairs.

Charlie sat in one of the chairs. She put her feet up on it.

Taking the other seat, Leo stared out at the port buildings. He assumed the view would improve once they left port. Reaching a hand across the table, he smiled at his wife.

Charlie took his hand. She squeezed it tenderly.

Clearing his throat, Leo said, "You know we have some time before the others start looking for us. We could…"

"Check out the T.V. Good idea," said Charlie hopping up to go inside.

Leo groaned. He stood to follow her. "That's not what I had in mind."

"I know."

Grabbing her, Leo kissed her passionately. He released her delighted by how she was out of breath.

Charlie smirked, "On second thought, too much T.V. is bad for you."

Magnolia Ruby slid her keycard into the lock of her balcony cabin. She opened the door then gestured for the others to enter.

Gloria and Lydia bounced inside. They chattered with excitement about all the fun they were going to have on the cruise ship.

Genevieve motioned for her to go first.

Leaving Genevieve in the hallway to enter when she was ready, Magnolia walked into the cabin.

The cabin had two twin beds covered in orange and white bedding. An orange leather couch sat beside the beds near the cabin door. Above the couch, a pull-out bed hung with a ladder hooked to it. A dresser with three drawers waited across from the couch. A flat screen television hung on the wall above the dresser. The bathroom was stationed on the opposite wall across from the twin beds.

Magnolia set her carry-on bag on the bed by the glass door.

"I would prefer being near the window," Genevieve said.

Surrendering, Magnolia picked up her bag. She moved to the bed near the couch. Sitting down, she focused on the girls both sitting on the couch. "Who wants the upper bunk?"

Lydia giggled, "Me, silly."

"You don't mind being up high?" asked Gloria.

Climbing the ladder, Lydia said, "It's better than my old room in the attic."

Magnolia and Gloria exchanged a glance.

Genevieve cleared her throat. "Not to alarm you, but I don't do well in a strange place. I may…befoul the bathroom at inopportune times."

Not turning to look at her, Magnolia wrinkled her nose. She nodded, "I'm sure it'll be fine. Shall we freshen up? Our luggage will be delivered later so we can unpack tonight. Maybe we can tour the ship first."

Lydia clapped her hands.

Gloria nodded with a smile.

Clearing her throat, Genevieve said, "I only mentioned it because I believe I'm about to have one of those moments now."

Magnolia tensed at what the older woman was saying.

Genevieve marched into the bathroom. She flicked on the light then closed the door.

Magnolia leaned closer to the girls. "We may have to go sit on the balcony for a bit before we freshen up."

As the girls giggled, Magnolia led them to the balcony. She slid open the double glass doors.

A big round table with four orange chairs was set on the balcony. Magnolia sat down in one of the chairs. She closed her eyes. The smell of salty sea air tickled her nose. Her body relaxed at the warm weather.

"False alarm, but it's coming."

Magnolia pursed her lips at Genevieve. She forced her eyes to remain shut. *Nine days of this? At least the ship is huge. Surely, I can get away from Genevieve and Lucretia most of the time. Other than dealing with them, what else could happen?*

Ophelia Hart climbed out of the yellow taxicab. She paid the driver then grabbed her bags. She marveled at the massive cruise ship's beauty. *I can't believe I'm spending nine days here.*

Ophelia smirked at how well her plan to steal the painting was going. She had changed her appearance and her name to get closer to the artist. No one would recognize her.

Scanning the loading area, Ophelia spotted her prey.

The artist stood beside his luggage. He snapped at two workers trying to carry a flat crate.

Ophelia focused on the crate. The painting had to be in it. She strolled over with her head down. She needed to pretend to be shy and harmless.

"May I help you, ma'am?"

Ophelia's head snapped up at the gruff voice. *It can't be.*

Reuben Malone stood in front of her with his hands on his hips. He had been the police detective at the Amateur Art Expo when she had stolen Sweet Freedom. Why was he there? Would he recognize her?

"It's okay, Malone. She's my new assistant."

Ophelia smiled weakly at the artist. She pursed her lips as he tapped his watch.

"You're late…What was your name again?"

"Viridian Greene…Viri…I'm sorry I'm late, Mr. Capone."

Unaware he was talking to the woman who had stolen six of his paintings and had her sights on a seventh, the artist said, "Call me Raphael."

CHAPTER 2

COARSE COMPANY

Weldon Hitchcock walked down the hallway with Ellison. The two men had examined their cabin then decided to check on the ladies. Maybe they could explore the ship for awhile.

Stopping at the correct cabin, Weldon knocked on the door. He waited for an answer. As the door opened, he smiled warmly at Nolia. His nose wrinkled at a foul stench exiting the room.

Nolia hurried the girls out of the cabin. She slammed the door behind her with a sigh. "Don't ask."

"Aunt Genevieve?"

Nolia nodded at him.

Lydia groaned, "She stinks."

Ellison leaned toward his daughter. He scolded, "Everyone does in the bathroom. Be polite."

"Okay, but I don't smell like her even in the bathroom."

Weldon suppressed a chuckle. He glanced over at Nolia.

Nolia mouthed. *It is bad.*

Weldon winked at her. His heart soared at the smile she gave him. He had hoped they would be able to spend time together on the cruise. Maybe their friendship would return to something more. *I just can't mess it up this time.*

Magnolia Ruby shouldered her purse. She had been in such a hurry to get out of the cabin that she had almost forgotten it. Luckily, she had remembered to grab it before the door closed.

"Excuse me?"

Magnolia turned toward the speaker.

A middle-aged man wearing a gray uniform stood near them. He had short black hair and blue eyes. His hands clung to the handle of a cart of supplies. Taking a deep breath, he released the cart and pulled a white card out of his jacket pocket. "Welcome. My name is Jonas Archer. I'll be your cabin steward. If you need anything like ice or towels or anything else, please let me know. I'll be glad to help."

Magnolia tilted her head at the rehearsed script. She waited for him to say more. At his silence, she said, "Thank you, Jonas. I think we're fine for now."

Jonas glanced at the men. "And you, gentlemen?"

"Everything's great. Thanks, Jonas," Ellison answered.

Jonas turned to leave. He pushed his cart down the hallway.

An older woman marched out of a room. She slammed into the cart.

Jonas jerked the cart to the side to soften the hit. A book fell from the cart hitting the floor. "Sorry, ma'am."

The older woman glared at him. She snapped, "Raise your head and speak clearly when you talk to someone, young man. You're being rude."

Jonas struggled to lift his head. He opened his mouth then closed it again. Pushing the cart down the hallway quickly, he tried to escape.

Magnolia stared at the woman.

"What are you gawking at?"

"A rude woman lecturing someone else about being rude," Magnolia replied.

Magnolia ignored the mutters and grunts from the rest of her group. She could imagine how her friends felt about her bluntness.

The other woman snarled, "How dare you! Do you have any idea who I am?"

"Not in the least. Who are you?"

"Doretta Brewster."

Magnolia did not recognize the name. "And?"

Doretta scowled, "And I have wasted enough time on you."

Turning toward the other end of the hallway, Doretta stormed away.

Magnolia turned back to her group. She narrowed her eyes at their shocked expressions. "What?"

Mumbling incoherently, her friends averted their gazes pretending nothing had happened.

Gloria stepped forward. She picked up the book from the floor. "Jonas dropped this. Can I return it to him?"

Magnolia nodded, "Of course. We'll wait for you here."

Gloria Fairbanks hurried down the hallway. She hoped she would be able to catch the steward before he reached the elevator. It would be impossible to find him on the large ship if that happened. *I guess I could wait until he checks in with us again.*

Walking around a corner, Gloria halted. She smiled brightly at Jonas standing a few feet away with his cart. Glancing down at the book in her hand, her smile grew. *And Then There was None by Agatha Christie.*

Gloria had read the book several times. It was one of her favorite mysteries. She returned her gaze to the steward. "Excuse me, Jonas?"

Jonas lowered his head. He turned toward her keeping his eyes staring at the floor. "Yes, ma'am. What do you need?"

"Nothing. You dropped your book."

Jonas glanced up at her. He reached out a hand.

Gloria stared at the scars on his wrist.

Noticing her scrutiny, Jonas pulled his hand back. He used his jacket sleeve to cover the scars. Reaching for the book again, he mumbled, "Thank you."

"You're welcome. Have you finished reading it yet?"

"I only have a few more pages."

Grinning, Gloria said, "Well, when you finish it, let me know what you think. It's one of my favorite books."

Nodding, Jonas averted his gaze. "Okay. Thank you, ma'am."

"Gloria."

"Gloria."

Recalling how impatient Lydia tended to be, Gloria hurried back down the hallway. She rounded the corner then jogged faster at Lydia's crossed arms.

"Hurry, silly."

Joining the group, Gloria asked, "What about Mr. Leo and Mrs. Charlotte?"

Magnolia exchanged an amused glance with the men. "Oh. I think we will let them catch up to us when they are ready."

Gloria rolled her eyes. *Why do adults act like teenagers don't know anything?*

"Let's go," Lydia demanded.

Ellison said, "Be nice, Lydia."

"Let's go please."

Laughing with the rest of the group, Gloria headed down the hallway to begin exploring the cruise ship. *Let the fun begin!*

Sitting in her car across the street, Frankie Lemmons stared at the apartment building where Jontray Scott lived. She scanned the area. Maybe she would see him. Then she planned to follow him. If she were lucky, she would catch him committing a crime. *I'll bust him.*

"What are we doing here?"

Frankie winced at the whiny voice. She had tried to get London busy on another case. However, her temporary partner refused to stay at the precinct without her. With no other choice, she had allowed London to come with her on her stakeout.

"There has been some gang activity here. I wanted to stake it out for a bit to see if something happens," Frankie explained.

"I thought we were homicide detectives. Why are we staking out a gang? Has there been a murder?"

"Yeah. I've been working on it for a while."

"Oh. Well, that's different. Who was the victim?"

Frankie tensed at the question. She did not want to talk about it with her. "A kid."

"I hate when kids are the victims."

Frankie lowered her head. Her mind flashed to Dillon. He had been such a great friend. None of the other kids at school had given Frankie a chance. Dillon had become like her brother. They had spent countless hours playing together.

London said, "There was a kid killed around here when I was a kid. He was shot on a basketball court."

Frankie jerked her head toward her. It had to be a different kid. She took a deep breath. "What was his name?"

"Dillon something. My mom and I moved after it happened. She wanted to get me away from the violence…I haven't thought about it in a long time."

The image of Dillon lying on the court with a bloody back flashed into her mind. Frankie blinked away tears. She picked up her soda cup with a shaky hand. Her eyes flicked to the other woman.

London stared out the window not paying any attention to her.

Frankie took a sip of her soda. She struggled to regain her composure.

"What's the name of the kid killed by the gang?"

Frankie stared out the windshield. Her mind debated with whether she should explain the situation. Could she trust London with the truth?

"Lemmons?"

Frankie turned toward her. She decided to take a chance. After all, she had kept the incident trapped inside herself for too long. "Dillon Pickler. He was my best friend."

Ophelia Hart grumbled under her breath at the size of the cabin Raphael Capone had reserved for her. She sneered at how it was more like a closet. The only furniture in the cabin was a twin bed with blue and white bedding. There wasn't even a television. Instead of a window, there was a small porthole with no curtains. She would probably have to change clothes in the bathroom.

Ophelia opened the bathroom door. She stared at a tiny room with a toilet and sink. The faucets for a shower hung on the wall beside the toilet. A white shower curtain hung on a curved pole. To take a shower, she would have to pull the curtain around her with barely any room to scrub.

Slamming the bathroom door, Ophelia stared at the main part of her cabin again. She had helped Raphael Capone with some paperwork in his fancy suite. Money was clearly no issue. Why couldn't he have reserved her a normal sized cabin?

Shaking away her disgust, Ophelia focused on the task at hand. She needed to tweak her plan now that she had discovered Reuben Malone on board. It would have been hard enough to steal a painting on a cruise ship. However, it would be nearly impossible to steal the painting with the police detective lurking around.

Sitting down on the twin bed, Ophelia folded her hands on her lap. Maybe she should abort her mission. She could wait to get Raphael Capone's next painting.

Ophelia rubbed a hand over her face. She hated the idea of letting one of the paintings escape from her grasp. But how could she steal it without getting caught?

Frankie Lemmons waited for London to understand what she had said. She could tell the news shocked her. *Maybe I shouldn't have told her.*

"He died when we were kids?"

"Yeah. Shot on a basketball court."

London rubbed her arms with a shiver. "Small world. That's weird...We probably lived in the same neighborhood."

"I lived on Elm."

"Pine."

Frankie recalled how Pine Street was one street over from Elm. She stared out the window silently.

"Is he your reason?"

"What?"

"You know. Your reason for becoming a cop."

Frankie lowered her head. She had never thought Dillon was the reason. "I guess. I became a cop to stop people like Dillon's killer."

"What happened to him?"

"His name's Jontray Scott. He got away with it because the police never had enough evidence…I didn't see Dillon get shot…I only saw Jontray Scott kill…"

Frankie's eyes bulged at the truth. She flicked her gaze to the building. Could this be the way to bust Jontray Scott?

"What?"

"I saw Jontray Scott kill a Hispanic man."

Frankie's mind whirled. She placed her hands on her face. "I'm an idiot."

"What? Why?"

Frankie started her car's ignition. She needed to get back to the precinct to do some research. "I always focused on how he killed Dillon. I never even told my…the police about the other guy. I witnessed Jontray killing him."

"And?"

Frankie smirked. Her mind filled with a new plan to take down Jontray Scott. "And there's no statute of limitations on murder in Missouri."

Cherishing the warm, salty breeze, Magnolia Ruby leaned back in the blue and white striped lounge chair beside the pool. She adjusted her sunglasses to protect her eyes from the piercing sunlight. Her smile grew watching Gloria and Lydia splashing each other in the turquoise water of the pool. Ellison waded nearby supervising the young ladies.

Magnolia picked up a glass of sweet tea and took a sip. Since it was only the first day, she had decided to sunbathe instead of swimming. Maybe she could finish reading the mystery novel she had started at home.

"Do you think we'll see the newlyweds on this trip?"

Magnolia turned her head toward Weldon. She winced at his hurt tone. Knowing he wanted to spend time with his daughter, she bit back a lecture at how the whole trip was supposed to be Leo and

Charlie's honeymoon. Smiling, she said, "Try to be understanding, Weldon. What were you like as a newlywed?"

"Busy."

"Me too. They'll join us when they're ready."

Weldon shrugged, "I guess. I just don't want them to miss all the fun."

"They won't. It's just the first day."

"I'll be patient."

"Good. Besides, you didn't only come to spend time with Charlie, did you?"

Weldon smiled warmly at her. He picked up her hand then kissed it. "No."

Magnolia blushed. She had not meant only her. Clearing her throat, she said, "I mean you did invite your aunt to come."

Weldon wrinkled his nose. He dropped her hand. Crossing his arms, he grunted, "I didn't invite her. She invited herself."

"Maybe she wants to spend time with her little nephew."

"Very funny, Nolia."

A shadow shaded her from the sun.

"And what is wrong with wanting to spend time with my nephew?"

Looking up, Magnolia used a hand to shield her eyes. She smiled weakly at Genevieve. She should have been more alert to her surroundings before speaking. "Nothing. I think it's wonderful to have someone to spend time with here."

Genevieve snorted. She struggled to sit in a lounge chair. Her face looked flushed. She patted her stomach with a wince. Opening a straw bag, she pulled out a magazine. She paused to look around then motioned to a worker walking by with a tray of drinks.

Magnolia exchanged a glance with Weldon.

Weldon leaned closer. He whispered, "Don't worry. She'll have to visit the bathroom again soon."

Suppressing a giggle, Magnolia returned her focus on the pool. Not seeing Gloria, she scanned the area around the pool finding her standing on the deck. Her eyebrows lowered at her daughter's frown. "What's wrong with Gloria?"

Climbing out of the pool, Gloria adjusted her swimsuit then headed toward the bar to get a couple of sodas. She winced at the heat radiating off the wooden paneled deck. Maybe she should slip her flip-flops on before going to the bar.

"You should have more modesty, young lady."

Gloria turned toward the gruff voice. She stared at Doretta Brewster sitting in one of the blue and white striped lounge chairs. "Excuse me?"

"A woman should not dress like a harlot when she's in public."

Gloria looked down. Why was she calling her a harlot? She wore a dark green one-piece swimsuit. Her body was properly covered. She did not see the problem. "I'm not dressed inappropriately."

Doretta pointed a finger at her. She snapped, "You should wear a shirt over that suit. That's what a lady would do."

Gloria put her hands on her hips. "If you were a lady, you'd mind your own business."

"Gloria."

Magnolia walked over to her. She shook her head at her.

Gloria lowered her head. She recalled how her adopted mother always told her to be polite even when others were rude. Looking back at Doretta, she said, "I'm sorry for being rude, ma'am."

"I should say so," Doretta said.

Gloria returned her gaze to her mother. "Lydia's waiting for her soda."

Magnolia motioned for her to go to the bar.

Walking away, Gloria brooded on how Doretta had treated her. Why didn't the older woman have to apologize for saying she looked like a harlot?

Waiting in line for the sodas, Gloria turned to see if Lydia was waiting patiently.

Magnolia stood in front of Doretta. "Gloria should not have talked to you that way. She was raised better."

Gloria lowered her head. She did not want to shame her adopted mother.

"But she's right. You should mind your own business."

Gloria jerked her head up. She smiled at how Magnolia defended her without knowing she was watching her.

Doretta said, "I beg your pardon."

"Gloria's clothing choices are my business and hers. It does not concern you. Please keep your busybody words to yourself in the future."

Magnolia turned away from the other woman. She started at Gloria watching her. Winking, she raised her voice to make sure Doretta could hear. "I do love that swimsuit on you, Gloria. Such a lovely shade of green."

Gloria giggled, "Thanks, Mom."

Ophelia Hart carried a clipboard into the exhibit room. She had been told Raphael Capone was going to display the painting for the remainder of the cruise to show off to the people on board. Once they reached the Bahamas, the painting would be sold to an art collector. *I must get it before it gets off the ship.*

Ophelia walked around the exhibit room. She searched for clues to help her steal the painting later when there were no people around. Her gaze fell on Reuben Malone.

The police detective stood near the doorway speaking with three security guards from the ship's security.

Ophelia turned to look at the large flat crate. Her heart pounded at how close she was to getting the painting in her possession. In her research, she had discovered that the painting was a landscape with the dimensions of 40 inches by 36 inches. She would need a way to transport the painting discreetly when she obtained it, but she already knew the perfect place to hide it.

Ophelia gritted her teeth at having to wait. However, she had to be patient. *The timing must be perfect.*

Raphael Capone strolled over to the crate. He clapped his hands to gain the attention of the small crowd gathering. "Ladies and gentlemen, it's time to unveil my latest masterpiece."

Ophelia stepped closer. She smiled warmly at some of the bystanders.

Two workers walked over to the crate with crowbars. They opened the crate. Setting the crowbars down, they picked up the painting and set it on a large easel.

Ophelia stared at the painting. Saloon girls were entertaining cowboys while they were drinking and playing poker. Her nose wrinkled at the risqué appearance of the women. *He didn't leave much for the imagination.*

"Ladies and gentleman, I present for your pleasure. Rowdy Howdy," Raphael announced.

The small crowd clapped. They moved closer to look at the painting.

Raphael strutted through the crowd mingling with the people. He seemed to absorb their praise.

Ophelia pursed her lips. She wished the people knew the truth about the artist. *If they did, they wouldn't be exalting him so much.*

"Ms. Greene?"

Ophelia turned toward the police detective. She smiled innocently at him. "Yes, Detective."

"Have you noticed anyone acting strangely?"

"No. Everyone seems excited by the painting, but that's normal, isn't it?"

Reuben scanned the area. He returned his attention to her. "I guess. Keep an eye out. Let me know if you notice anything…unusual."

"Of course…Detective, is there a reason someone might act unusual?"

Reuben stared at her. He remained silent for a moment.

Ophelia forced herself to stay in character. She could not act like anything was wrong.

"What do you know about Raphael Capone?"

Ophelia hugged her clipboard to herself. "Not much. I needed a job. He needed an assistant. Of course, I didn't know I would get to be on a cruise to do my job. It's so exciting."

"That's a nice surprise for sure…Well, keep me informed."

Ophelia nodded. She glanced over at the artist.

Raphael motioned at her to join him.

Ophelia marched toward him eager to play the assistant part flawlessly. Her mind raced with tweaks to her plan. She could almost feel the canvas in her hands. *Nothing will stop me.*

CHAPTER 3

DETAILED DINNER

Entering the main dining room, Magnolia held back a gasp. Crystal chandeliers hung from the ceiling radiating light on the massive room. Several round tables with white tablecloths were scattered throughout the room. Blue and white cushioned chairs surrounded the tables. Silver utensils were placed strategically on the table for the guests. Quiet music drifted through the air.

The hostess smiled warmly at the group. "Good evening. How many are in your party?"

Ellison replied, "Five please."

Grabbing five menus, the hostess led the group to an empty table. She set the menus on the table. "Enjoy your meal."

Magnolia sat down thankful for time to relax and eat. She had been relieved when Genevieve stated she would stay in the cabin and order room service. Perhaps the family could enjoy a peaceful dinner.

"There's Aunt Lucretia."

Magnolia suppressed an eye roll at how she would have to deal with Lucretia during dinner. She turned her head to look at where Gloria was pointing.

Lucretia strutted to a table dressed in a golden gown. She looked like she was at a ball instead of a semi-formal dinner. She talked excitedly with three other ladies dressed in equally fancy attire.

Magnolia wrinkled her nose at how one of the women was Doretta Brewster. She recalled meeting Doretta on the middle-class hallway. Why had Doretta been in their area of the ship if she was so rich?

Shaking away the question, Magnolia smiled at how she would not have to eat with Lucretia after all. She turned her attention to their server.

"Good evening. My name is Tina. May I start you with some drinks?"

Magnolia ordered a sweet tea. She listened as the others ordered their beverages. Her phone buzzed in her purse. Pulling it out, she read a text from Charlie. "Charlie says they are going to order room service and eat it on their balcony together."

Sitting on the left of her, Weldon picked up his menu. "Of course, they are."

Ignoring his whiny tone, Magnolia looked around the table at the rest of her group. Sitting on her right side, Gloria explored her dinner options. Ellison sat on the teenager's other side. Lydia played with her silverware on the other side of her father. Three empty seats were across from the group.

"Excuse me?"

Magnolia glanced at a redheaded man with glasses. She smiled warmly at him.

The man lowered his head. "Do you mind if I sit at your table? I'm alone."

Magnolia turned to look at the hostess station. Why didn't someone escort him to a table like her group? Maybe he had snuck past the hostess while she was busy. *Always so suspicious, Magnolia Ruby.*

Nodding at him, Magnolia said, "Please join us."

"Thank you. I'm Norman Chalker."

Magnolia introduced herself. She examined her menu as the others introduced themselves. Glancing at Norman, she tilted her head.

Norman had a small notebook on the table. He wrote frantically with a blue pen. What could he be writing?

"May we join you?"

Magnolia turned her head at the pleasant voice. She smiled at a middle-aged couple dressed in matching yellow shirts and khaki pants. "Of course."

"Thank you so much. The hostess set us over there by ourselves, but we love to meet new people. I'm Shirley Kimble. This is my husband, Nelson."

As the introductions started again, Magnolia returned her attention to the menu. Her stomach swooned at the choices. *Sweet and Sour Shrimp. Roasted Chicken. Vegetable Lasagna.*

Tina returned with the drinks. She scribbled down the drink orders of Norman and the Kimbles. "And do we know what we want to eat?"

Magnolia ordered the Sweet and Sour Shrimp with a salad. She stacked her menu with the others. Waiting for Tina to leave to put in their orders, she tasted her sweet tea. Her nose wrinkled at the strong caffeinated taste. She reached for a packet of sugar.

Shirley said, "What do you do with your time, Mrs. Ruby?"

"I paint. I'm an artist."

"Oh, how wonderful. I am a fan of all art, but I am currently obsessed with pop art. The pieces are so unique and captivating."

Magnolia preferred nature art over the occasionally odd pop art. However, it was nice to talk to someone else who enjoyed art like she did.

"Art trafficking ranks third, behind drug and arms trafficking among worldwide criminal enterprises. You should always insure your artwork."

Magnolia turned her attention to Nelson waiting for him to continue to speak.

Nelson folded his hands on the table without another word. He stared at the table.

Shirley nodded, "I'm a telemarketer. It can be hard dealing with rude people."

Magnolia pursed her lips at the odd change of topic. She nodded at her.

"I hate telemarketers."

With wide eyes, Magnolia jerked her head toward Weldon. She kicked him under the table. Her eyebrows raised at his startled glance.

Clearing his throat, Weldon said, "I mean the pushy ones. I'm sure you're not like that."

Shirley smiled weakly at him. "Well, I'm not. Anyway, I like to sketch in my free time. One of my sketches was published in Sunshine Monthly. It's a children's magazine. I drew a swan driving a car."

Magnolia opened her mouth to compliment her on her success. She closed it as Nelson cleared his throat.

"12.6% of drivers don't have car insurance."

Magnolia assumed the man's job had something to do with insurance. Her gaze moved to Norman. She wanted to ask him about his career. Her eyebrows lowered.

Norman scribbled in his notebook. He turned the page then kept writing. His attention never lifted to the other people at the table.

Shirley said, "Nelson and I enjoy our hobbies. Art is mine. Nelson has been obsessed with collecting antiques since he was fresh out of college."

Magnolia smiled at Nelson. "What kinds of antiques do you collect, Mr. Kimble?"

"Knives. Most collectors give up because they don't learn the proper way to maintain their knives. The best way to guard your collection against environmental elements is to keep them in an enclosed box. Heat and moisture are two of the biggest enemies of metal and wood. Eliminate all modes of contamination and make sure the blades get plenty of sunlight to kill any termites or bugs."

Magnolia blinked her eyes to wake herself up. She suppressed a yawn not wanting to be rude. Glancing over at the others, she could tell they were pretending to be interested in Nelson's knife discussion as well.

"Your daughters are so polite and well-behaved, Mr. Knight," Shirley said.

Ellison nodded, "Thank you. They better be."

"You do not have daughters. You have me. Leo is not a girl," said Lydia with her head tilted.

Ellison chuckled. He leaned closer to her then whispered in his daughter's ear.

Lydia nodded. She leaned forward to see around her father. "You're my sister now, Gloria."

Magnolia smiled at the sweet sentiment. She glanced over at Shirley. *She doesn't seem aware of the mistake.*

"Nelson and I never had any children, but I always wanted them," Shirley said.

Nelson added, "Insurance rates increase for each dependent you claim."

Magnolia gritted her teeth at the odd couple. Turning at movement, she smiled warmly at Tina carrying a tray of plates. *Good. Maybe we can eat in silence for a bit.*

Entering the main dining room, Reuben waved a hand of dismissal at the hostess. He did not have time to sit at a table with a bunch of strangers. He planned to grab dinner and return to the exhibit room. He had left a security guard on shift to watch the painting. *I hope nothing happens while I am gone.*

Reuben marched toward the kitchen. His stomach growled at how he had not eaten since breakfast. He motioned to a server walking toward the kitchen doorway.

"Yes, sir?"

"Detective Malone. I need to see a menu."

"Yes, sir. I will get you one."

Reuben nodded. He turned to scan the main dining room while he waited. He stopped at the sight of a familiar face. His smile grew at how improbable it was to see her here of all places. Strolling toward the table, he thought about what he could say. *What a small world.*

Magnolia Ruby stuck her fork into her piece of apple pie. She made sure there was plenty of vanilla ice cream on the bite before she brought it to her mouth. Savoring the sweet dessert, she told herself she had earned the treat for enduring the awkward and boring conversation at the table.

"As I live and breathe, Magnolia Ruby."

Magnolia jerked up her head at the familiar voice. She could not believe her eyes. "Reuben Malone, what are you doing here?"

"Apparently, I was destined for a clandestine reunion with you."

Magnolia blushed at the compliment. She put her fork down then gestured at him. "This is Reuben Malone. He's a police detective I met when I went to the Amateur Art Expo…I can't believe you are here."

As the rest of the table introduced themselves to Reuben, Magnolia stared at him. She had not known how much she missed him until this moment. Though she knew it was foolish to be so enamored with a man she only spent time with on a murder case, she couldn't help herself. She liked Reuben. Her heart soared at how it could not be a coincidence. *What are the odds of him being on the same cruise ship as me?*

Weldon Hitchcock watched Nolia hating the happy expression on her face as she talked to Reuben Malone. His temper flared in jealousy as she asked him to join them.

Reuben looked around for an empty chair.

Standing, Ellison said, "You can have my seat, Reuben. The girls and I are going to go to the theater. They're showing Jaws. We've seen it many times, but never at sea."

As Ellison and the girls left, Reuben sank into Gloria's chair instead.

Weldon grimaced at how close he sat to Nolia.

Nolia turned her body to talk to Reuben. She seemed to have forgotten Weldon was there.

Weldon cleared his throat. "I'm a police detective too. How long have you been retired from the job?"

"Oh. I'm not retired. I can still chase a perp like any good cop. Are you retired?"

Weldon shrugged, "Officially. I still get called in when there's a case no one else can solve."

"I see. Well, I'm sure you'll agree there's no one better at solving difficult cases than Magnolia."

Laughing, Nolia patted Reuben on the arm.

Weldon narrowed his eyes. He did not like the idea of losing his second chance with Nolia to another man. *I better keep an eye on him.*

Magnolia Ruby smiled brightly at Reuben as he ordered his dinner. She could not believe how happy talking to him made her. Her past with Weldon had been full of lies, deception, and uncertainties. She never knew if she could trust him.

Magnolia picked up her fork to finish her pie. Reuben was different. Though she had only worked with Reuben briefly, she recalled how they had become close during the murder case at the Amateur Art Expo. He had treated her like a feeble woman at first, but then they had solved the crime together.

"Why are you on the cruise, Reuben?" asked Weldon.

Magnolia focused on Reuben. She longed to hear the answer to the question too. It seemed odd that they were on the same cruise. Could Reuben be following her for some reason?

"I'm on the job. There's an artist on board. Raphael Capone."

Magnolia's eyes widened. She recalled the name. "Isn't he the artist of Sweet Freedom?"

"Yep. He's also the artist of five other stolen paintings."

Magnolia remembered how Ophelia Hart had used her to steal Sweet Freedom. Could she be the thief of the other paintings? It seemed unlikely that more than one thief would target the same artist.

"Uh, oh."

Magnolia looked at Reuben. "What?"

"Your wheels are turning. I can see them."

"Just thinking about the past...Raphael Capone is on board. So what?"

"He has a new painting with him. It is on display in an exhibit room next to the nightclub. I'm here to make sure it doesn't get stolen," Reuben explained.

Magnolia nodded. Things were starting to make sense.

Weldon grunted, "Then why aren't you there protecting it?"

Turning toward him, Magnolia gave him a stern look.

Weldon shrugged. He focused on eating his praline cake.

"I have to eat too. One of the ship's security guards is watching it now," Reuben said.

Magnolia returned her attention to him. "Well, you are welcome to eat with us."

Weldon grumbled under his breath.

Reuben smiled warmly, "Thanks...Oh, there's the artist. He's a real jerk."

Magnolia turned her head to see a middle-aged man with slicked down black hair.

Raphael strutted around the dining room. He stopped at each table speaking briefly before moving on to the next one. Snapping his fingers at a server, he ordered a drink.

Lucretia waved at him. She motioned for him to join her group at their table.

Raphael charmed the ladies by kissing each of them on the hand. He spoke for a moment.

The ladies giggled except Doretta Brewster who glowered at him.

The server brought a tray with a drink to the artist.

Raphael took the glass and sipped the drink. His nose wrinkled. Slamming the glass back on the tray, he snapped, "I deserve better than that substandard slop."

As the server trudged away, Raphael turned back to speak to the ladies.

Doretta wagged a finger at him. She said something Magnolia could not hear.

Magnolia rolled her eyes at how the woman was probably lecturing him on his rudeness. *She needs to take her own lessons to heart.*

Raphael laughed loudly. He waved a hand of dismissal at her. Gesturing toward the door, he announced, "I'm returning to the exhibit room if anyone would like to see my newest masterpiece. I will also be offering autographs."

Lucretia and two of her friends stood to follow him.

Doretta stared after them. She picked up her wine goblet and chugged the rest of the contents. With a scowl, she rose to her feet and marched out of the dining room.

"Would you like to go see the painting, Nolia?" Weldon asked.

Magnolia returned her attention to her table. She wanted to see the painting, but she did not want to abandon Reuben. Looking at the empty seat beside her, she asked, "Where did he go?"

"Who cares?" Weldon grumbled.

"You be nice, Weldon Hitchcock."

"Yes, ma'am."

Returning to the table, Reuben said, "I've made arrangements for a server to bring me my dinner when it's ready. Come on. I'll show you Rowdy Howdy."

Magnolia stood to follow him to the exhibit room averting her gaze from Weldon's pouty face. *Sweet Freedom. Rowdy Howdy. Those seem like two quite different names.*

Slamming down the phone, Frankie growled under her breath. She had hoped the district attorney would jump at the opportunity to use her witness testimony to bring down Jontray Scott. However, he had doubted her testimony would hold up in court since she was only ten years old when the crime occurred.

Frankie leaned back in her chair. She needed to find a witness who was older than her. Her mind raced with who else was at the basketball courts. She assumed none of the Black Skulls would testify against Jontray Scott. Maybe one of the other Flames would want to get the guy who killed their leader.

Picking up her phone, Frankie dialed the extension for the Gang Unit. "This is Detective Lemmons, homicide. I need some information on a gang called the Flames."

"Detective Beckett has a lot of experience with that gang. Could you meet with him?"

"Absolutely. I'll head on down. Thanks."

Hanging up the phone, Frankie stood. She pushed her chair into her desk.

"Where are you going?"

Glancing over at London exiting the break room, Frankie said, "I need to talk to a detective in the Gang Unit downstairs."

"You mean we need to talk to him. Let's go."

Magnolia Ruby entered the exhibit room excited for the opportunity to see another of Raphael Capone's works. Sweet Freedom had enthralled her. What would this masterpiece look like?

"How dare you!"

Magnolia halted right inside the doorway. She stared at the other side of the room.

Doretta Brewster pointed a stern finger at Raphael Capone. "I have never seen such crude work in my life. That painting is obscene and vulgar. How dare you portray women like that! You will rot in hell for your heinous work."

Doretta marched toward the doorway.

Magnolia moved out of the way before the enraged woman could push her. She waited until Doretta was gone before walking over to the painting. Her curiosity rose at what had caused the outburst.

As the others in the room stepped to the side to talk to the artist, Magnolia faced the painting. *I can see why Doretta was disgusted.*

Saloon girls dressed in low-cut satin dresses straddled drunk cowboys. Not much of their bodies were left for the imagination.

Magnolia averted her gaze. Her face flushed warmly at the provocative painting. She had expected the painting to resemble Sweet Freedom which had been a beautiful piece showing the joy of slaves being granted their freedom. How could Raphael Capone, who painted such a memorable scene, paint this risqué piece?

Magnolia scanned the room to find the artist eager to discuss his works.

Raphael stood off to the side flirting with a blond-haired lady. Leaning closer to her, he whispered in her ear. The woman giggled and nodded. Raphael kissed her hand. He strutted over to the other ladies.

Magnolia approached him motioning to gain his attention.

Raphael smiled warmly at her. He walked over to join her. "Yes, my dear lady."

"Mr. Capone…"

"Raphael."

"Raphael, what art techniques did you use to make the dresses look so realistic?"

Raphael's smile faltered. He regained it a moment later. "I would love to tell you all about my techniques, dear lady, but I'm afraid it is quite complicated. You wouldn't understand."

Magnolia forced her smile to stay on her face. Her temper flared at how he believed her to be too simple to understand his process. "Well, I have used fabric rendering in a few of my works when trying to make clothing look more realistic. However, those dresses seem to have something more done to them."

"I'm afraid I am too busy to explain my work to an amateur. Excuse me," said Raphael moving away from her.

Magnolia narrowed her eyes at him. Why was he being so rude? She had asked him a simple question.

"Maybe you should ask his assistant. I don't see her now, but her name is Viri Greene," Reuben said.

Magnolia nodded.

"What does it matter?" asked Weldon.

Remembering the man had accompanied her and Reuben, Magnolia turned to look at him with pursed lips. She could not believe his indifference to her love of art. *He's known me long enough to understand why I would want to know more about the painting.*

Reuben said, "Well, she's an artist. It's like us cops needing to know about each other's cases. Professional curiosity."

Magnolia smiled warmly at him. She appreciated how he understood her interest.

"Shall we take a walk around the deck, Nolia?" asked Weldon offering his arm.

Magnolia glanced at Reuben to see what he thought.

Reuben motioned for her to go ahead. He walked over to the security guard.

Magnolia intertwined her arm into Weldon's. She allowed him to escort her out of the exhibit room. Her temper flared at how jealous he was acting. *We're just friends. We haven't even started dating again yet. Maybe we won't if he doesn't straighten up.*

Stepping out of the exhibit room, Magnolia noticed movement in the shadows. She turned to get a better look. Nothing. *I must be seeing things.*

⚓

Ophelia Hart adjusted her glasses. She strolled toward the exhibit room. Her plan floated in her mind. It was going to be perfect. Stepping into the doorway, she halted in surprise. Without a sound, she backstepped out of the room and hid in the shadows. *What is she doing here?*

Ophelia stared at Magnolia Ruby. She had not seen the amateur detective since the case at the Art Expo. Could Magnolia have joined forces with Detective Malone to trap her? Maybe they were on to her scheme. Why else would they be on the same ship at the same time as her?

Biting her lip, Ophelia recalled her perfect plan. It shattered with the added knowledge of Magnolia being there. Her plan might have worked with only the police detective and ship security, but Magnolia Ruby was extra clever.

Watching Magnolia leave the exhibit room with her arm linked in a man's, Ophelia stepped further into the shadows. If Magnolia saw her, it would all be over. She needed to revise her plan before she attempted to steal the painting. *I can't let anything stop me. Not even Magnolia Ruby.*

⚓

Frankie Lemmons scanned the information in Detective Beckett's file on the Flames. She bit her lip at how most of the gang members were either dead or in prison. Only one man was left from the gang. "What can you tell me about Mateo Castillo?"

Detective Beckett took a sip of his coffee. He set the mug down. "You mean Father Castillo."

Frankie did not like the sound of that.

"Is he a priest?" London asked.

"Yeah. He's the priest at the Cornerstone Catholic Church downtown."

Frankie stared down at the file. She knew that church. It was located near the park where Dillon had died.

"What do you want to do, Lemmons?"

Staring at the picture of the man, Frankie could feel he was her only hope of taking down Jontray Scott. "I think I need to go to confession."

⚓

Magnolia Ruby walked down the hallway to her cabin. She had excused herself from Weldon wanting to return to her room to get settled for the night. She slowed down as she spotted her cabin.

Jonas Archer stood near her door. What could the cabin steward need?

Magnolia's heart pounded at the unwelcome news he could be bringing them. Could something have happened to Ellison and the girls? Maybe it was Charlie and Leo. "Do you need something, Mr. Archer?"

Jonas looked over at her. He lowered his head. "No, ma'am. I was hoping to see Gloria return to her cabin."

Magnolia did not like the idea of the middle-aged man being attracted to the eighteen-year-old. She would become ruder than Doretta if he wanted to pursue a romantic relationship with her daughter.

Jonas held up a book. "She saw I was reading this book."

Magnolia nodded at the Agatha Christie novel. It was one of Gloria's favorites.

"She said she wanted to talk about the book when I finished it…I'm sorry. I didn't mean anything by being here," added Jonas turning to walk down the hallway.

Magnolia mentally kicked herself for assuming the worst. It had become a habit over the years as she dealt with suspects in murder cases. "Wait, Jonas."

Jonas halted. He turned back keeping his eyes lowered. "Ma'am?"

"Maybe you could meet with Gloria on deck tomorrow. It might look better if you were near more people."

"I don't like people," Jonas mumbled.

Magnolia opened her mouth to insist.

Jonas shook his head. "Yes, ma'am. Thank you."

Shaking away her suspicious nature, Magnolia entered the cabin. She closed the door behind her. Her nose wrinkled.

A strong odor wafted from the bathroom. Light shone under the bottom of the door. Assuming Genevieve was using the facilities, Magnolia headed for the balcony. She needed some fresh air. Opening the door, she left it open to help air out the cabin.

Sitting in a chair, Magnolia enjoyed the warm salty breeze floating over her. Her mind recalled the evening with Weldon and Reuben. She wished she could talk to Charlie about her conflicted feelings. *Maybe tomorrow.*

CHAPTER 4

ENRAGED EFFECTS

Frankie Lemmons stared up at the massive Cornerstone Catholic Church. She had driven past the church many times over the years. Yet now it towered over her like the answer to her prayers. Inside, she could find the key to bringing Jontray Scott to justice.

"Are you Catholic?" London asked.

Shaking her head, Frankie said, "Baptist. At least when I was a kid. You?"

"Baptist too. Do you know how to act in a Catholic church?"

Opening her car door, Frankie shrugged, "I'm a cop. I'll act like I always act."

"Boy, are we in trouble."

Ignoring her, Frankie slid out of her car. She slammed the door shut and marched toward the church's front entrance. All she had to do was convince Castillo to function as a witness against Jontray Scott. How hard could that be?

Pulling the large wooden door open, Frankie entered the sanctuary. Colorful stained glassed windows depicting the saints of the Bible aligned the walls. Shiny wooden pews lined both sides of the sanctuary with a red carpet dividing the two areas of the room. At the front, a stage with red carpet held a wooden pulpit and a communion table covered in a red and gold cloth. The beauty of the sanctuary was astounding.

Shaking away her awe, Frankie scanned the sanctuary for her target. She spotted two priests dressed in black entering from a side room. One was an older man who looked like he would have been a young adult when she was a child. The other priest looked fresh out of seminary.

Pulling out her badge, Frankie walked toward the two priests. She called, "Father Castillo?"

The two men turned to her. The older priest smiled warmly, "Yes, Officer. How can I help you?"

"It's Detective actually. Detective Lemmons. Can we have a word? Privately."

Nodding, Father Castillo leaned toward the younger priest whispering. He pointed toward the side door the priests had come from. "We can talk in my office, Detective."

Frankie glanced back to see if London was following them. The other woman sank into a pew. She gestured for Frankie to go with him.

Frankie turned to follow the priest. She entered the office and took the seat Father Castillo indicated for her. Scanning the office, she noted there were no other ways out of the room except the main door.

"Would you like a cup of coffee?" Father Castillo said, standing next to a table with a coffee pot on it.

Frankie shook her head. She did not need any distractions from her task.

Sitting in the chair behind his desk, Father Castillo asked, "What can I do for you, Detective?"

"First, you can tell me how a gang member becomes a priest."

Father Castillo's smile faded. He cleared his throat. "God works in miraculous ways."

"And how did He work on you?"

"I was initiated into The Flames when I was seventeen. I didn't have much of a choice. In my neighborhood, you joined a gang or became a victim of one. Saying no was not an option," explained Father Castillo.

Frankie nodded, "I know the neighborhood way. So, why did you leave the gang?"

"When I was twenty, Santiago Montoya was murdered. He was our leader."

"So? Gangs get new leaders. They don't break up because the leader died."

Father Castillo lowered his head. He stared at his lap. "He wasn't the only one who died that day."

Frankie froze. Her heart pounded at the image of Dillon dead on the basketball court. She clenched her fists at the horrible reminder.

Father Castillo added, "There was a…boy. He was innocent. Just there to play basketball. He was killed for being in the wrong place at the wrong time."

"And who killed them?"

Father Castillo raised his gaze. He wrinkled his forehead. "Why does that matter? I thought you wanted to know why I left the gang and became a priest."

Frankie dropped her arms to her side. She leaned forward in her chair. "I want to know if you'll stand as a witness to get justice for Santiago and Dillon."

Father Castillo stared at her. "How did you know his name was Dillon?"

Frankie mentally kicked herself for letting her emotions cause her to slip in her interrogation. She shrugged, "I'm a cop. I do my research."

Father Castillo leaned back in his chair. "You said Detective Lemmons, right?"

Averting her gaze, Frankie nodded.

"You're that cop's granddaughter. You were there when the shooting happened…Your grandpa died a few weeks later, right?"

Tears blurred her vision. Frankie blinked them away. Her heart wrenched at the reminder of her dead grandpa. Not wanting anyone to see her weakness, she stood. "I have to go."

Frankie hurried out of the office. She winced at the rushed footsteps behind her.

"Detective Lemmons, wait! Please."

Shaking her head, Frankie looked toward the pew where she had left London. She motioned to her to get ready to leave.

London looked in the direction of Father Castillo then followed Frankie as she passed her.

"Your grandpa visited me before he died."

Frankie halted at the priest's exclamation causing London to knock into her back. Turning back to Father Castillo, she took a deep breath. Why had her grandpa met with the young gang member? What had he found out?

Placing her hands on her hips, Frankie said, "And?"

"And we should talk in my office."

Magnolia Ruby hummed softly to herself at the table in the main dining room. She had ordered a breakfast of scrambled eggs, bacon, and toast. Now, she scanned the cruise restaurant brochure to see her choices. Which one would be a good one to try for lunch?

"Hey, Mags."

Magnolia glanced up with a smile. She was thrilled at not being alone after all. "Good morning, honeymooners."

Leo pulled a chair out for his bride and then pushed it forward. He sank into the chair next to his wife. "Where is everyone?"

"Well, let's see. Gloria and Lydia are sleeping in. They got home late from a shark movie marathon. I assume Ellison is sleeping in as well. I don't know about Weldon. Lucretia abandoned us for some new ritzy friends," Magnolia explained.

Charlie asked, "And Aunt Genevieve?"

Magnolia wrinkled her nose. It had been a long night. She mumbled, "She's still adjusting."

"To what?"

"You don't want to know. Let's just say she is planning to stay near the bathroom this morning."

Leo and Charlie exchanged a glance.

As the server took the couple's order, Magnolia picked up her cup of hot tea, blew on it, and took a sip. She scanned the dining room hoping to see Reuben. It would be nice to talk to him without Weldon breathing down her neck or inserting rude comments.

Magnolia spotted Raphael Capone eating alone. Where was his fan club?

The blond woman he flirted with last night strolled toward the table. Glancing around, she sat in the seat beside him. Leaning toward him, she stroked his cheek with the back of her hand.

Raphael dropped his napkin. Waving her away, he stood to leave the table.

The blond woman rose to her feet. "Wait. Where are you going?"

Ignoring her, Raphael sauntered toward the dining room exit.

Grabbing his arm, the woman screamed, "I thought you loved me."

Raphael jerked his arm out of her grasp. "That's what they always think."

"But I chose you over my husband. He has no idea what we did last night," the woman hissed.

"Look, Elise, you were fun, but I've moved on. Get over it."

Elise slapped him hard on the face.

Glaring at her, Raphael's focus on leaving seemed to have changed.

Magnolia bit her lip at the scene. "Leo, maybe you should see if you can break it up before it gets worse."

Nodding, Leo stood and marched across the room towards them.

Raphael turned to leave.

Grabbing his arm, Elise pulled him toward her. "No! You won't get away with this!"

Turning, Raphael shoved her backwards.

Elise fell to the floor.

Magnolia and Charlie rushed over and knelt beside her.

Magnolia scowled at Raphael. What kind of man treated a woman so disgracefully?

Leo moved to stand between the woman and Raphael. "That's enough, sir."

"Mind your own business," Raphael snapped.

"I'm a cop. This is my business…Why don't you go about your day now?"

Cursing loudly, Raphael stomped out of the main dining room.

Magnolia looked at Elise. "Are you okay?"

"Yes. Thanks. I'm just an idiot. I fell for his lies."

Charlie said, "You don't have to talk about it. We respect your privacy."

Magnolia agreed. She could imagine what had happened between the man and woman last night. There was no reason to have Elise relive her mistake.

Elise sighed, "No. It's okay. I was deceived into thinking he loved me. We…Well, you know."

Magnolia averted her gaze. She did not condone a woman cheating on her husband. Yet, Raphael was just as guilty.

Elise struggled to stand and accepted help from the other women. "Thanks, girls. I'm Elise Quincy."

"Magnolia Ruby."

"Charlotte Knight."

47

Leo joined the group.

Elise batted her eyelashes at him. "I don't usually like cops, but you're alright, Handsome."

Charlie crossed her arms. She scowled, "And he's Leo Knight, my husband."

Elise jerked at the news. Stepping away from Leo, she glanced at Charlie. "Sorry, sugar. Bad habits."

Leo stepped closer to Charlie. He put an arm around her waist. Looking at Elise, he said, "Maybe you should report this assault to ship security."

"No way. The Quincys take care of their own problems. Patton will take care of him."

"Patton?" asked Magnolia.

"My husband. He's a professional boxer. He'll deal with that creep," Elise said strutting toward the dining room exit.

Magnolia shook her head. She glanced at Leo. "What do we do now?"

Leo motioned toward the table. He shrugged, "Nothing if neither of them will file charges. Let's mind our own business and eat breakfast."

As she followed Leo and Charlie back to their table, Magnolia halted.

Norman Chalker sat at a table watching her as he scribbled in his notebook. Noticing her attention, he lowered his head though he did not stop writing.

"Mags?"

Returning to the table, Magnolia sat down just as the server arrived with their breakfast. Folding her hands on the table, she closed her eyes. "Lord, we thank You for this food to nourish our bodies. We thank You for this wonderful vacation on such a beautiful ship. Please bless us today. In Jesus' name. Amen."

"Amen."

Magnolia picked up her fork to begin eating her breakfast. She glanced over at Leo and Charlie. "So, what are you two planning to do today?"

"I promised to hit the gym with Dad," Leo said.

Charlie added, "Which means I need a partner in crime."

Magnolia smiled warmly at the news. She longed to spend time with her best friend. She needed some advice and encouragement. "What a coincidence. I'm alone this morning as well."

"Great! What do you want to do?" Charlie asked.

Magnolia picked up another brochure. It had a list of activities available on the ship. "There are endless options."

Charlie took the brochure from her. She scanned the list. "We could go rock climbing, ziplining, or skydiving."

Magnolia opened her mouth to suggest they try something a little calmer. She remained silent at Charlie's wink.

Leo coughed on his scrambled eggs. He drank some orange juice. Shaking his head, he said, "You can't be serious."

"What?" Charlie asked forcing her face to stay solemn.

"You two are not going to do any of those risky adventure activities."

Joining in the fun, Magnolia asked, "Why not?"

Looking back and forth at them, Leo stammered, "Because you're…and you're…You should be swimming or relaxing in a lounge chair not risking your lives."

Magnolia and Charlie laughed at his stuttering explanation.

Charlie pointed at her husband. "You should have seen your face."

Magnolia nodded, "I wish I had a picture."

Rolling his eyes, Leo returned to his breakfast. "Nice. Do you have to torture me?"

"Yes," Charlie said kissing him on the cheek.

Magnolia reached over and patted his arm. "We appreciate your concern, Leo, but we can plan our own day. We promise to be careful whatever we do."

"And what are you going to do?"

Charlie opened the brochure again. "How about a trip to the spa?"

"Absolutely. Mud baths, massages, and seaweed body wraps. Sounds dangerous," Magnolia agreed.

Leo chuckled, "Okay. That won't give me nightmares."

"Until you see a picture of me wrapped up in seaweed with mud on my face," Charlie giggled.

Laughing, Magnolia picked up the restaurant brochure. "Maybe we can meet up for lunch. We can text the others to join us…The Rock 'Til You Drop Diner sounds fun. It has a 50's theme."

"Cool," said Charlie.

Nodding, Leo added, "I'm in."

Magnolia returned to eating her breakfast. She could not wait to enjoy time with her best friend. *We could use some girl talk.*

Gloria Fairbanks closed the cabin door behind her. She placed her towel around her waist. Her heart raced with the excitement of going back to the pool. She had tried to get Lydia to go with her, but her friend had wanted to sleep and watch television. Genevieve had volunteered to keep an eye on her.

Gloria had texted her adopted mother for permission to go alone. She needed to stay where there were a lot of people, but she could go. Now, she walked down the hallway in her lime green flipflops ready to enjoy her swim.

Gloria hurried down the hallway at seeing Jonas with his cart. "Hi, Jonas."

Jonas turned to look at her. He smiled weakly then lowered his head. "Hi, Gloria."

"Did you finish And Then There Were None?"

"Yes."

"Do you have time to talk about it now?"

With his smile fading, Jonas shook his head. "Sorry. I have a lot of work to do. Maybe later?"

"Sure. I'm headed to the pool, but I'll check in with you when I get back."

Jonas nodded. He reached for a pile of towels on the cart.

Gloria spotted the scars she had seen on his wrists yesterday. Where had he gotten them? It would be rude to ask him. Shaking away her nosiness, she headed toward the elevator. Her heart pounded at how the rude lady had insulted her yesterday. She did not like the idea of facing her alone. Maybe Doretta Brewster was sleeping in like Lydia. *If I'm lucky.*

⚓

Leo Knight stepped onto a treadmill while waiting for his father to arrive at the gym. The news broadcast was on one of the televisions hanging above the exercise equipment. Annoyed by all the shocking news in the world, he reflected on his honeymoon and the fun he intended to have on the cruise. His mind focused on Charlie. Was she missing him during their brief time apart?

"That's quite a smile, son. Married life must be agreeing with you."

Leo turned his head with a nod. "Hi, Dad. It is. Did you enjoy sleeping in?"

"I can't believe I slept so late. Ten o'clock? Who has ever heard of sleeping that late on a cruise?" Ellison said stepping onto the treadmill next to his son.

Leo chuckled, "I'm sure it is a common occurrence here. It's a vacation after all."

"I suppose. Where's your bride?"

"At the spa with Mags."

Nodding, Ellison tapped around on the treadmill buttons. He began to walk as the machine stirred to life.

Leo listened as his father talked about how much fun he had with Lydia and Gloria at the pool and then at the movie marathon. He thanked God for the chance to spend father and son bonding time together.

"Capone!"

Leo stopped his treadmill at the enraged shout. His cop mode activated although he longed to mind his own business. He turned to find the source of the commotion.

The man from the dining room, Raphael, stood near the weight-lifting area. He stared with wide eyes and a frown.

A muscular man with a bald head stormed over to him. He pointed a finger at him. "I heard you've been messing with my wife."

Raphael crossed his arms. "Who's your wife?"

"Elise. I'm Patton Quincy."

Sighing, Raphael said, "Look. Elise and I had a quick fling last night."

Leo snorted at his boldness. He gritted his teeth at the fury on the muscular man's face.

Patton balled his hands into fists.

"Don't worry. I'm done with her. She's all yours," Raphael added.

Patton swung a fist at him.

Raphael dodged to the right. He fell to the floor as Patton's other fist slammed into his face.

Leo rushed over to the two men stationing himself between them. Facing Patton, he held up his hands. "Take it easy, Mr. Quincy."

"Are you a friend of his?" Patton snarled.

"Not a chance. I have higher standards. I'm a cop."

Patton stared at him as if trying to decide if he believed him.

Ellison patted a hand on the big man's shoulder.

Patton glared at him with raised fists.

"You don't want to go to jail for this clown, do you?" Ellison asked.

Patton shook his head. He lowered his fists.

Raphael wiped his bloody lip with a gym towel. "I'm pressing charges."

Leo turned his back on Patton while positioning his hands on his hips. "That's your right, Mr. Capone, but I have witnessed two incidents today involving you. Ship security might be curious about the trouble you have stirred up. I'm sure they would want to ask lots of questions."

Shaking his head, Raphael cursed loudly. Standing, he snarled, "Fine. I'll let it go."

Pointing at him, Patton growled, "You're going to pay for seducing my wife."

"Like I've never heard that before," snorted Raphael marching toward the exit.

Patton clenched his fists. He stared after Raphael for a moment then stormed into the boxing area of the gym.

Leo thanked God the fight had not escalated any further than it did. However, he had a feeling the dispute was not completely over. Looking at his father, he said, "I thought cruises were supposed to be relaxing."

"Only if you don't act like a cop."

Leo wished he could stop himself from being a cop sometimes. However, it was in his nature to step in and help people, even weasels like Raphael Capone. "How about we try weightlifting?"

Ellison nodded, "Yes. I want to get as strong as that big boy. His muscles were as round as tires."

"We could lift weights for the rest of our lives and never get that big, Dad," Leo laughed.

Ellison walked over to the rack of weights. He snorted, "I'll bet D'Angelo could take him."

"Only if Frankie didn't shoot them both first," Leo added. *What are you up to now, Partner?*

Sitting in the priest's office, Frankie waited for London to sit down in the chair next to her. She focused her attention on Father Castillo as the priest returned to his desk chair.

Sitting down, Father Castillo said, "I attended Dillon's funeral."

Frankie did not remember seeing him at the funeral. However, she had not been in a good place then. Most of that day was a blur. "And?"

"I left near the end before everyone headed outside to go to the cemetery. Your grandpa followed me out. He said I must be remorseful to come to the funeral. He asked if I was present at the basketball court when the shooting occurred. I told him I couldn't talk to the police. But your grandpa was very persistent. He asked if I would testify against Jontray Scott," Father Castillo explained.

Frankie recalled how determined a cop her grandpa had been. She admitted his story made sense. "What did you say?"

"I was scared because anyone who testifies against a gang is killed, and their family suffers. I didn't want any part of that mess."

"So, you let a killer walk," Frankie mumbled.

Father Castillo lowered his gaze to the desk. He said, "I wasn't going to. Your grandpa harassed me for a week. I finally agreed to testify."

"To get him off your back?" London asked.

"No, because I didn't want that boy to have died in vain. I wanted the violence in our neighborhood to stop."

Frankie snorted, "Then you chickened out?"

"No."

"Then why has Jontray Scott been free all these years if you testified?" Frankie asked.

Father Castillo said, "It wasn't my idea to back out. Lamont said…"

Frankie's eyes bulged at the name. Her grandpa had never allowed anyone to call him anything other than Lemmons.

"Who's Lamont?" London asked.

Frankie whispered, "My grandpa…What did he say?"

"He said to forget the whole thing."

Leaning forward, Frankie glowered at him. She had never known her grandpa to give up seeking justice for a crime. "He would never say that."

"But he did. He said he was dropping the case, and I should forget everything I saw that day," Father Castillo said.

Standing, Frankie shook her head. She stomped out of the priest's office. Her temper flared at the news her grandpa had dropped the case. Could it be true?

"Lemmons!"

Ignoring London, Frankie stormed out of the church. She marched toward her car. Nothing made sense. She needed more information.

London raced to catch up with her. She panted, "Where are you going?"

Frankie unlocked her car. She could only think of one person left in her life who could answer her questions. "To talk to my mother."

In the dim waiting room at the spa, Charlotte Knight sat in a lounge chair wearing a fluffy white robe. She listened to the quiet music drifting from the intercom above. Her body relaxed from the divine massage she had enjoyed. Waiting for Mags to return from her massage, she thumbed through a fashion magazine left in the waiting area. Manicures and pedicures were on their itinerary next.

Staring at a couple holding hands in the magazine, Charlotte smiled warmly. Was Leo missing her as much as she missed him?

"Excuse me?"

Charlotte looked up at the voice.

A woman with black hair and caramel skin stared down at her wearing glasses. She held a book against her chest.

"Yes?"

"I'm sorry to bother you. Are you Charlotte Pearl the author?"

Charlotte tilted her head at the woman. How could she know her? She did not have any writing materials with her. "Yes. How did you know?"

The woman's smile grew. She folded her hands into a quiet clap. "I knew it. I've read your book. It was amazing."

Charlotte blushed at the compliment. "And you are?"

"Viri Greene. I have my copy of *Fiery Frenzy* with me. Will you please autograph it for me, Ms. Pearl?"

"It's Charlie. Sure. I appreciate your kind words," Charlotte said taking the book and pen out of Viri's hands.

Charlie opened the front cover of the book. Other than friends, she hadn't signed any books for her fans. In fact, she doubted she had fans.

Ophelia Hart held back a squeal at having an author sign her book. She could not believe her luck. What were the odds of meeting Charlotte Pearl on the cruise ship?

Taking back her book, Ophelia said, "Thank you so much, Charlie. Will you be writing a new mystery soon?"

Charlie returned the book and pen to her. "I'm not sure. Maybe."

Ophelia would love to read another mystery novel by her. Fiery Frenzy had been captivating and really kept her on her toes. She had not put it down until she had read the entire book.

Charlie looked past her smiling warmly, "Hi, Mags. This is Viri. She's read my book."

Ophelia turned around with a smile which faded as she came face to face with Magnolia Ruby. Recalling how she was disguised as Viri Greene, she forced a weak smile on her face. Would the clever amateur detective recognize her?

Clearing her throat, Ophelia lowered her head. "Well, I must run. Nice to meet you both. Thanks again for the autograph."

Clutching the book, Ophelia rushed out of the room. *Charlotte Pearl knows Magnolia Ruby. Maybe my luck is not as good as I thought.*

Magnolia Ruby's eyes followed Viri as she made a quick exit from the spa. Why had Viri left so abruptly?

"That was weird."

Magnolia turned back to Charlie. "Yes, it was. I wonder what frightened her away."

"No clue," Charlie shrugged.

Sitting down in the chair beside her, Magnolia put her feet up on an ottoman. She adjusted her robe to make sure her body was covered appropriately.

Charlie said, "An attendant dropped by a little while ago. She said it'll be about twenty minutes before they're ready for us. They're running behind…I think there was an issue."

"Probably Lucretia and her ritzy friends commandeering the spa," snorted Magnolia.

Giggling, Charlie offered her a magazine to peruse while they waited.

Magnolia accepted the magazine. She set it on her lap not wanting to read right now. This seemed like the perfect opportunity to discuss what was on her mind with her friend. Taking a deep breath, she said, "Charlie, something amazing happened last night."

Charlie glanced at her waiting for her to share.

Magnolia said, "Reuben Malone is on this cruise."

Charlie sat up straighter. She tossed her magazine onto the table. Turning her body to face her friend more completely, she said, "No way. What's he doing here?"

"He's on a job protecting the painting of that odious artist from the main dining room."

Charlie smirked, "And?"

"What?"

"How do you feel?"

Magnolia wrung her hands on her lap. She shrugged, "Confused."

Charlie nodded.

Magnolia stared at her hands. She recalled how Charlie offered to make her wedding a double wedding so Magnolia and Weldon could get married. Clearly, Charlie wanted her best friend and her newly found father together. How would she feel about her feelings about Reuben?

Charlie said, "Go on."

"I like him."

Silence. Magnolia focused on her lap. She did not want to see Charlie's hurt expression.

"More than Pop?"

Magnolia shrugged without a word. She examined her left ring finger. Her wedding ring had been removed shortly after she met Weldon. She had decided Edward would want her to move on with her life.

"Mags, there's no wrong answer. I'm your friend no matter who you date."

Magnolia relaxed at the warm smile on her friend's face. "Thanks, Charlie. You know I thought I was in love with Weldon before he lied to me. Since we have started to spend time together again, I find myself liking him as a friend, but I'm not sure it will ever be more than that."

"And Reuben?"

Magnolia leaned her head back against the chair. She stared at the ceiling. "I don't know. I felt a connection to him at the Art Expo. At first, he was rude and patronizing which infuriated me. We butted heads every step of the way on the case. Yet, I hated to say goodbye when it was time to go home."

"And last night?"

Magnolia closed her eyes remembering Reuben joining their dinner group and talking with him at the table. Her mouth rose into a smile at the flutters in her stomach as she listened to his voice. "I can't explain it. Being with him felt…right."

Silence. Magnolia opened her eyes. She raised her head from the back of her chair. Glancing at her friend, she waited for her to speak.

Charlie said, "I don't think you're confused, Mags. Based on that smile on your face as you talked about him, I would say you've made a decision."

"Which is?"

"To get to know Reuben. See where it leads."

Magnolia shook her head. "It's not that easy."

"Why not?"

"Weldon."

Charlie tilted her head. "You're not married to him, Mags. In fact, you're not even dating. He has no claim over you. If you want to spend time with Reuben, then do it."

"But Weldon is sticking to me like glue. You should have seen him last night. He was clearly jealous of Reuben. We could barely talk without him butting in."

Charlie pulled out her cell phone from the pocket of her robe. She began to type frantically.

"Who are you texting?" Magnolia asked.

"Pop."

"Why? What are you telling him?"

Charlie stopped texting. She set the phone on her lap. "I'm asking him to spend the afternoon with me playing miniature golf. I'm sure you will find someone to spend your afternoon with too."

"Thanks, Charlie."

"Of course. Pop and I are supposed to get to know each other on this trip anyway."

"And Leo?"

Charlie jerked upward from her chair. She began to text on her phone again.

"Now, what are you doing?"

"Telling my husband that the afternoon belongs to Pop. We can have dinner alone and spend time together this evening."

Magnolia did not want to stir up trouble between the newlyweds. "Will he be okay with that?"

"He'll have to be because Pop has already agreed to golf."

Magnolia leaned back and closed her eyes. She did not want to create a problem for Leo and Charlie. Shaking away her worry, she tried to relax. *They'll be fine. I'm the one trying to start a new relationship.*

⚓

Ophelia Hart strolled through the exhibit room pretending to write notes on her clipboard. Her disguise as Viri Greene had been working like a charm. She had even managed to escape Magnolia Ruby before she recognized her.

Ophelia observed the guests viewing the painting. Her face flushed warmly at what a group of men joked about concerning the cowboys and the saloon girls in Rowdy Howdy. As she strolled through the room, she made a mental note of the exhibit room's atmosphere for what seemed like the hundredth time. Her plan would work if she could provide the proper distraction for the security guard.

Smiling at the current guard on duty, Ophelia walked over to the doorway. She took in a deep breath of salty air. *Today, that painting will be mine.*

CHAPTER 5

FISHY FINDINGS

Gloria Fairbanks climbed out of the pool. A cold soda would be refreshing. Before going to the outdoor bar, she considered wrapping a towel around herself before she walked across the pool's deck. She did not want trouble with anyone who had an opinion about her swimsuit.

As a man slammed into her, Gloria fell to the wooden deck. Her body jolted at the impact. "Hey!"

Spinning toward her, the man glared at her. He snapped, "Why don't you watch where you're going?"

Gloria wanted to snap back at the man. She took a deep breath to calm her temper. There was no reason for her to be as rude as the man.

"She didn't knock into you, Raphael Capone."

Gloria turned her head toward the familiar voice.

Doretta Brewster sat on a lounge chair pointing a stern finger at the man. "You attacked that poor girl. Shame on you. She ought to call ship security and report you…Jimmy, help her up."

A young man wearing a black suit and sunglasses approached her extending a hand.

Accepting it, Gloria allowed the help to stand. She thanked him.

Raphael stepped toward her. He held his hands up in surrender. "Now, there's no reason to overreact. No one is hurt. Ship security's not needed. Right, dear?"

Gloria could not believe how his tone had changed. Maybe he was afraid of being in trouble. "I guess not. I'm not hurt."

Raphael said, "Good. Sorry for bumping into you. I need to go."

Gloria watched the man leave the pool deck. She turned toward Doretta. "Thank you for your help, Mrs. Brewster."

"You're welcome, girl…I still think you're not dressed appropriately," Doretta said with a raised eyebrow.

Gloria forced her smile to stay in place. "I understand. Excuse me."

Rushing over to her own lounge chair, Gloria grabbed her towel. She wrapped it around her body. Maybe she should head back to the cabin before anything else happened.

Magnolia Ruby headed to the exhibit room hoping to find Reuben available to spend some time with her. Hearing footsteps behind her, she slowed down. Maybe Charlie had changed her mind about seeing the painting before lunch.

Magnolia turned around. She tensed.

Norman Chalker followed her.

Magnolia stepped to the railing. She looked out at the ocean. Glancing around, she let out the breath she was holding.

Norman walked past her. He kept walking not looking back.

Magnolia shook her head at her overreaction. *I'm getting paranoid. He isn't after me. He has a right to enjoy the cruise ship as much as me.*

Focusing on her task at hand, Magnolia entered the exhibit room. She spotted the woman she had met at the spa. "Hello, Viri."

"Hello," Viri mumbled then hurried out of the room.

Magnolia reflected on the odd behavior. Why would Viri be in the exhibit room? If she came to see the painting, then why did she rush away when she saw Magnolia? "There's something up with that girl."

"Always so suspicious."

Smiling, Magnolia turned toward Reuben. "Yes, you are."

Reuben chuckled, "Takes one to know one…She's Capone's assistant by the way."

At least, it made sense for Viri to be in the exhibit room if she was Raphael's assistant. She still did not understand why Viri left so quickly.

Shaking away the suspicions, Magnolia said, "Well, I came to see you not her."

"Oh?"

"Yes. I was wondering if you'd like to have lunch with me," Magnolia explained.

"Sure. Kevin is on shift for another two hours. I was just checking in. Shall we?"

Magnolia followed him out of the exhibit room. "Where would you like to eat?"

"We have lots of choices. There's a 50's diner that might be fun."

Magnolia could imagine the drama she would have to face if they met up with the rest of her friends and family at the Rock 'Til You Drop Diner. She blurted, "No! Anywhere but there."

Reuben raised his eyebrows. "Are you wanting to forget the 50's?"

Averting her gaze, Magnolia blushed at how she had not meant to speak loudly in such a dramatic manner. "Sorry, but my group is eating there today."

"And you don't want them to be angry at the handsome man you ditched them for?" Reuben asked with a smirk.

Magnolia laughed, "Something like that."

"I understand. They would probably want to hog all our time asking me deep probing questions. How about Shelly's Shrimp Shack?"

Magnolia agreed to visiting the seafood restaurant. She hoped none of her group had strayed to a different restaurant. *Get a grip, Magnolia Ruby. You're a grown woman. You can eat lunch with a man without telling anyone if you want.*

⚓

Charlotte Knight sat in the turquoise leather booth at the Rock 'Til You Drop Diner. She liked the 50's music resounding from a juke box. The servers skated around the restaurant in old-time roller skates. The waitresses wore turquoise blouses and black skirts with turquoise poodles on them. Their bouffant hairstyles were perfection. The waiters wore turquoise bowling shirts and black pants with the cuffs rolled up. Their hair was slicked back Elvis-style.

"I want to roller skate," Lydia whined.

Charlotte turned to look at her sister-in-law with a warm smile. She had to admit it would be fun to roller skate.

Ellison handed a plastic menu to his daughter to distract her. He said, "That's part of their job, Lydia. We'll see if we can roller skate later. What do you want to eat?"

Lydia looked at the plastic menu. She mumbled to herself while pointing at the pictures of the food.

Charlotte smiled weakly at her father. She could tell Weldon was not enjoying the outing. His scowl had nothing to do with the food on the menu he was glaring at. "What are you going to get, Pop?"

"I don't know. Why isn't Nolia joining us?" Weldon grumbled.

Charlotte did not want to lie to him. However, she knew he would overreact to the truth. Staring at the menu, she said, "She said she would join us later."

"But where is she?"

Charlotte shrugged, "I don't know." *It's true. I don't know where they went for lunch.*

Leo elbowed her gently. He raised his eyebrows at her. Clearly, the police officer knew something was going on. After all, his wife was planning to spend the afternoon with Weldon instead of him.

Glancing over at the juke box, Charlotte said, "Leo and I are going to pick a song from the juke box."

Weldon continued to glower at his menu.

Sliding out of the booth, Charlotte walked toward the juke box at the other end of the diner. She waited for her husband to join her. As he came to her side, she stared at the list of songs.

Leo said, "Subtle. What's up?"

Charlotte glanced over at the table. No one was paying them any attention. "Mags is having lunch with Reuben Malone."

"The detective from the Art Expo? Why is he here?"

"He's on a case to protect a painting from that jerk we met in the dining room this morning. Anyway, she likes him. I'm keeping Pop busy this afternoon to give her a chance to spend time with him," Charlotte explained.

"Wow. That sounds deceitful."

Charlotte placed her hands on her hips. "Are you going to squeal on me?"

"Not if you go dancing with me tonight."

Charlotte wrinkled her nose at him. She hated the idea of dancing. She had never learned more than a few basic steps, so it did not sound like a fun experience to her. "I don't dance."

"That was before you had a husband. Now, you can dance."

Charlotte giggled, "Oh really? Is that some kind of marriage magic?"

"Of course."

Nodding, Charlotte said, "Okay, husband. I'll go to dinner and dancing with you tonight if you'll help me distract Pop."

"Deal…Now, what song do you want to hear?" Leo asked, focusing on the juke box list.

Charlotte studied the list of songs again. She smiled, "Well, you can't go wrong with the King."

Leo reached forward to press a number into the juke box. He nodded, "Elvis it is…Now, let's distract your father."

⚓

Frankie Lemmons pulled her car into the driveway of her childhood home. Her mind raced with how the visit would go. She had not been home since she left to attend the police academy. Her heart pounded at the oppressiveness she had experienced in the house especially after her grandpa's death.

"Do you think she's home?" asked London.

Frankie snorted, "She's always home. She runs a beauty parlor out of her basement."

"So, what's the plan?"

Frankie closed her eyes. She placed her head on the steering wheel. Her temper had cooled as she drove. Now, she dreaded facing her mother.

Frankie had always been a huge disappointment to her mother. Dominique Lemmons had wanted a prim and proper daughter who wore dresses and acted like a lady. She could not stand Frankie's boyish ways. Their differences had led to more fights and eventually less visits. Frankie had even stopped calling over the years. She only sent cards on Christmas, Mother's Day, and her mother's birthday.

"Lemmons?"

Opening her eyes, Frankie sat up straighter. "Why don't you wait here, Bridges? I need to talk to her alone."

"Okay, but I'm not staying in the car. I'll take a walk in the neighborhood."

Frankie asked, "Do you think it's safe?"

"For me. I'm a cop. The rest of the neighborhood may be in danger with me around."

Frankie marveled at how London's response sounded like something she would say to Leo. Opening her car door, she climbed out ready to get the ordeal over with. She paused at the lack of cars near her mother's house. There had always been a lot of ladies getting their hair done, especially in the middle of the day. *Where is everyone?*

Frankie walked toward the porch. She climbed the three concrete steps. Listening, she gritted her teeth at the lack of noise from inside. She raised a fist then knocked on the door.

"Who is it?"

Frankie tilted her head at the harsh voice. It sounded like her mother, but Dominique usually did not sound so angry. Even in their arguments, her mother never sounded like that. Could something have happened?

Taking a deep breath, Frankie said, "It's me, Mom."

Silence. Frankie debated with herself about leaving. She turned to head back to the car.

Just then, the front door swung open. Frankie turned back forcing a smile on her face trying to look friendly.

Dominique stood in the doorway wearing a fluffy pink bathrobe. Her hair looked disheveled. "Francesca?"

Frankie forced her smile to stay in place. "Hi, Mom. How are you?"

Dominique placed a hand on her heart. She whispered, "Oh my word. What's happened?"

Frankie stared at her confused by the question.

"There's no way you would be here for a social call. Now, what's happened?"

Frankie rolled her eyes at her mother's dramatic nature. "I need to talk to you about Grandpa."

Walking through the door Reuben held open for her, Magnolia Ruby entered Shelly's Shrimp Shack. The owners had gone overboard with the seaside theme. The walls were painted in shades of blue. Anchors, plastic fish, nets, and lifesaver rings hung on the walls. The booths were shaped like boats with bright blue seats and a table in the center.

"I feel like I need to talk like a pirate," Reuben snorted.

Magnolia laughed, "Please don't."

A young woman dressed in a white and blue sailor dress bounced over to them. She smiled brightly, "Welcome to Shelly's Shrimp Shack. How many in your party?"

"Two please."

The woman grabbed two plastic menus. She led them to an empty boat booth. The name on the side of the boat read: Shark Bait.

Reuben mumbled, "That's not a good sign."

The hostess laughed as she placed the menus on the table. "Your server will be with you shortly."

Magnolia took Reuben's offered hand. She used him for balance as she stepped into the boat booth. Sitting down, she held her breath as Reuben hopped over the side into the booth. "Careful, Reuben. You don't want to have a boating accident."

Reuben waggled his eyebrows at her. "I'm always careful, Magnolia."

Magnolia picked up her menu. She scanned the drink menu knowing the server would ask their drink order first. Movement drew her attention to their server.

A young man dressed in a white sailor suit complete with a hat approached their table. "Ahoy, folks. Welcome to Shelly's Shrimp Shack. My name is Davey, and I will be your server today."

Reuben held up a hand. "It's not Davey Jones, is it? That would be too funny."

"No, sir. Davey Peele. Jones would be awesome though. May I start you with some drinks?"

"I'll have a sweet tea," Magnolia said.

Reuben nodded, "I'll have the same."

Davey walked away to get their drinks.

Magnolia leaned back against the seat. "Do you really like sweet tea? Or did you order that to make it look like we have something in common?"

"I love sweet tea. The sweeter the better. My family's from the South where sweet tea is mandatory."

"Where South?"

Reuben said, "My grandparents lived in Savannah, Georgia. My parents moved to Missouri shortly after I was born, but I spent every summer with my grandparents."

Magnolia nodded still looking at the menu.

"And where in the South are you from?"

Magnolia stared at the list of food. She forced her face to remain solemn. "Who says I'm from the South?"

"Oh, come on, Magnolia. I'm a police detective. I've heard your Southern accent when you get excited."

Magnolia lowered the menu. "Okay. You caught me. I'm from Fulton, Mississippi. I moved here when I was eight years old. It was after the…"

Magnolia grew quiet. She had not meant to talk about the fire that took her family.

"The what?"

Surrendering, Magnolia said, "My family had a fire. My brother and I moved up here after they were killed."

"I'm sorry…I would like to meet your brother someday."

Magnolia smiled weakly as she reflected on her dear Wally. Though they were not related by blood, she considered him her brother. She missed him so much. "He died a few years back."

Reuben slapped a hand on his forehead. "I'm sorry again. I keep putting my foot in my mouth. Maybe we should focus on the menu."

Magnolia lifted the menu. She smiled at the odd seafood choices. "It's okay. Let's see. There's Captain Cobb's Cod BLT."

"Bacon and fish sound weird together. How about the Sea and Land Platter. It comes with fish and chicken."

Magnolia could not imagine eating both in the same meal. "There's Leona Lobster's Mac and Cheese. I'll bet that's rich."

Davey returned with their drinks. He set them on the table then pulled out his pad and pen. "Are you ready to order?"

Magnolia smiled at their server. "I'll have Captain Cobb's Cod BLT with fries."

Reuben wrinkled his nose. He cleared his throat. "I'll have the Caribbean Sea Salmon with hushpuppies and fries."

Davey scribbled down their order. He took the plastic menus with a smile. "I'll put your order in right away."

As Davey hurried away, Magnolia folded her hands on the table. She said, "Tell me about yourself, Reuben."

Leaning back against his seat, Reuben smirked, "Why don't you tell me about myself? You're the amateur detective after all."

Magnolia nodded at the challenge recalling the time she spent with him at the Art Expo. "Okay. You're an aging police detective nearing retirement age."

Reuben narrowed his eyes at her. "Be nice. Your turn is next."

Magnolia laughed. She held up a hand. "Let me try again. You're a distinguished detective nearing retirement age."

"Better."

"You're not married though you have been married in the past."

"And how do you know that?"

"If you were currently married, I doubt you would be having lunch with me."

Reuben shrugged, "Unless I'm a cheating jerk…What makes you think I've been married before?"

Magnolia took a sip of her sweet tea. She wrinkled her nose at the lack of sweetness. Picking up a packet of sugar, she said, "At the Art Expo, I noticed a lighter area on your left ring finger. So, either you lost your wife recently or you recently decided to take the ring off."

Reuben touched his left ring finger. "She died three years ago. I put the ring in my dresser drawer about a week before the case."

"I'm sorry."

Reuben shrugged, "Anything else?"

"You love your job, but you hate when civilians interfere. You patronize old women until they must bully their way into your cases."

Reuben chuckled, "You're not an old woman."

"Thank you. Now, do you have any children?" Magnolia asked.

"I've had three children."

Magnolia tensed at his response. She cleared her throat. "Maybe we are getting too personal."

"Well, that's what you do on a date," Reuben said.

Magnolia blushed at the sentiment.

Reuben said, "My son, Grant, died thirty-five years ago in the army."

"I'm sorry."

"Thank you. My older daughter, Abigail, was killed in a car accident five years ago."

Magnolia folded her hands on her lap. She could feel the mood sink with the conversation. "I'm sorry again."

"My youngest daughter, Savannah, is in her late twenties. We had her a long time after the other two children. In fact, she was quite a surprise."

"Savannah?"

"In honor of my summer home. She's a single mother to my two granddaughters," Reuben said pulling out his cell phone.

Magnolia leaned forward to look at a picture of a young woman with two redheaded girls. The smiling family stood in front of the St. Louis Arch. "They're beautiful."

"Autumn is seven and Amber is four. I see them at Christmas and a couple of weeks in the summer. Do you have any children?"

Magnolia bit her lip. She had longed to have children of her own throughout most of her marriage to Edward. However, she had been unable to get pregnant. She still found times when it hurt her not to have children. "No. My husband, Edward, and I couldn't have children. When my brother died, I adopted his daughter, Gloria. She's grown up with me, so I feel like she is my daughter."

Reaching into her purse, Magnolia pulled out her cell phone. She clicked around until she found a good picture of Gloria. Holding it out for Reuben to see, she thought about the blessing of being in Gloria's life. What would life be like when she went off to college in the fall?

"Lovely lady," Reuben said.

Davey returned to the table with their meals. "Let me know if you need anything else."

Magnolia thanked him. She glanced down at their plates. Both dishes looked delicious.

Reuben raised his tea glass in the air. He said, "Here's to our first date."

Blushing, Magnolia picked up her glass. She tapped it lightly to his glass. She had never said it was a date. However, she could not help but believe it was exactly that.

Frankie Lemmons sat down at the kitchen table waiting for her mother to join her. How could she start the conversation?

Dominique grabbed two cans of diet soda from the refrigerator. She set one in front of her daughter.

Frankie hated diet soda. However, she decided to choke it down and not start an argument. "Thanks…So, are you closed today?"

"Today and forever."

Frankie opened the soda can. "You closed the shop? What happened?"

Dominique shrugged, "If you would call occasionally, you'd know the answer to that."

Frankie gritted her teeth. She did not want to answer rudely. It would only make things more difficult.

"Why do you want to talk about Lamont?"

Frankie stared at her soda can. She replied, "It's about a case."

"What case?"

Remaining silent, Frankie took a sip of her soda. She winced at the diet soda taste.

Dominique grunted, "Oh no. Please tell me this is not about Dillon Pickler."

Frankie tensed at how her mother said her best friend's name with disgust. She looked up at her. "So, what if it is?"

"Francesca, you've got to move on with your life. Dillon died almost twenty years ago."

"I know when he died. I was there, remember?"

"Yes. I know it was a horrible day, but Lamont tried to catch the killer and failed. Let the dead rest in peace."

Frankie slapped her hands on the table. Rising to her feet, she snarled, "I'm not after the dead. I'm after the one who put them in their graves."

Dominique placed her head in her hands. She released her breath in a loud huff. "I can't go through this again, Francesca. Losing Dillon was bad enough, but then Lamont and your father. It's too much. Don't go bringing it all up again."

Frankie sank back into her chair. She placed her hands on her lap. Her heart ached at her mother's words. Jontray Scott had destroyed her family. First, he murdered Dillon. Then the stress of trying to convict him had caused Grandpa to die a few weeks later. To make matters worse, her father, Jordan, started drinking heavily after his own father's death. He died a year later from alcohol poisoning.

Shaking away the great loss in her family, Frankie refocused on the task at hand. "I need to know why Grandpa dropped the case."

Silence. Frankie raised her head to look at her mother. She tensed at the tears dripping down her face.

Dominique wiped away the tears. "I don't know why he dropped it, but there's still a box in the attic with his police stuff in it. Maybe you'll find what you are looking for."

"Thanks, Mom."

Frankie left the kitchen. She headed for the stairs.

"Francesca?"

Frankie froze at her mother's strained voice. She glanced back toward the kitchen.

Dominique leaned against the door frame in the open doorway. She wiped a hand over her face. "Take the box with you. I'm going to take a nap. Lock the door when you leave."

Frankie tensed at how her mother talked to her like she was a visitor not her daughter. "Sure, Mom. I'll be quick."

⚓

London Bridges strolled through the park where the shooting had taken place twenty years ago. She smiled at how peaceful the park had become. Her eyes focused on some kids playing basketball. She stepped out of the way of two mothers pushing their strollers with babies. A boy played Frisbee with a dog.

London marveled at the difference. There were no gangs hanging around. No one seemed to be fussing or fighting. Everything looked peaceful.

Spotting a table near the short bleachers, London read the sign taped to the front of it. *Please help send our kids to summer camp this year.*

A middle-aged African American man stood behind the table. He talked excitedly with a couple of women. As they placed money into a large jar, he thanked them with a warm smile.

London walked over to the table. She stared at the large amount of money in the jar.

"Good afternoon, ma'am. Would you like to donate to help our community center kids?"

"Summer camp, huh?" London asked reaching into her pocket.

"Yes, ma'am. It costs $150 per child to go to Camp Paradise. We started early in hopes of being able to provide admission for as many of our at-risk kids as we can."

London pulled out a twenty-dollar bill. She placed it into the jar. "That's a noble cause. On behalf of the city police, thank you."

"You're a cop?"

"Detective London Bridges."

London held out her hand.

The man shook her hand with a bright smile. "Jontray Scott."

CHAPTER 6

GIFTED GUISE

Frankie Lemmons sneezed at dust rising in the air as she moved some boxes around in her mother's attic. She found a box labeled: *Lamont*. Opening the top, she spotted a picture of her grandpa in his police uniform. It had been take many years ago before he became a police detective.

Frankie caressed a finger on her grandpa's smiling face. Her eyes swelled with tears. She had missed him more than she would have liked to admit. Closing her eyes, she recalled how he told her endless stories about his police adventures. *You always knew how to make a story more exciting, Grandpa.*

Opening her eyes, Frankie returned the top to the box. She picked it up ready to take it with her and study it more carefully back at the precinct. Stepping carefully down the attic steps, she stopped outside of her mother's room.

Dominique had closed her door. No light came from under the bedroom door.

Frankie shook her head at how her relationship never seemed to improve with Dominique. *We're just too different.*

Frankie headed for the front door. After opening it and making sure the door's lock was turned, she exited the house closing the door behind her. She walked down the porch steps balancing the box in her hands. She halted abruptly when she saw London sitting on her car kicking her feet like a child..

Narrowing her eyes, Frankie said, "Do you always put your butt on other people's cars, Bridges?"

London slid off with a shrug. "Sorry, Lemmons. Let's get back to the precinct."

"What's the hurry?"

"I need a computer."

Frankie opened her back door. She set the box on the seat. Climbing into the driver seat, she said, "Why?"

London mumbled, "I've got to do some major research."

Frankie buckled her seatbelt. Glancing at the house, she froze.

Dominique stood at her bedroom window. She peeked through the curtains then closed them with a frown.

Frankie started the ignition of her car. She had a hunch her mother was hiding something. Shaking away her suspicions, she put the car into reverse. She needed to get back to the precinct, too. London had research to do, but she did too. She could not wait to see what Grandpa had in the box about the case.

⚓

Charlotte Knight swung her golf club slamming it into her pink golf ball. She held her breath as it rolled toward the clown's mouth. As the ball rolled through the mouth, she turned to celebrate with her father. Her good mood soured instantly.

Weldon stood a few feet away. His head was lowered staring at his cell phone screen. He had not even noticed her shot.

Charlotte walked over to the clown to pick up her ball before joining her father. Her temper was very close to rising because this was not the way she had pictured their afternoon together. Why couldn't he forget about everything else and enjoy the game?

Weldon looked up at her. "Still no texts from Nolia. Where could she be?"

Charlotte bit her lip. She wanted to be understanding, but his obsession with Mags grated on her nerves. "I thought you wanted to spend time with me."

"I do."

"Then can we enjoy the afternoon together without worrying about Leo or Mags or anyone else?"

Weldon shoved his cell phone into his pocket. "Sure, Charlie. I'm sorry. What's next?"

"The windmill."

As the father and daughter strolled to the next hole on the miniature golf course, Charlotte thanked God for being able to talk to Weldon without showing her annoyance.

"Leave me alone!"

Charlotte spun in the direction of the shout.

Raphael Capone shoved a young man dressed in a black suit with sunglasses. The young man fell to the concrete ground.

"Who's the jerk?" Weldon asked.

Charlotte mumbled, "Raphael Capone. He's a real piece of work. I don't know the younger guy."

"That's Doretta Brewster's bodyguard. She's a rich lady who is in everyone's business. I saw him at the pool with her yesterday."

The young man struggled to his feet clenching his hands into fists.

Storming away from him, Raphael headed toward the miniature golf course exit.

The young man screamed, "You're not even worth it!"

Charlotte turned back to the windmill. She waited as Weldon placed his yellow ball on the ground. She thought about the other run-in with Capone she had witnessed. *Does that artist get along with anyone?*

⚓

Magnolia Ruby whacked the mallet onto the toy mole's head. She laughed at the creatures popping up and down in different holes. After lunch, she had wanted to spend more time with Reuben. He had checked in at the exhibit room then suggested they try out the arcade. Magnolia had looked at her cruise map finding the arcade far away from the miniature golf course. She had agreed with the activity.

Reuben whacked his mallet rapidly on the heads of the moles. He grumbled under his breath about the hyper beasts.

A loud bell rang out above their heads. Magnolia looked up to see her mallet color shining on the points screen. She whooped in victory at conquering the moles and beating Reuben.

"Act your age, Magnolia."

Laughing, Magnolia set her mallet down. She wagged a finger at him. "Don't be a sore loser, Reuben. Just because you wanted to come to the arcade and lost doesn't mean you should act like that."

75

Reuben set his mallet back in its place. "I didn't know you were going to be so competitive."

"Well, Mississippi is known for raising some competitive people. You Georgians wouldn't know anything about that," Magnolia teased.

"I disagree. My own Georgia Bulldogs tend to excel in college football…How about a walk on the deck? That seems more my speed."

Magnolia took his offered hand. She blushed at how he tenderly squeezed it then led her out of the arcade.

"So, tell me your darkest secret, Magnolia."

Magnolia snorted, "I don't think we've known each other long enough to share the darkest secrets."

"I'll tell you mine," Reuben whispered.

Nodding, Magnolia walked around a corner. She gasped at a sudden shove that knocked her to the deck. A laundry cart was the unseen culprit.

A maid dressed in a gray dress looked down at her from behind dark sunglasses. Her long black braids bounced around her scarred face. "Oh, ma'am. I'm so sorry. I can't believe I didn't look before I came around that corner. Are you hurt? I can fetch a doctor."

Magnolia held up her hands. "I'm not hurt. It's okay. Accidents happen."

The maid reached down to help her to her feet. She grabbed one of her arms.

Reuben took her other arm. He worked with the maid to help her stand. "Are you sure you're okay?"

Magnolia nodded, "I'm fine. Really."

The maid brushed her braids out of her face. She stammered, "Can I get you anything?"

"No, dear. I'll be fine. Don't worry about it anymore," Magnolia soothed her.

"Yes, ma'am. Thank you, ma'am. I need to get these linens to the laundry."

Reuben and Magnolia stepped out of her way.

The maid pushed the cart past them. She hurried away without a look back.

Reuben muttered, "It's not even safe to walk on the deck."

"At least, no one was hurt," Magnolia said. *I hope I didn't jolt my body too much. I may feel that in the morning.*

⚓

Smirking, Ophelia Hart spied on Detective Malone and Magnolia Ruby as they continued their walk on the deck. She pushed her fake braids out of her face pleased at how the detective duo had not recognized her. She had staged the "accident" to see if her disguise was good enough to work. It had also been a successful way to locate the two crime-solvers.

Ophelia hurried to a nearby elevator and pushed the cart inside. Choosing a button, she waited for the elevator to drop down a floor to where the exhibit room was located. Her plan was true brillance. She could not wait to have Rowdy Howdy in her clutches.

At a soft ding, the elevator doors opened. Ophelia pushed the laundry cart out of it. She strolled past the open door of the exhibit room. There was only one person in the room, the security guard, standing in front of the painting.

Passing the windows of the exhibit room, Ophelia turned a corner. She stopped her cart at a trashcan. Glancing around, she scanned the area for witnesses. No one.

Pulling a bottle of nail polish remover from the cart, Ophelia opened it. Her nose wrinkled at the strong alcohol odor. She poured it into the trashcan. Glancing around one more time, she lit a match then dropped it into the trashcan. The flames burst up quickly.

Ophelia pushed her cart back toward the exhibit room. *Time to use my acting skills.*

⚓

Frankie Lemmons pulled her car into a parking spot outside their precinct. She turned off the car then looked over.

London quickly unbuckled her seatbelt then exited the car without a word. Rushing across the parking lot, she headed toward the front door.

Frankie could not believe London had not questioned her about her visit with her mother or the box she had retrieved from her childhood home. It was not like the other woman to not be in her business. What could be going on?

Shaking away her suspicions, Frankie grabbed the box setting it in the passenger seat. She decided she would rather look at its contents privately in case she became emotional again. Opening the lid, she pulled out the picture of her grandpa. She set it to the side then reached in to see what else she would find.

Feeling another picture frame, Frankie lifted it out of the box. Her heart wrenched at her family smiling back at her. She touched her father's face. Her eyes swelled with tears. *We were so happy then.*

Placing the photo on the other one, Frankie pulled out a hunk of clay shaped like the world. It was painted with blue and green splotches. Her mouth slid up into a smile.

Frankie had made the art sculpture in art class when she was in kindergarten. She had given it to her grandpa for his birthday that year. Grandpa had treasured the piece of junk. He had said it would make the best paperweight on his desk at work.

Frankie placed the paperweight on her dashboard. She could not believe he had kept it until his death. Maybe she could secure it to her dashboard as a reminder of her grandpa.

Returning her attention to the box, Frankie found a little black notebook. It reminded her of the one she used as a police detective. Could it be full of Grandpa's notes about the case?

Frankie opened the notebook. She smirked at his messy handwriting. Her mother used to nag her often about writing too fast. Apparently, it ran in the family.

Frankie read the first few pages. None of the notes matched Dillon's case. Scanning the dates at the top of the pages, she turned until she found the date of Dillon's death. She read her grandpa's notes carefully.

Took J.S. in for questioning. J.S. refused a lawyer. J.S. said innocent people don't need one. Gave alibi of being at the movies with his girlfriend Andrea Pepper. Asked what movie. J.S. said Aliens Massacre 2. Asked more questions about case. No useful information. Informed J.S. alibi would be checked. Let J.S. leave.

Frankie turned the page. She read the next entry of notes.

Visited A.P. at work. A.P. gave same story. When asked what movie, A.P. said A Love to Recall. A.P. changed to say Aliens Massacre 2. A.P. became nervous and asked if she needed a lawyer.

Frankie nodded. She flicked her eyes across the page to the next entry. Her eyes widened at the initials F.L. *He even wrote notes about me.*

Spoke to witness F.L. for more details about case. F.L. mentioned The Flames. Going to check in with The Flames weakest link M.C.

Frankie assumed M.C. was Mateo Castillo. Turning the page, she braced herself for what happened when her grandpa talked to Castillo.

Took lots of convincing but M.C. has agreed to testify that J.S. killed S.M. and D.P. Going to arrest J.S. as soon as a warrant is approved to check his home and car for murder weapon.

Frankie clenched the notebook tighter. She mumbled, "Then what happened? Why didn't you arrest him, Grandpa?"

Turning to the last page written on, Frankie read her grandpa's final notes.

Received new information. F.L. in danger. Informed M.C. there is no case.

Frankie stared at the notes. Her heart pounded at how her grandpa believed her to be in danger and then dropped the case. Why did he think she was in danger? Had he received a threatening call or note?

Frankie searched the notebook for answers. She found none. With a shriek, she threw the notebook into the box. How had Jontray Scott forced her grandpa to drop the case? His actions may have been the reason Grandpa stressed out and died of a massive heart attack three weeks later.

The car door opened. Frankie jerked back startled. "What?"

London picked up the box. She set it on her lap as she sank into the passenger seat. Taking a deep breath, she said, "We need to talk."

Ophelia Hart rushed toward the exhibit room doorway. She stopped her cart right outside out of the way. Stepping into the room, she screamed, "There's a fire!"

The security guard spun toward her. "What? Where?"

"A trashcan. Down there," Ophelia said pointing the way she had come.

The security guard grabbed his walkie talkie out of its holster. Pushing the button on the side, he shouted, "Code Red at second floor east."

As the security guard left the room, Ophelia waited until he was out of sight. She pushed the cart over to the painting. Moving the linens in the cart, she picked up Rowdy Howdy and placed it gently into the cart. She covered the painting with the linens thrilled at the perfection of her plan.

"Hey!" yelled Raphael Capone entering the room.

Ophelia held her breath. Her eyes darted around to find a weapon to defend herself. She spotted the security guard's baton waiting on a table next to her. A new plan quickly came to mind. Nothing would stop her from getting the painting.

⚓

Magnolia Ruby held Reuben's hand as they strolled along the second-floor deck. She had enjoyed her afternoon with him. Her feelings for him had already grown. She wished to spend more time with him. However, first, Reuben needed to check in with the security guard stationed in the exhibit room.

Screams floated down the deck toward them. Gray smoke rose into the air.

Reuben released her hand. He hurried forward to see what was causing the commotion.

Magnolia followed him. A fiery trashcan came into view. She placed a hand on her mouth at the smoky air surrounding her. A security guard worked to put the fire out with a fire extinguisher. How could the fire have started?

Reuben approached the security guard. He grabbed the man by the shoulder. He barked, "Who's watching the painting?"

The security guard turned in the direction of the exhibit room. "Uh…Nobody. I came to see the fire and called it in."

"Then you should have returned to the painting," Reuben snapped pulling his Glock pistol from a hidden holster.

As he rushed toward the exhibit room, Magnolia hurried after him. Her fear grew at how a fire must have been started as a distraction. She reached the open doorway of the exhibit room behind Reuben.

The easel where Rowdy Howdy had sat was empty. There was no sign of the painting anywhere. No one else was in the exhibit room. There was a puddle of blood on the floor.

Ophelia Hart opened the door of her cabin. She glanced up and down the corridor. No one. Moving the linens, she pulled the painting out of the laundry cart. She put it inside her cabin then closed the door.

Ophelia scanned the corridor again. Satisfied at its emptiness, she pushed the cart farther away from her cabin. She abandoned it in a different hallway then returned to her cabin.

Opening her cabin door, Ophelia entered quickly then shut the door. She used the extra lock at the top to make it more secure. Turning toward her bed, she lifted the mattress then turned it over. The Velcro straps had been added as soon as she boarded the cruise ship. Placing the painting on the mattress, she secured it with the straps. *A perfect fit.*

Ophelia gently replaced the mattress. She smirked at the success of her plan. Now, she needed to work on how to get the painting off the ship when they reached port in a few days.

Ophelia pulled her fake braids off her head smiling at how her disguise had worked. Raphael Capone had almost ruined her plan when he caught her with the painting. Smiling, she tossed the braids into her suitcase. *He won't be able to squeal on me now.*

CHAPTER 7

HOPEFUL HUNT

Frankie Lemmons sat down in her usual booth at Alice's Diner. She had ordered an Apple Pie Burger to try to relieve the stress of the day. What did London want to tell her? She knew her temporary partner had been inside the precinct doing some kind of research. What could she have been up to?

D'Angelo lumbered over with their plates of food. He set London's salad in front of her then placed Frankie's specialty on the table. He turned to leave them to their meals.

"Hang around, D'Angelo. We need to talk," Frankie said.

With a nod, D'Angelo pulled a stool to the end of the table. He sank down onto it then focused on her.

Looking across the table at London, Frankie said, "D'Angelo is a good friend. He occasionally helps with cases. He is going to help me bust Jontray Scott."

"Then he needs to hear this," London said.

"Hear what?"

London took a deep breath. "While you were visiting your mother, I met a man at the park. He was collecting money to send underprivileged kids to summer camp."

"That's nice of him," D'Angelo said.

Frankie shrugged, "Cool. And?"

London picked up her glass. She took a sip of her soda then set it back down. "It was Jontray Scott."

Frankie snorted, "Then it's a scam. He's probably using the money for his gang."

"Actually, he isn't. That's what I wanted to research. There's a lot more about Jontray Scott you don't know," London replied.

Crossing her arms, Frankie glowered at the other woman. How could she not be on her side? "I don't care. All that matters is he's a murderer who didn't pay for his crimes."

London pursed her lips. She glanced around briefly then focused on Frankie. Lowering her voice, she said, "The truth is he did pay for his crimes."

⚓

Magnolia Ruby stepped carefully through the exhibit room not touching anything. She absorbed as many details as she could hoping to find a clue to the identity of the thief who must have caused the fire to get the security guard away from the painting. She stared at the puddle of blood. Could it be the thief's blood? Maybe he or she was hurt during the theft, but how?

Reuben joined her with a frown. He mumbled, "What do you think?"

"It's odd. With this much blood, I would expect to find a body or someone stumbling around looking for help," Magnolia replied.

"We have neither. I called the infirmary. No one has reported any wounds that could cause this amount of blood."

Magnolia froze at a firm voice resounding from the other side of the exhibit room. She glanced over at the security guard being chewed out by a tall man dressed in khaki pants and a navy-blue polo shirt. "Who is that?"

Turning his head in the direction she was looking, Reuben replied, "Chief Dwight Jackson. He's the head of ship security. I wouldn't want to be Kevin right now."

Magnolia observed the repentant expression on Kevin's face. "Have you questioned Kevin?"

"Not my jurisdiction. Everything that happens on the ship is Chief Jackson's jurisdiction."

Magnolia walked toward the two men. She paused at a hand on her arm.

"Magnolia, it's not your jurisdiction either."

Pulling her arm gently away from Reuben, Magnolia continued toward Chief Jackson. She smiled warmly at his sudden attention. "I'm sorry to disturb you, sir."

Chief Jackson beamed at her. He held out a hand. "No disturbance, ma'am. I'm Chief Jackson. And you are?"

"Magnolia Ruby."

Magnolia shook his hand. She hoped the chief would not be offended by her interference.

"How can I help you, Mrs. Ruby?"

"Well, Chief, I was wondering if Kevin could tell me what happened."

Chief Jackson silently stared at her for a moment. Was he unsure about granting her request? With a shrug, he gestured toward Kevin.

"Thank you for your kindness, Chief. Kevin?"

Kevin glanced at the chief. At his firm nod, he said, "I was at my post. A maid ran in screaming there was a fire. I went to put it out. I called the incident on the walkie talkie. That's all I know."

Placing his hands on his hips, Chief Jackson glared at him.

Lowering his head, Kevin averted his gaze from his boss.

Magnolia reflected on the information. "What did the maid look like?"

"She was African American with long braids. She wore her gray uniform and sunglasses," Kevin answered.

Magnolia stared at him. Her eyes widened at the description. She turned back to Reuben. She could tell he was thinking the same idea.

"It's the maid who bumped into you on the upper deck," Reuben said.

Magnolia bit her lip. It did not make sense. Why would a maid be involved in the theft? She glanced at the puddle of blood. Could the maid be injured?

Reuben grunted, "If we can find the maid, then we might be able to get some answers."

Chief Jackson pulled out his cell phone. He clicked around on it. "I'll call our employment services and give the description. They should be able to give me her name."

As Chief Jackson walked away to make his phone call, Magnolia focused on Reuben. "Has anyone talked to Raphael Capone yet?"

Shaking his head, Reuben pulled his cell phone out of his pocket. "Not that I know of. I'll call him now. I'll probably get an earful about incompetence and failure. Lucky me."

Magnolia stepped over to look at the bloody puddle. It was stationed right in front of the easel. She closed her eyes trying to picture the painting on the easel. There had not been anything on the painting that could cut a person and cause this much blood. *What in the world happened here?*

Frankie Lemmons leaned back against the booth seat. She tried to listen to everything London had discovered about Jontray Scott. Her interest grew at the statement that he had paid for his crimes.

London pulled out a printout. She set it on the table then pushed it toward her.

Frankie ignored the printout. She waited for London to tell her what it said.

Picking the printout back up, London said, "Jontray Scott confessed to shooting Santiago Montoya as part of a gang war. He went to prison for twenty years. He recently was granted parole due to no crimes or violent tendencies in prison."

Frankie assumed his time in prison was why she had not seen Jontray Scott since the crime. Her temper flared at how he had been granted parole. Why would they let him out to hurt others?

"What about killing Dillon? He didn't serve any time for that," Frankie hissed.

Holding up her hands, London said, "I know, but there wasn't any evidence of Jontray being the one to shoot Dillon."

Glowering, Frankie bit back a harsh response. How could London be on the side of the killer?

A hand touched her arm. Frankie flicked her gaze to the side.

D'Angelo pulled his hand back. He mumbled, "You were running, Lemmons. Did you see him pull the trigger that killed your friend?"

Frankie could not believe what she was hearing. Was no one on her side? Though it was true she did not see Jontray Scott shoot Dillon, she believed it had to be him. "He killed him."

London leaned forward. She lowered her voice not allowing their private conversation to be overheard by the other customers in the diner. "Look, Frankie. I know you want to bust this guy, but he's not a threat to anyone anymore. He spends his time trying to help gang members get out of that life and trying to stop teens from joining up with the gangs. He leads Bible studies and collects money for charities to help the poor. Face it. He's changed his ways."

Frankie slapped a hand on the table. She slid out of the booth. Pointing a finger at London, she yelled, "No! He's a monster and I'm not going to let him get away with killing Dillon."

Frankie marched toward the exit. Her heart pounded in rage at how she would have to deal with the murderer by herself.

"Lemmons!"

"Frankie, there's more."

Ignoring them, Frankie pulled the diner door open hard causing the bell to ring louder than usual. She slammed it behind her then stormed across the parking lot toward her car. *I won't let him get away with this.*

Magnolia Ruby walked along the deck outside of the exhibit room. She scanned the area for any clues the thief could have mistakenly left behind. Nothing appeared to be out of order.

"We have a problem."

Magnolia turned around to face Reuben. She tensed at the scowl on his face. What could have happened now?

Reuben held up his cell phone. "Raphael is not answering. I sent a guard to check his cabin. There's no sign of him."

Magnolia tilted her head at the news. Where could the artist be? She glanced through the open doorway of the exhibit room. Staring at the puddle on the floor, she assumed it could be Raphael's blood since he was missing.

Reuben said, "I know what you're thinking. Let's not jump to any conclusions. Raphael could be enjoying himself on the ship and ignoring his phone calls."

Magnolia knew it could be true. Maybe Raphael had seduced another woman. He could be spending his time showing off to his fans unaware anything had happened to his painting. "What are we going to do?"

Reuben raised his eyebrows at her. "We? This is not my jurisdiction, remember?"

"Protecting the painting and keeping the artist informed is why you are on this ship, isn't it?" asked Magnolia.

Reuben glanced over at the security guards meandering in the exhibit room. Returning his attention to her, he snorted, "I forgot about not arguing with you...I guess we can talk to Capone's assistant. Maybe she knows where he is right now."

⚓

Charlotte Knight strolled down the hallway toward the women's cabin. She had agreed to go and check on Aunt Genevieve with her father. Their father-daughter afternoon had improved after she got Weldon to stop talking about Mags.

Walking around the corner, Charlotte slowed down. She glanced at her father then back down the hallway. What could she do now?

Mags and Reuben walked ahead of them at the other end of the hallway.

Weldon hissed, "What in the world?"

Charlotte placed a hand on his arm. She pointed to the women's cabin door. "This is the right one, Pop."

Weldon shoved her hand off his arm storming down the hallway.

Charlotte rubbed a hand over her face. She jogged to catch up to him. "Pop!"

"Nolia!"

⚓

Magnolia Ruby stopped outside of the cabin belonging to Capone's assistant. She marveled at how it was in the same hallway as her own cabin. Raising a fist, she prepared to knock on the door.

"Nolia!"

Magnolia spun around at the angry shout. "Weldon, what are you doing?"

Stomping toward her, Weldon gestured at Reuben. "What are you doing with him?"

Magnolia reflected on the question. How could she explain about their day together? Though she only wanted to be friends with Weldon, she did not want to hurt his feelings.

Reuben said, "We're on police business."

Magnolia hoped the explanation would be enough for him for now. She needed time to sort things in her mind.

"What police business?"

Magnolia said, "The painting has been stolen. No one can find Raphael Capone. We're checking in with his assistant."

Weldon stared at her.

Magnolia held her breath wanting to tell him more, but it was not a suitable time to talk about their relationship. Her duty had to be with the case for now.

Nodding, Weldon shoved his hands into his pockets. "Okay. Sorry."

Charlie stepped forward. She pointed back down the hallway. "We're going to visit Aunt Genevieve."

Magnolia released the breath. Her annoyance at Charlie faded at the knowledge they were not checking up with her. "I'm sure she would love to visit with both of you."

Weldon looked back and forth between Reuben and Magnolia. He stepped closer to her. "Do you want to have dinner tonight, Nolia?"

"Of course. I'll even let you pick the restaurant."

Weldon grinned causing his bushy white mustache to rise comically. "Sounds good. See you later."

As Weldon and Charlie walked back down the hallway towards the women's cabin, Magnolia turned back to the task at hand.

Reuben stared at her with raised eyebrows.

Magnolia shrugged, "What?"

"I think your other boyfriend is suspicious."

"I don't have boyfriends. We went to lunch, Reuben."

Reuben stepped closer to her. He leaned forward. "It was more than lunch…at least to me."

Magnolia looked away. Her cheeks flushed warm at the sentiment. "It was nice."

"Nice?"

Magnolia cleared her throat. She focused on Capone's assistant's door. "Let's get back to work."

⚓

Ophelia Hart sat on her bed dreaming about how she would display the newest painting with her collection. She had been victorious over Raphael Capone again.

A knock resounded on her door. Ophelia was not expecting anyone to visit. Putting on her glasses, she made sure her Viri Greene disguise was ready. She walked over to the door.

Opening it, Ophelia peeked out. Seeing Magnolia and Reuben, she prepared for her next performance. "Yes?"

Reuben held up his badge. "Ms. Greene, we need to talk to you."

Ophelia opened the door wider. "Of course, Detective and Mrs…"

"Ruby. Magnolia Ruby. We met at the spa this morning. Viri Greene, isn't it?"

"Yes. I remember you now, Mrs. Ruby. Please come in," Ophelia said moving back to let them enter her cabin.

As the detective duo entered the cabin, Ophelia glimpsed at the bed. She assumed the painting was safe. However, she did not like having it in the same room as Magnolia and Reuben. She closed the door with a fake smile. "What can I do for you?"

Reuben turned to face her. "Do you know where we can find Raphael?"

Ophelia forced herself to breathe. They had not found the artist yet. Stepping over to the porthole, she said, "No. I haven't seen him since this morning."

"Isn't that odd?" asked Magnolia.

"Not really. Mr. Capone usually gives me an order then disappears for hours. He told me this morning to work on articles about the painting to be published in different major newspapers. I've been stuck in here all day writing them," Ophelia explained turning back from the porthole.

Magnolia sat down on the bed facing her. "Why do the articles have to be different?"

Ophelia shrugged, "Because he said so."

Snorting, Reuben walked around the bed. "That sounds like him."

Ophelia held her breath. She assumed Magnolia's weight would not strain the mattress or hurt the painting. However, the plump police detective would probably cause damage if he sat on the bed too.

"We need to know if you hear from him, Ms. Greene," Reuben added remaining standing.

"Of course. Is something wrong?"

"Yes. The painting is missing."

Ophelia placed a hand on her mouth. She gasped, "That's terrible." *Who could have done such a thing? The woman standing right in front of you.*

⚓

Magnolia Ruby found Viri Greene's behavior odd. First, she had talked facing the porthole. Now, she seemed nervous. Could Viri know more than she was telling?

Reuben said, "We need to know if you hear from him, Ms. Greene."

Viri's eyes darted to Magnolia then quickly back to Reuben. "Of course. Is something wrong?"

"Yes. The painting is missing," Reuben answered.

Viri raised a hand to her mouth. She gasped, "That's terrible."

Magnolia observed her not certain she believed her reaction. Something seemed off about the girl.

Reuben's walkie talkie beeped. "Malone, this is Chief Jackson. Over."

Reuben pulled the walkie talkie from his belt. He raised it to his mouth. Pushing the button on the side, he said, "Malone, here. Over."

"Malone, we talked to employment services. No maid matching that description. Over."

"Copy. Over."

Lowering the walkie talkie, Reuben looked over at Magnolia. "That's odd. Then who was the maid?"

Magnolia admitted it was strange. Obviously, the maid must have been in disguise, but who could she be?

Turning her attention to Viri Greene, Magnolia examined her from head to toe. Her eyes stopped at a scar on the young woman's arm. It was a squiggle between her wrist and elbow. It seemed familiar.

Raising her gaze to the young woman's face, Magnolia imagined Viri without glasses. She pictured her hair in different lengths and styles. Her gaze returned to Viri's arm.

Standing, Magnolia said, "Ophelia Hart."

CHAPTER 8

ILLUSIVE IDOL

Magnolia Ruby stepped farther away from Ophelia Hart. She could not believe she was facing the deceitful woman again. She recalled how Ophelia had lied to her at the Art Expo leading to her theft of the Sweet Freedom painting.

Reuben pulled his service weapon from his holster. He pointed it at the young woman.

Ophelia removed her glasses. She tossed them onto a table near the wall. Focusing only on the older woman, she smirked, "Well played, Magnolia."

Magnolia moved to stand behind Reuben. She did not want to give Ophelia a target to use to distract the police detective. "It's not a proud moment, Ophelia."

Reuben snapped, "Where's the painting?"

Sighing, Ophelia walked over to the bed. She glared at the police detective. "Take it easy, Detective. I don't know which is worse you accidentally shooting me or the painting."

Magnolia pursed her lips.

Reuben lowered the gun slightly.

Ophelia grabbed the side of the mattress. "Will you help me flip the mattress, Magnolia? It's much heavier with the painting strapped to it."

Magnolia looked to Reuben for permission. At his nod, she walked to the opposite side of the bed. She grabbed the mattress and helped lift it up.

The two women flipped the mattress over to reveal Rowdy Howdy secured with Velcro straps.

Magnolia returned to her original spot behind Reuben.

Reuben raised the gun again. "And where is Raphael Capone?"

"No idea," shrugged Ophelia holding her hands up.

Reuben motioned for her to turn around.

Ophelia obeyed without a word. She put her hands behind her back.

Reuben handed the gun to Magnolia. "If she moves, shoot her."

Ophelia tensed.

Magnolia took the Glock pistol. She aimed it at Ophelia keeping her finger off the trigger.

Using his hadcuffs, Reuben snapped them onto Ophelia's wrists. "Ophelia Hart, you are under arrest for theft. You have the right to…"

"Don't waste your breath, Detective. I know my rights. Magnolia can be your witness that I decline the recitation," Ophelia said.

Reuben pulled his walkie talkie out of his belt. He pushed the side button. "Chief, Malone. Over."

"Go ahead, Malone."

"I found the thief and the painting. Send guards to cabin…What cabin is this?"

Ophelia snorted, "It doesn't have a number because it is a converted closet."

Reuben scowled.

"Tell them to meet you at the B level elevator," Magnolia suggested.

Reuben spoke into the walkie talkie. "Send guards to the B level elevator. I'll meet you there. Over."

"On the way. Over."

Reuben led Ophelia out of the cabin.

Magnolia unstrapped the painting. She carried it carefully out of the room feeling victorious over Ophelia Hart. She enjoyed the satisfaction of getting the woman back for tricking her at the Art Expo. *Now, she won't be able to steal any more paintings.*

Frankie Lemmons headed to her apartment. She had stopped by the church, but Father Castillo had already gone home. She decided to go back in the morning. There were more questions to be answered.

Entering the apartment, Frankie's nose wrinkled at a strong chemical smell. Walking to the open bathroom door, she peeked inside.

Humming, Jolie knelt by the tub. She scrubbed it with a blue sponge. The rest of the room looked spotless.

Frankie had been Jolie's foster mother for only a week. It had already been quite an experience trying to adjust to another person in her life.

Leaning on the door frame, Frankie sighed, "Jolie, what are you doing?"

Jolie turned her head to look at her. She smiled brightly, "Hi, Frankie. I thought I would do some cleaning."

"Again? Girl, you clean more than any teenager I've ever known."

"I like to stay busy."

"Try watching T.V. or surfing the Internet like normal teens."

Lowering her head, Jolie's smile faded. Dropping the sponge in the tub, she mumbled, "That's what Mom always told me."

Wincing, Frankie mentally kicked herself. Her mouth tended to get her into trouble. She hated to have upset the girl with a reminder about her dead mother.

Jolie shrugged, "I guess it's built into me. I was always helping at the Knight manor. It's hard to break old habits."

"Well, my apartment has never been cleaner. Thanks."

Jolie's smile returned. "You're welcome. I'm almost finished. What do you want to do for dinner?"

Frankie tensed. She had meant to eat dinner at the diner though she had left before enjoying her burger. How could she have forgotten about feeding Jolie? Maybe she was not meant to be a foster mother.

Starting toward the kitchen, Frankie said, "I'll see what we have."

Jolie replied, "Not much. It's a little late to go to the store. We could order a pizza?"

Frankie turned back to her. "Now, you sound like a teenager. Let's get pizza." *Hang out with Jolie tonight. Finish the case tomorrow.*

Magnolia Ruby freshened up for her dinner with Weldon. She brushed her silver hair then put it into her usual bun. She thought about the two men in her life. She had enjoyed her lunch with Reuben. It had been refreshing to talk to someone who was not afraid to tell the truth. Spending time with Reuben was different than spending time with Weldon. She did not feel like she had to be on her guard with Reuben.

"Are you okay, Mom?"

Turning around, Magnolia smiled warmly, "I was just thinking, Gloria. How was your day?"

"Good. I slept in then went to the pool. It was fun."

"Sounds like a vacation to me. Did you get to talk to Jonas about that book yet?"

"No. He was extra busy today. Maybe tomorrow."

Magnolia secured her gold earrings into her earlobes. "Sounds like a plan."

Gloria sat on the edge of the tub. She stared at her for a moment. "Are you going out?"

"Weldon and I are having dinner."

Magnolia looked into the mirror at her adopted daughter.

Gloria wrinkled her nose. Her smile had changed into a frown.

Magnolia turned around to face her. "And what is that look, young lady?"

Lowering her head, Gloria shrugged, "I don't think he's right for you."

"Why?"

"It's not my place. You're an adult. You can date whoever you want."

Magnolia stepped over to her. She touched her chin then raised her head. "You're my daughter, Gloria. You're also an adult. I treasure your opinion."

"Thanks, Mom."

"Now, why do you think Weldon is not right for me?"

"It's a feeling I have. He keeps lying. I don't think you could ever fully trust him. I wouldn't want to date someone who acted like that. You need a nice man who is honest like Mr. Edward. He would never have treated you that way."

Magnolia sat next to her on the edge of the tub. Her heart wrenched at the reminder of her deceased husband. She had to admit their relationship, though not perfect had been an honest and loving one. "You're wise beyond your years, Gloria."

Gloria hugged her. "Thanks for not being mad at my opinion."

Magnolia returned the hug. She kissed her head. How many more moments would they share together once Gloria started her adult life?

"The child makes more sense than any of you."

Magnolia and Gloria turned toward the bathroom entrance.

Genevieve stood in the doorway.

"What?" Magnolia asked.

"You're too good for my nephew, Magnolia. Free yourself while you still have a chance."

Magnolia asked, "Did you give me a compliment?"

"I suppose…Now, get out of the bathroom before I befoul more than the air."

Magnolia and Gloria rushed out of the bathroom.

Genevieve closed the door.

Magnolia leaned over to Gloria. She whispered, "Maybe you should make dinner plans too."

Gloria giggled, "I did. Lydia and Mr. Ellison invited me to go to El Casa de Queso."

"The house of cheese? Sounds fun."

Gloria walked over to the couch. She picked up her hot pink purse. "They wanted to meet at the elevator."

Magnolia grabbed her own purse. She headed toward the door. "I'll walk with you."

As Gloria opened the door, Magnolia turned back to the bathroom door. "Do you need anything, Genevieve?"

"Just peace while I do my business," Genevieve snapped from inside the bathroom.

Magnolia and Gloria exchanged a smile. They headed into the hallway.

Magnolia shut the door. She turned to walk down the corridor to the elevator.

Doretta Brewster stomped out of a cabin mumbling to herself. Walking to a laundry cart against a wall in the hallway, she grumbled, "Stupid fool. Jewelry is ruined in the laundry."

Magnolia escorted Gloria around the cranky woman and the laundry cart. They headed toward the elevator.

Doretta shrieked.

Magnolia spun around at the sudden shrill sound. She placed a hand on her chest.

Doretta stood staring at the cart. Her hands covered her mouth.

Magnolia took a step forward then stopped. "Mrs. Brewster, what is it?"

Pointing at the cart, Doretta backed up against the opposite wall with her eyes closed.

Looking at Gloria, Magnolia said, "Stay here."

At Gloria's nod, Magnolia strolled toward the laundry cart hoping the woman was not overreacting to something trivial. It would annoy her if it were a spider or something.

Reaching the laundry cart, Magnolia leaned over to look inside. She gasped averting her gaze in horror. Taking a deep breath, she forced herself to look again. *Dear Lord, help me not to vomit.*

A body had been stuffed into the cart. Blood stained everything. There was no head on the body. Yet, Magnolia recognized the clothes which she had seen that morning when she was in the main dining room.

Pulling out her cell phone, Magnolia clicked on a new number in her contacts. She turned away from the cart not wanting to see the headless body anymore.

"Malone."

"Reuben, you need to get to my hallway."

"I thought you had dinner plans."

Closing her eyes, Magnolia swallowed the bile rising in her throat. Taking a deep breath, she mumbled, "I found Raphael Capone."

Ophelia Hart sat in her brig cell marveling at how it was not much worse than her closet cabin. It was a small room with a locked door to keep her from escaping. The walls were painted navy-blue. There was a bed with white sheets and a pillow as well as a blue blanket. No other furniture was in the cell. There was not even a bathroom. She had been told to knock when she needed to use the bathroom.

Ophelia stared at the blank wall. She could not believe her perfect plan had been destroyed. Her heart wrenched at how Magnolia had revealed her identity. If only she had kept her back to the detective duo throughout the questioning.

Now, Ophelia would go to prison for the painting theft. The police would probably locate her apartment. Then they would find the other six stolen paintings. *That will be seven counts of theft.*

Ophelia heard the lock on the door being unlocked. She turned her body to face the door.

Opening the door, Chief Jackson stepped right inside the brig. "Ms. Hart, I wanted to let you know about an update in the charges."

Ophelia reflected on how the theft charges could be updated. Had they found the other paintings this quickly? It seemed unlikely. "Oh? What's that?"

Chief Jackson said, "You're being charged with the theft and the murder."

Gasping, Ophelia rose to her feet. "Murder? Who?"

"Like you don't know."

"I don't know. I didn't kill anyone."

"Fine. Stick to your story, but you should know we have found his body."

"Who?"

Chief Jackson turned to leave the brig. He said, "The artist."

"Capone is dead?"

Leaving the cell, Chief Jackson closed the door with a curt nod.

Ophelia placed her hands over her face. She could not believe Raphael Capone was dead. Though the news would usually make her glad, she needed a way to prove her innocence. But who would believe her?

Dropping her hands from her face, Ophelia rushed to the closed door. She pounded her fists on it. Hearing the lock click, she stood back wringing her hands in front of her.

The door opened. Chief Jackson glared at her. "Well?"

"I need to make a phone call. Please."

Chief Jackson motioned for her to step into the hallway. "Calling a lawyer sounds like a good idea."

As he escorted her down the hallway, Ophelia walked eagerly to make her phone call. *It won't be to a lawyer. I need real help.*

Charlotte Knight stood outside of their suite waiting for Leo to put the keycard in the lock. She had enjoyed their romantic dinner at the elegant That's Amore Ristorante. The food was delicious, but the atmosphere was amazing.

Leo opened their suite door. He gestured for her to enter first.

"Aren't you going to carry me across the threshold?"

Leo groaned, "No way. I'm too full to do any heavy lifting."

Raising her eyebrows, Charlotte placed her hands on her hips. "Heavy?"

"That's not what I meant. You're not heavy."

Charlotte lightly slapped his arm. She walked into the suite kicking off the high heel shoes that pinched her feet.

"I ate too much," Leo groaned falling onto the bed.

"Well, you did devour six breadsticks with your Pasta Puttanesca."

Leo closed his eyes. "How are you not full? That serving of Chicken Marsala was huge."

Grabbing her flat shoes, Charlotte shrugged, "But I only had two breadsticks."

Leo sat up on the edge of the bed. "You could have had more."

"Only if I wanted to lose a hand…Look. If you're too full, we can go dancing tomorrow night."

Leo shook his head. "Not a chance. You're not getting out of keeping your part of the deal."

Charlotte sat down on the sofa. She rubbed her feet then put the black flats on them. "Okay. I'll freshen up then we can go. Just don't puke on the dance floor."

Leo lay back down with a groan. He covered his face with his hands. "Please. Don't say puke."

The suite phone rang. Charlotte reached over and grabbed the receiver. She held it to her ear. "Hello?"

"Charlie, you have to help me."

Charlotte frowned at the unfamiliar voice. "Who is this?"

"Viri Greene…well, Ophelia Hart. Please let me explain, Charlie."

Charlotte tilted her head at the name. She recalled how Mags told her about an art thief named Ophelia Hart. Could Viri be the woman who manipulated and deceived Mags so she could steal a painting from the Art Expo?

Not willing to listen to someone who had treated her friend like that, Charlotte said, "Ms. Greene…Ms. Hart…whatever your name is. I would appreciate if you wouldn't call me again."

"Please, Charlie. I stole the painting, but I did not kill Raphael Capone."

Charlotte tensed at the news. Had the jerk artist been killed? She could not blame anyone for murdering him based on how he had acted. However, it was not her business to get involved. She was on her honeymoon.

Charlotte turned toward the bed.

Leo sat up with a bewildered expression on his face. He mouthed, "What's up?"

Shaking her head, Charlotte said, "I don't know what you think I can do for you."

"Get Magnolia Ruby to talk to me. She's the only one who can prove I'm only a thief not a killer."

The call ended. Charlotte hung up the phone. She stared at it for a moment. Should she get involved? Mags would probably not like her helping Ophelia. Yet, she did not know if she could ignore Ophelia's plea for help. What if she was telling the truth?

"What's going on, Charlie?"

Charlotte stood from the couch. Though she was not sure if she believed Ophelia Hart, she decided she needed more information about the crimes before she could do anything. "I need to talk to Mags."

Changed into her pajamas, Magnolia Ruby hung her formal clothes back on the hanger. She hated that she had canceled dinner with Weldon. However, after seeing Raphael Capone's body, there was no way she could eat dinner. Her mind replayed through her conversation with Weldon. She had explained why she needed to cancel their dinner then listened as Weldon whined about how he had not spent any time with her today. Weary of his whining, she had promised to meet him for breakfast in the morning without the others. Finally appeased, Weldon ended the call.

Magnolia sat down on her bed. She did not like how possessive Weldon seemed to be growing. They were supposed to be renewing their friendship. Yet, he was acting like they were engaged or married. Maybe it was time to have a serious talk with him.

"I'll handle him, Magnolia."

Magnolia turned her head to regard Genevieve. "What do you mean?"

Genevieve picked up the cabin phone. She typed in a cabin number then waited.

Aware the other woman must be calling Weldon, Magnolia opened her mouth with a protest. She could not imagine what Genevieve would say to the man about her. "Genevieve…"

Scowling, Genevieve held up a stern finger. "Weldon, this is your aunt. I want to have dinner with you unless you have other plans…Good…Yes. I can manage at the main dining room. They have a roasted chicken my stomach can handle…Alright. I'll meet you there in about half an hour…Goodbye."

Genevieve hung up the phone. She walked over to the closet. Rummaging through it, she mumbled to herself. She appeared to have forgotten about Magnolia.

"Thank you. Why did you do that?" Magnolia asked.

"He's my nephew. Why wouldn't I want to have dinner with him?"

Genevieve grabbed an outfit. She headed toward the bathroom. Stopping at the doorway, she turned back toward Magnolia. "Just make sure you don't come to the main dining room…I don't want you messing up my time with my nephew."

Magnolia's smile grew at how the woman was trying to help her. "I'm not planning to go anywhere. I think I'll order room service." *I could use a peaceful evening after today's craziness.*

Charlotte Knight knocked on Mags' cabin door. She considered all Ophelia had said on the phone. She hoped to discover more details to help her decide whether to help the arrested woman.

Charlotte knocked again at no response.

"I told you I'd meet you in the dining room, you incompetent fool."

Charlotte took a step back at Genevieve's shout.

Opening the door, Genevieve paused. "Oh, Charlotte. I'm sorry. I was expecting…someone else."

"It's okay. Is Mags here?"

Genevieve stepped back. She gestured for her to enter the cabin. "Please come in. I would stay to chat, but I'm having dinner with…someone."

As Charlotte entered the cabin, Genevieve left shutting the door behind her.

Charlotte walked farther into the cabin. She pasted on a smile at the sight of Mags sitting on the bed in her pajamas. "Hey, Mags. Sorry to bother you."

Mags patted the end of the bed. "You could never bother me. I thought you were spending the evening with Leo."

"I was, but then I got a weird phone call…What happened today with the Rowdy Howdy painting and Raphael Capone?"

Charlotte sat down on the bed hoping she did not look too nervous.

Mags answered, "The painting was stolen and then recovered. Then Raphael's body was found. The criminal has been arrested."

"And it was Viri Greene who is really Ophelia Hart?"

"How would you know that?"

"Well, Leo and I had dinner. We went back to our suite to change before going dancing. I got a call from Ophelia begging me to talk to you. She said she's the thief, but she didn't kill anyone," Charlotte explained.

Mags stood then walked to the balcony door. Staring out at the ocean, she said, "She's manipulating you, Charlie. She probably started in the spa when she pretended to be a fan and got your autograph. She's a con artist with lots of practice."

Charlotte admitted to herself it could be true. However, it hurt to think her one fan was using her. Recalling Ophelia's desperation on the phone, she said, "That could be true, Mags, but it's possible she's telling the truth. What could hurt by hearing her out?"

Mags turned back to her. "Why is this so important to you?"

"I want the killer caught. If it's Ophelia, then great, but what if she isn't? We can't let a killer run free on a cruise ship."

Mag returned her attention to the ocean. Her shoulders slumped. She nodded, "Okay, Charlie. I'll make you a deal."

"Uh oh. I need to be careful with you dealmakers. That's how Leo got me to agree to go dancing with him. What is it?"

"I'll talk to Ophelia in the morning if you will go dancing with Leo tonight," Mags said turning back to face her.

"Deal. Do you want to go with us? You could invite Reuben."

Laughing, Mags shook her head. "Not a chance. With my luck, Weldon would see us and add to the chaos of this crazy day."

⚓

Gloria Fairbanks followed Lydia down the hallway to their cabin. She listened to the other girl talk non-stop about the menu at El Casa de Queso. There had been too many choices for them to pick so they ended up ordering a sampler platter with small portions of everything.

"The tacos were too messy. They should have had diapers on them," Lydia said.

Gloria giggled at the idea. She opened her mouth to answer. However, she changed her mind at movement down the hallway. Her smile grew.

Jonas pushed his cart toward them.

"I'll be back, Lydia," Gloria said hurrying toward the steward.

Lydia stopped at their cabin door. She waited for Gloria to return with the keycard.

Gloria stopped in front of the steward's cart. "Hi, Jonas."

Jonas kept his head down. He turned away from her. His hat was pulled down shielding some of his face. He studied the contents of his cart not looking at her. "Do you need something, ma'am?"

Gloria considered his odd response. Why was he calling her ma'am again? "I was wondering if you had time now to talk about the book."

"I don't have time to read, ma'am."

Gloria said, "But you just finished reading And Then There Were None. You said we were going to talk about it."

Jonas guided his cart around her. He snapped, "I have work to do. Leave me alone, kid."

As he pushed his cart down the hallway, Gloria stared after him. She did not understand what she had done to upset him. Why was he acting so strangely?

Lydia stuck out her tongue and blew a loud raspberry. "Grumpy man."

Nodding, Gloria walked toward their cabin. She shrugged, "We can all be like that at times. Maybe he had a rough day." *Maybe he found out about the dead man. That would upset anyone.*

CHAPTER 9

JUMBLED JUDGMENT

Frankie Lemmons walked into the Cornerstone Catholic Church. She scanned the sanctuary for Father Castillo. Not seeing the priest, she headed toward his office. She needed to get him on board for testifying against Jontray Scott.

Knocking, Frankie opened the office door. She peeked in nodding at the priest.

Father Castillo sat at his desk. Though he was on the phone, he motioned for her to enter and be seated.

Frankie sank into the same chair she had used yesterday. She waited as patiently as she could for the priest to finish his phone call. Pulling out her little black notebook, she prepared to take notes of their conversation.

Ending his call, Father Castillo said, "Detective Lemmons, what can I do for you?"

"You can help me put Jontray Scott in prison for killing Dillon."

Father Castillo leaned back in his chair. He folded his hands on his lap. "I can't help you."

Frankie took a deep breath trying to remain calm. She wanted to give him a chance to do the right thing. Maybe he was scared of what would happen if he testified.

Closing her notebook, Frankie asked, "Did Jontray Scott threaten you?"

"No. I'd talk to you even if he threatened me, but he didn't."

"Then why won't you testify against him?"

"Because it would be a lie. I didn't see him kill Dillon Pickler."

Frankie leaned forward not liking how he was being difficult. She snapped, "But you did. You were there when it happened."

"Look, Detective. All I saw was Jontray Scott kill Santiago. When he shot him, we all ran so he wouldn't kill us too. I never saw who killed Dillon. There were others shooting from both gangs. I'm sorry."

"You're lying."

Father Castillo held up a hand toward her. "I'm sorry you think that, Detective, but I'm telling you the truth. I didn't even know Dillon was dead until the next day on the news."

Frankie tried to figure out if he was telling the truth. It made sense that he did not see Dillon die. The gang members did scatter. All she saw was Jontray pointing the gun toward him. Maybe he wasn't the only one.

Frankie closed her notebook. She could tell she was getting nowhere with the priest. Standing, she headed for the door.

"Maybe you should talk to Jontray," Father Castillo said.

Frankie spun back toward him. "And what would that accomplish?"

"He's changed, Detective. Maybe he can tell you what happened that day."

Shaking her head, Frankie left the office. She did not want to hear Jontray explain why he killed Dillon. Her original plan of revenge flashed into her mind. Maybe it was time to get rid of Jontray like he did Santiago and Dillon.

As she headed to her car, Frankie mumbled to herself, "I think I will have a talk with Jontray Scott."

⚓

Magnolia Ruby took a bite of her toast. She had ordered a light breakfast since her stomach still lurched at the image of finding Raphael Capone's body. Her conversation with Weldon had been light and happy to her relief. She wanted to keep her mood lifted as much as possible.

"How was your evening, Nolia?"

Magnolia winced at the reminder of her horrible evening. She shrugged, "I ordered soup from room service, but I struggled to eat it after seeing that body. I went to bed shortly after."

"And what did Reuben do?" Weldon asked picking up his coffee cup.

Magnolia did not like being interrogated by the man. Did he really think she had cancelled dinner with him to spend time with

Reuben? "I don't know what Reuben did with his evening. That would be his business."

Weldon sipped his coffee. He continued eating as if he had not offended her with his question. Pulling a folded piece of paper out of his pocket, he said, "I thought we could go to Lois Barnhardt's Comedy Show at ten. Then we could have lunch at Southern Bliss. It has comfort food like fried chicken and meatloaf. I thought you would like it. After lunch, we could go to the pool. Then dinner at That's Amore Ristorante followed by a walk on the deck."

Magnolia set her toast on her plate. Her appetite faded at his planned itinerary. She did not like how he thought he could occupy her entire day. He had not even asked if she wanted to do any of those things. She planned to visit Ophelia at some point. She had promised Charlie she would.

Holding up a hand, Magnolia said, "I have plans for part of the day, Weldon."

Weldon set his paper on the table. "What plans?"

"That's my business."

"You're meeting him, aren't you?" Weldon grumbled.

Magnolia decided it was time to set things straight. She could not let Weldon continue to believe that their relationship was more than it was. Lifting her napkin off her lap and setting it on her plate, Magnolia said, "Weldon, we need to talk."

Staring at the table, Weldon waited without a word.

Magnolia took a deep breath. She said, "I agreed you and I could renew our friendship, but I never said we were renewing anything else. You're acting like a possessive boyfriend, but I'm not your girlfriend."

Weldon raised his head. He peered at her with sorrowful eyes. "I love you, Nolia."

"We can't be more than friends, Weldon. I don't feel that way about you."

"I thought you would give me another chance over time."

"I'm sorry if I gave you that impression. It's not going to happen. Please understand."

Standing, Weldon threw his napkin on the table. He marched away.

"Weldon!"

Ignoring her, Weldon stomped out of the main dining room. He did not even look back.

Magnolia rubbed a hand over her face. She believed she did the right thing. It was important to tell him the truth before things went any further. However, she hated to upset him so deeply. Her heart ached at his pain.

Dropping her hand, Magnolia tilted her head.

Norman Chalker sat a table next to hers. He scribbled in his notebook.

Magnolia hated how paranoid she could get. She had no proof Norman was doing anything but writing during breakfast. *How vain am I to think he must be writing about me.*

Averting her gaze, Magnolia scanned the rest of the dining room.

Reuben stood at the other end of the room. He talked to Chief Jackson at a table.

Rising, Magnolia walked over to talk to them. How could she convince them to let her talk to Ophelia Hart?

Seeing her, Reuben left the chief's table. He strolled over to her with a bright smile. "Good morning, Magnolia."

Magnolia blushed at how her name sounded when he said it. "Good morning, Reuben. Any news about the case?"

"It's out of my jurisdiction, remember?"

Magnolia waited because she could tell he was going to say more.

"But I did convince Chief Jackson to let me talk to our suspect," Reuben added.

"Good. I want to go with you."

"Why?"

"To satisy my curiosity."

Reuben stared at her as if trying to gauge what she wanted. "The chief won't allow that. You're a civilian."

Magnolia opened her mouth in protest.

Holding up a hand, Reuben said, "I could leave my phone on the table during my questioning if you promise not to talk and get me busted."

"Deal."

"Really?"

"I can be quiet if I want."

Reuben laughed. He forced himself back into a serious composure. "Sure, you can. I will call you in about twenty minutes."

Magnolia shouldered her purse then headed out of the dining room. She needed to get back to her cabin in time for the phone call. *I can't wait to hear what Ophelia Hart has to say for herself.*

⚓

Weldon Hitchcock stood behind a pillar in the main dining room. He had left after Nolia's breakup speech then returned to try to convince her to change her mind. However, as he entered the dining room, he spotted Nolia talking to Reuben Malone.

Weldon leaned around the pillar. He could not hear what the two adults were saying. However, it was evident they were enjoying each other's company by the smiles on their faces.

Nolia's face shone with excitement. She walked away from Reuben and headed out of the dining room.

Reuben stared after her for a moment before he headed back to the chief's table.

Weldon glared at the man. How had he let Reuben drift in and steal Nolia away from him? *I won't let her go easily.*

⚓

Magnolia Ruby sat on her bed waiting for Reuben's call. She liked how no one else would be around during the interrogation. Gloria and Lydia went to the pool again. Genevieve decided to try out the spa with Charlie. Leo and Ellison went to play some basketball. Lucretia was still off with her wealthy friends.

Her cell phone rang. Magnolia answered it quickly. She put it on speaker. She did not want to miss anything.

Reuben's voice spoke without addressing her. "Ms. Hart, I wanted to talk to you about what happened. I assume you've heard Raphael Capone's body has been discovered."

"Yes."

Magnolia tensed at the soft voice. It reminded her of when Ophelia talked to her at the Art Expo explaining her life was in danger. She struggled with the innocence of the voice. She had been deceived by her before.

"What did you do with his head?" Reuben asked.

"What?"

Magnolia leaned closer at Ophelia's strangled voice.

Reuben explained, "His body was found in a laundry cart with no head attached. Where is his head?"

A loud slap hit the table. Magnolia assumed Ophelia had hit it with her hand.

Ophelia gasped, "Are you kidding me? I'd never kill anyone especially by cutting off their head."

Magnolia closed her eyes. She listened to the panic in Ophelia's voice. *She sounds surprised and horrified, but she's quite the actress.*

"Did they tell you that you're being charged with the theft and the murder?" Reuben asked.

Sighing, Ophelia said, "I stole the painting. I stole several paintings, but I didn't kill him. When I last saw him, he was…"

Magnolia leaned forward. She picked up the cell phone straining to hear the rest of the sentence.

Ophelia grew silent.

Not thinking, Magnolia asked, "He was what?"

Silence. Magnolia placed a hand over her mouth. She mentally kicked herself for asking the question. *I promised not to talk.*

Getting louder, Ophelia said, "Is that Magnolia? Magnolia, please listen to me. I set the fire in the trashcan. I went into the exhibit room and told the security guard. He went to put out the fire. I took the painting and put it in my laundry cart. Capone came into the room. He started to yell at me thinking I was that maid. He came at me. I knew he would hurt me. The guard left his baton on a table. I hit Capone with it. He fell. His head was bleeding, but Capone was alive when I left the room."

110

Magnolia glared at the phone. Ophelia's story sounded like a fantasy she had cooked up to stay out of trouble. "Why should I believe you? I know how good your acting skills are, remember?"

"Please, Magnolia. You must help me. I didn't kill him. If there is anyone who can prove my innocence, it's you."

Ophelia's voice faded away.

Magnolia listened silently.

Clearing his throat, Reuben said, "Our time was up. The guard took her back to the brig."

"Okay. Thanks for letting me listen in."

Reuben chuckled, "And join in the questioning...I knew you couldn't stay quiet."

"Well, you didn't ask fast enough," Magnolia retorted with a giggle.

Ending the call, Magnolia set the cell phone back on her bed. She replayed what she had heard in her mind. Ophelia sounded sincere and desperate to be believed. Could she be telling the truth?

Magnolia did not know what to believe. She had been tricked by the sneaky woman in the past. Her suspicions grew at what to believe. She did not want to be deceived and humiliated again. *I can't let a brutal killer go free either.*

Walking toward the pool, Leo Knight held his wife's hand. He had enjoyed playing basketball with his father while Charlie bonded with Aunt Genevieve at the spa. Now, he was eager to spend time swimming with Charlie before lunch.

Slowing down, Charlie pulled her hand away from him.

Leo peered at her. He did not like the frown on her face. "What's wrong, Charlie?"

"Mags."

Leo turned his head in the direction she was looking.

Mags sat in a lounge chair. She focused on a pad of paper on her lap. Her hand grasped a pen. She looked like an artist drawing by the pool except her face was cemented in a deep frown.

Leo watched her for a moment. His cop mode activated telling him something was wrong with her. He headed toward the lounge chair with Charlie by his side.

Reaching their friend, Leo asked, "What's up, Mags?"

Mags' frown transformed into a weak smile. "Good morning. How are the newlyweds?"

"Good. Now, answer my husband's question. We can tell something is wrong," Charlie said.

Sighing, Mags said, "I'm trying to decide what to do about Ophelia Hart."

Charlie walked over to the lounge chair beside her friend. She sat on it sideways facing Mags.

Leo sat down beside her. He tensed at how the chair wobbled as if it was going to collapse or fall over. Steadying it, he exchanged an amused glance with his wife.

"Did you talk to her?" Charlie asked.

Mags nodded, "Reuben questioned her and I listened in…Well, I took over about halfway through."

"Of course, you did," chuckled Leo.

Charlie slapped him lightly on the arm. Returning her attention to Mags, she said, "And?"

Mags held her pad toward them.

Leo stared at a pro and con list scribbled on it. He could tell Mags had been working on it for a while.

"And I'm spending this beautiful day trying to figure out if I believe her or not," Mags answered.

Charlie muttered, "Looks like you're struggling with that decision."

Nodding, Mags set the pad of paper back on her lap.

Leo considered how he handled suspects when they claimed they were innocent. He clapped his hands together. "Okay. Let's say Ophelia is telling the truth. Who else would have a reason to kill Raphael Capone?"

"Elise Quincy. We saw her slap Raphael for not wanting her after their affair," Charlie answered.

Mags flipped to a fresh page. She jotted down notes of their discussion. "She did say her husband would take care of him."

"Which gives us another suspect. Dad and I saw Patton Quincy fight with Capone in the gym yesterday. He threatened to make him pay."

Mags wrote the new information on her paper. "Then there's Doretta Brewster. She threatened him after she saw his painting. She didn't like how the women were dressed showing too much."

"Do you think she would kill him over that?" asked Charlie looking skeptical.

"He also knocked Gloria down at the pool yesterday. Doretta chewed him out and threatened to have him arrested."

Charlie nodded, "Pop and I saw her bodyguard fighting with Capone at the miniature golf course too. Maybe she sent him to take care of him."

Leo said, "Wait. He knocked Gloria down? He's lucky I didn't know or I'd be a suspect."

Mags and Charlie shot him a startled glance.

Leo held up his hands. He did not like their solemn expressions. Could they really think he would kill someone even to protect Gloria? "I said I didn't know."

Charlie giggled. She leaned her head on his shoulder.

Leo muttered, "You two tease too much."

"You make it too easy. Any other suspects," Charlie replied.

Leo looked back and forth between the two women. He could not think of anyone else to add to the list. "I guess we have some investigating to do."

"We?" asked Mags.

Charlie said, "Sure. Leo and I can see what we can find out about our other suspects."

"What about me?" Mags asked gathering her things and placing them in a beach bag.

Leo replied, "You're going to talk to Ophelia face to face. You need to find out why she targeted Capone for her thefts. There's a story there."

Mags asked, "And what makes you think Chief Jackson will let me talk to her?"

Leo and Charlie exchanged an amused glance.

"Experience. You'll figure out a way," Leo smirked. *She always does.*

Entering the cruise ship casino, Magnolia Ruby searched the crowded area. Her eyes focused on Reuben standing near a blackjack table. She did not like to think of him as an addicted gambler. That kind of life could be dangerous and unpredictable. She could not see herself in a relationship with that kind of man.

Magnolia walked over to him. "Reuben."

Reuben turned to look at her with a warm smile. "Hello, Magnolia. What is a sophisticated Christian woman like you doing in a den of gambling?"

"Looking for you. I didn't know you gambled."

"I don't. I like to people watch. A casino is a great place to see interesting things."

Relieved, Magnolia said, "I could never be in a relationship with…not that we're in a relationship…I mean…"

Stepping closer to her, Reuben chuckled, "I like when you're flustered."

"I'm sure you do. It must be a nice change from your own flustering moments."

"Absolutely. Now, why were you looking for me?"

Magnolia covered her ears as several of the crowd whooped in victory. She motioned out of the casino. "Maybe we can talk somewhere quiet."

Reuben led the way to the exit. Outside, he walked over to the railing of the ship.

Magnolia joined him placing her hands on the railing. She stared out at the endless sea. Warm breeze caressed her face. Her nose wrinkled at the strong salty aroma. If she wasn't investigating a murder, it would be a romantic moment.

Magnolia said, "I need to talk to Ophelia."

Reuben leaned on the railing. "It's not my jurisdiction. Chief Jackson calls all the shots."

"Then I'll have to see if I can get him to let me talk to her."

"Why do you want to talk to her?"

Magnolia shrugged, "I want the whole story before I decide if I believe her or not."

Reuben placed his hand on hers.

Glancing down, Magnolia blushed at the sentimental gesture.

"I don't know if I can get the chief to let you talk to her, but I will definitely try," Reuben said in a soft voice.

Magnolia pulled her hand free then started to walk along the deck. "How would you describe Chief Jackson?"

"He's a stickler for the rules. He expects everyone to do things by the book. He treats everyone especially women with respect. He's a manly man," Reuben said walking beside her.

Stopping, Magnolia formed a plan in her mind. Her smile grew at the genius idea. "Then I have the perfect way to get in to see Ophelia, but first I need to stop by one of the shops."

⚓

Unable to reach Frankie with his cell phone, Leo Knight picked up the cabin phone to call his police precinct. Getting an outside line, he dialed his precinct's main number. Asking for Lemmons, he waited for his partner to answer.

"Bridges."

Leo recognized the voice. "Wait. London Bridges?"

"Who's this?"

"Leo Knight."

"Well, if it isn't my knight in shining armor. Aren't you on your honeymoon? Is your wife okay with you calling women when you're supposed to spend time with her?"

"Look, Bridges. I don't have time for your teasing. Where's Lemmons?"

Silence. Leo waited for more teasing. Could the two women be planning to gang up on him together? He braced himself for whatever they had concocted for him.

"She's out right now, Knight. Maybe I can help you with something. I transferred to your precinct," London explained.

Leo gritted his teeth. He did not like the idea of dealing with London and Frankie all the time at work. However, he needed to focus on the task at hand. "I need information about a couple of suspects."

"Suspects? I think your cases can wait until you get back, Knight."

"It's a case on the cruise ship."

Leo waited for her next punchline.

"What kind of case?" asked London.

"Murder."

"Whoa. You all like to catch killers on your vacations, don't you? Who do you want info on?"

Leo suppressed a snort at how much London sounded like Frankie. "I need anything you can find on a couple. Patton and Elise Quincy."

"The boxer?"

"Boxer?"

London snorted, "Geez, Knight. Watch some sports, will you? Patton Quincy is last year's New York Metro Golden Gloves winner in the heavyweight division. He retired shortly after the competition. I'll see what else I can find out about him and his wife. Anyone else?"

"Doretta Brewster. She's a rich woman, but that's all I know," Leo replied.

"Got it. I'll do some research. Call me back in an hour."

"Okay. If you see Lemmons, tell her I called."

"Why?"

Leo smirked, "Tell her I was checking up on her. It will rile her up for fun."

"Will do," London said as she ended the call.

Hanging up, Leo sat on the bed.

Charlie exited the bathroom. "How's Frankie?"

"I don't know. She wasn't in. I talked to London Bridges instead."

Charlie sat down on the bed beside him. "What's she doing there?"

"She transferred. She's going to research for us. I'll call her back in an hour."

Leo put his arm around her. He leaned toward her ear. "We have an hour to kill. We could…take a nap or a bubble bath. Do you know what you want to do?"

"Yes."

Leo kissed her on the neck.

Charlie pushed him away. She stood with a smile. "I'm going to track down Elise Quincy. Maybe we can have lunch and girl talk."

Leo groaned, "What am I supposed to do?"

Charlie opened the suite door. She turned back with a smirk. "I guess you can take a nap or a bubble bath. See you later."

Leo waved at her in dismissal. He lay back on the bed. *We can't even have a honeymoon without a murder.*

Entering the Imperial Sun Cuisine restaurant, Charlotte Knight examined the red and gold décor. The red walls had Chinese symbols etched in gold on them. Red lanterns hung above round tables with white tablecloths.

Charlotte spotted Elise Quincy sitting at a table. She thanked God for helping her track the woman down. It had been a miracle to locate her on the large cruise ship. However, she had found the woman flirting with a young man near the pool.

Charlotte had reminded Elise how they had met the day before in the dining room when Raphael treated her dreadfully. She had invited her to have lunch with her.

Elise had accepted. She had told her to meet at the Imperial Sun Cuisine restaurant in fifteen minutes.

Now, Elise waved her arm into the air.

Charlotte waved back. She walked over to the table and sat down.

Elise picked up her menu. "I think we should start with an appetizer of Chicken Pot Stickers. I love those things, but I can't eat all of them."

"Sounds good," Charlotte said.

"Excellent. Now, what else do I want? Tea Smoked Duck. Yum. Beef and Broccoli Stir Fry. Not in the mood. You can never go wrong with Sweet and Sour Chicken Stir Fry."

Charlotte admitted it all sounded good to her.

Elise set the menu down. She folded her hands on the table. "How about I order Tea Smoked Duck and you order Sweet and Sour Chicken Stir Fry? Then we can share each of them."

Charlotte agreed. She did not care about the food as much as the answers to her questions. She decided to let the woman have what she wanted. Maybe Elise would be more forthcoming. "That's a wonderful idea, Elise."

"For dessert, we can order the Chocolate Sesame Bites and Chinese Almond Cookies. Of course, we'll get fortune cookies."

Dazed by all the food the woman wanted, Charlotte waited for Elise to order the food from their server.

As the server left to get the food, Elise said, "I guess you heard about that artist. The one who jilted me?"

"Yes. Isn't it terrible? I was worried about how you were taking the news."

Elise picked up her glass of soda. She sipped it. Her nose wrinkled. "Me? Why would you be worried about me?"

"Well, he obviously meant something to you."

Elise examined her fingernails. "Not really."

Charlotte leaned on the table. "Oh? You seemed so upset when he did not want to…spend time with you anymore."

Elise flicked her gaze at her. She examined her for a moment. Her lips were pursed. She stared at Charlotte's hands. "I see you're married, Charlie. How long?"

"Less than a week. We're on our honeymoon," Charlotte answered.

"Ah. Newlyweds. It's a wonderful time. You'll find, Charlie, that marriage becomes dull and stale."

"Is that what your marriage is like?"

Elise used a hand to flip her blond hair back. "Look, honey. I married Patton because I wanted to be the wife of a prized fighter. I'm not ashamed of it. I like money and fame. Patton and I would rarely see each other during his training and boxing season. I found company in other men over the years. I lost count of the number of men who have entertained me."

Charlotte bit her lip. She could not believe the woman was so remorseless about her affairs. How could she do that to her husband?

Sighing, Elise added, "Men are like tissues, dear. You can always find an endless supply."

Charlotte nodded without a word. She did not trust herself to speak kindly to the woman.

"Then Patton decided to retire. He started being at home all the time. I couldn't get a spare moment by myself. If I left the house, he wanted to go with me. It was suffocating."

Charlotte took a sip of her water. She could not imagine not wanting Leo around.

Elise added, "Raphael was a welcome distraction. I hoped we could repeat our time of passion a few more times on this cruise, but he dumped me after one time. I'm the one who is supposed to dump him when I'm finished with him."

Charlotte gritted her teeth. Her stomach twisted in disgust at Elise's shallowness. She did not know how much more she could listen to. "That would give you a motive to kill him."

"What?"

"Do you have an alibi for the time between the fire and the discovery of the body?" Charlotte asked.

Leaning forward, Elise hissed, "I don't have to tell you anything."

Charlotte shrugged. She leaned back in her chair. Reaching into her purse, she pulled out her cell phone. "I guess you can talk to my police detective husband. I'm sure he will want to question you next."

Elise slapped a hand on the table. She snapped, "Fine. I was in the bar looking for a rebound man for my next affair…Besides, if I wanted to kill Raphael Capone, I would have cut off something other than his head. Now, if you'll excuse me, I have an appointment."

Charlotte opened her mouth to protest. She thought about the huge amount of food Elise had ordered. How could she eat all of it?

Not waiting for an answer, Elise stormed out of the restaurant.

Charlotte clicked around on her cell phone. She tapped on Leo's name. She had a lot of information to tell him.

"I'm sorry, but Leo Knight is taking a nap because his wife abandoned him to have lunch with a suspect. You can try leaving a message, but he probably won't respond."

Charlotte interrupted, "Well, then I guess he doesn't want to have Chinese food with his wife. Maybe she will find a handsome man who does."

Silence. Charlotte waited for her husband to react to her invitation.

"Ignore that message. Some imposter made it…I'd love to have lunch with you."

"Then come to Imperial Sun Cuisine. I would hurry because our meal will be out shortly."

"You already ordered?"

Sighing, Charlotte replied, "It's a long story. I would love to tell it to you if you would get down here."

"Well, I called London and found out some interesting information. We can swap stories. I'm on my way."

Ending the call, Charlotte placed her cell phone back into her purse thinking about Elise. *She had no love for Raphael. A woman scorned could make a vicious killer.*

CHAPTER 10

KEEN KEEPSAKE

Following Reuben, Magnolia Ruby carried a red tote bag into the security area of the ship. She hoped she would be able to get in to talk to Ophelia.

A security guard sitting at the desk looked up at their approach.

Reuben waved at the guard. "Hey, Marty. This is Magnolia Ruby."

"Detective. Mrs. Ruby. What can I do for you?" Marty asked with a smile.

Reuben shrugged, "Mrs. Ruby would like to visit Ms. Hart."

"Not a chance."

Magnolia turned toward the voice. She forced her smile to remain on her face.

Chief Jackson stepped out of a side office. "I'm sorry, Mrs. Ruby, but it's against regulations."

Magnolia clutched the red tote bag closer. She pasted on a stern frown. "Is it against regulations for her to be treated respectfully as a woman?"

Chief Jackson scowled, "What do you mean?"

Magnolia stepped forward. She opened the tote bag. Motioning, she waited for his reaction to the feminine products she had bought at the shop.

Leaning forward, Chief Jackson looked into the bag. His face flushed red. Turning away, he motioned toward a door. "Marty, take the bag to her."

Closing the bag, Magnolia smiled sweetly, "Thank you, Chief. You are a true gentleman."

Chief Jackson marched into his office. He closed the door with a slam.

Magnolia turned her attention to Marty. She lowered her voice. "I'm sure you don't want to be around a couple of women with feminine products, Marty."

"Uh...not really, ma'am."

Reuben held out his hand. "Give me the key and I'll take her, Marty. It will only take a few minutes."

Marty opened a drawer. Pulling out a ring of keys, he handed it to Reuben. "Thanks, Detective."

Reuben and Magnolia headed down the hall to the brig cell.

Leaning toward her, Reuben muttered, "How did you know that would work?"

Magnolia shrugged, "I've never met a manly man who wasn't embarrassed by the natural processes of a lady."

Reuben chuckled. He unlocked the brig door. Opening it, he said, "You only have a few minutes so make them count."

Magnolia entered the cell.

Ophelia sat on a bed in an otherwise empty room. She looked up at the motion at the doorway. "Magnolia?"

Magnolia set the tote bag at her feet. "If you want my help, you better start talking."

Nodding, Ophelia placed her hands on her lap. She mumbled, "What do you want to know?"

"Everything."

Frankie Lemmons parked her car on the street running along the basketball court where Dillon had died. Opening her door, she grabbed the bag of food and her soda. She climbed out of the car and walked into the park. Her eyes flicked at every sign of movement. There were no threats, only people enjoying the park. *Spring is in the air.*

A chilly breeze slammed into her as if to contradict the statement. Frankie pulled her jacket closer. Walking to the basketball court, she found a group of young men playing basketball. She did not recognize any of them.

Frankie climbed onto the bleachers. She set her bag of food beside her. Reaching in, she pulled out a box of chicken nuggets and a container of ranch. Taking a bite, her mouth filled with a familiar taste she had not eaten in years.

Dillon and Frankie had enjoyed ranch sauce with their chicken nuggets every time they ate them. When he died, she had switched to every type of sauce to stay away from ranch. She could not imagine chicken nuggets and ranch without her best friend. Even as an adult, she found ranch left a sorrowful taste in her mouth.

Frankie took another bite. Today was different. She had chosen to get the familiar food to honor Dillon. He was the reason she would be risking her job and her life.

Laughter echoed through the sky. Frankie glanced over at the young men. Her heart ached at their basketball game across the court. She closed her eyes. *Don't worry, Dill Pickle. I'm going to find you justice tonight.*

⚓

Ophelia Hart scooted over on the bed. She patted it for Magnolia to join her. She winced at the conflict on the older woman's face.

Magnolia walked over to the bed and sat down. "We don't have much time. Start at the beginning."

Ophelia recalled how much had happened in her life since she had first heard about Raphael Capone. Taking a deep breath, she shared her story for the first time.

"I grew up in Chicago with my parents. My father was a lawyer with barely any time for us. My mother was an artist. She loved to create paintings. Her masterpiece was a painting she called Peace in the Storm. It showed a nest of baby birds perched on a rock in the middle of a storm. The mother bird shields her babies with her body. It was beautiful."

"What does this have to do with Raphael Capone?" Magnolia asked.

Ophelia wrung her hands. Her leg bounced. She stared at her lap. "My mother, Viridian Greene, had an affair with a handsome man who visited the local museum where she liked to take art classes. His name was Ralph. He gave her time and attention when my father did not. He was charming. After a short affair, my mother found Peace in the Storm missing. Ralph had stolen her masterpiece."

Magnolia rubbed a hand through her hair. Sighing, she said, "Ralph is Raphael."

Magnolia Ruby considered what she had already heard. She wanted to focus on the facts not on the feelings she was experiencing from Ophelia's story. Her heart softened at how Viridian had been deceived. However, she did not want Ophelia to con her with a sweet story to get her to help her deceive others. "Ralph is Raphael."

Ophelia said, "My father found out about the affair. He divorced my mother and left us both. I never saw him again."

"I'm sorry," mumbled Magnolia.

"Thanks. A few months later, Peace in the Storm appeared in a magazine. It was in an exhibit at a New York City Museum. It had won an amateur art competition. By then, Ralph had become Raphael Capone. My mother tried to tell the police and the museum that it was her painting, but she had no proof. Her life's work had been stolen and there was nothing she could do about it."

Magnolia's heart wrenched at what the real Viri Greene had experienced. She could imagine how much it would hurt if someone stole her artwork. Each piece was special.

"My mother became depressed. She could barely get out of bed. One day, I came home to find her dead. She had overdosed on sleeping pills."

Ophelia grew quiet. She wiped a tear from her face.

Magnolia reached out and took one of her hands. She patted it with her other hand. "I'm sorry, Ophelia. That must have been horrible."

Ophelia nodded without a word. She averted her gaze to the other side of the room.

Magnolia took a deep breath. Her mind filled with why Ophelia had turned to a life of crime. She could not condone her actions, but she understood her reasons. "So, you were getting revenge on Raphael Capone."

Ophelia pulled her hand away. She turned to face her more fully. "By stealing his paintings not by killing him. I stole my mother's painting first. Then I started researching to find his other works. Rowdy Howdy was going to be the last one. Now, it really is the last."

Standing, Magnolia walked over to the open door. Her gaze met Reuben's eyes. She could see the same sorrow and uncertainty. Turning back to Ophelia, she asked, "Why should I believe you didn't kill him?"

Ophelia placed around her own stomach hugging herself. "You shouldn't, but I still pray you will help me."

Charlotte Knight watched Leo devour the Chinese food. She had told him about her conversation with Elise while he ate. She could tell he was as shocked and disgusted by her flippancy as she had been.

Waiting for him to finish his meal, Charlotte picked up a fortune cookie. She prepared to break it then stopped at Leo's scrutiny. Smirking, she said, "You know these are fun, but not real, right?"

"Duh. I still like to hear them."

Charlotte opened the fortune cookie. She slowly looked at the folded paper making her husband wait for the fortune.

Leo continued to eat. He shook his head. "I think they expire if you take too long to read them."

Charlotte giggled. She unfolded the paper. "Be careful who you trust. Salt and sugar look the same."

"Wow. We need that on a T-shirt for everyone in our detective club."

Charlotte nodded. She dropped the paper on her plate. Pointing to the other one, she said, "Your turn."

"I'm still eating," Leo shrugged.

Picking up the fortune cookie, Charlotte asked, "Is it void if someone else opens it for you?"

"Not as far as I'm concerned."

Charlotte broke the cookie. She started to eat the pieces.

Leo held up a hand. "It will hurt our marriage if you eat my cookie."

Charlotte dropped the pieces on his plate. She opened the paper. "Now is the time to pursue a new love interest…Sorry. I think that's Elise's cookie."

Leo laughed. He took the paper and tore it into tiny pieces. "She can have it. I have my only love right here. No one else to pursue."

Charlotte reached across the table. She took his hand into hers. Squeezing it tenderly, she said, "Ditto. Now, tell me what London found out."

Leo set his fork down on the table.

Charlotte smiled at how he still could not use chopsticks.

Wiping his mouth with a napkin, Leo said, "As you know, Patton is a retired boxer and Elise is the shopaholic wife with a straying eye for anything male."

"Which reminds me. You're not allowed to be alone with her at any time."

Leo snorted, "Trust me. There's no interest in her at all."

"Good. Go on."

"Patton has been arrested seven times for assault. Each charge was dropped. London figures he pays off the victims."

Charlotte said, "That leaves Patton as a suspect. I assume he is strong enough to…you know."

"Definitely. I'll question him when we're finished here."

"What about Doretta Brewster?"

Leo replied, "She's an heiress with millions of dollars. She has no known criminal history. London dug deeper and found that Doretta has paid the bail for her son, James Brewster, several times. She sent me a picture of him."

Leo took his hand back. He reached into his pocket for his cell phone. Tapping around on it, he then handed the phone to her.

Charlotte looked at the picture. "Isn't that her bodyguard? I remember him when I played mini golf with Pop. He was having that fight with Raphael."

"Why would her son be pretending to be her bodyguard?"

"It's something to investigate. What was his charges?"

Leo pocketed his phone. "Aggravated assault, domestic violence, and drunk or disorderly."

"So, he could kill Raphael," Charlotte said.

"It's worth checking out, but I still think it's going to be Patton. He has a violent temper. I'm going to track him down now."

Charlotte took a sip of her water. Her mind raced with what she could do to help the investigation.

Observing her, Leo asked, "And what are you going to do?"

"Take a nap or a bubble bath."

Leo said, "Sure. Mags is going to relax and stay out of the case too."

Charlotte smiled sweetly at him without a word.

Sighing, Leo shook his head. "Why do I bother? Be careful when you question Doretta and her bodyguard."

Standing, Charlotte shouldered her purse. She smirked, "Of course, darling. Pay the bill, would you?"

Magnolia Ruby strolled down the hallway. Her mind filled with excuses of why she needed access to Ophelia's cabin. She hoped Chief Jackson would not find out. She had left Reuben to check on the painting. Rowdy Howdy had been returned to its crate and locked in a cargo hold with other valuable items. *Why didn't they do that in the first place? It would have saved us a lot of trouble.*

Seeing Jonas up ahead with his cart, Magnolia's smile grew at a plan forming in her mind. She waved at him. "Hi, Jonas."

The steward froze. He lowered his head. His hat covered most of his face. "Yes, ma'am?"

"I need to get into my friend's cabin, but she forgot to give me her keycard. Could you let me in?"

Jonas reached for his master keycard. "Which one?"

Magnolia gaped at him. She had not expected him to agree so easily. Thankful for her good luck, she led the way around the corner then pointed at the correct door.

Sliding the keycard into the lock, Jonas pushed the door open for her.

Magnolia put her hand on the door. She thanked the steward.

Jonas kept his head lowered. He walked back to his cart.

Watching him, Magnolia bit her lip. She did not like how standoffish he seemed to be today. Something about him seemed different yet familiar. Shaking away her suspicions, she muttered, "One case at a time."

Entering the cabin, Magnolia halted. "Reuben, what are you doing here?"

Reuben sat in a chair near the wall. "Waiting for you. What took you so long?"

"Funny."

Standing, Reuben said, "I figured you would want to look for clues here after your conversation with Ophelia."

"Did you find anything?"

"No. I just got here. I heard you in the hallway and thought I would have some fun with you."

Smiling at his silliness, Magnolia began her observations of the small cabin. She spotted Ophelia's suitcase. Walking over to it, she lifted it off the floor.

"Allow me, ma'am."

Magnolia surrendered the suitcase to Reuben. She sat on the bed.

Reuben placed the suitcase on the bed. He opened it.

The maid braids lay on top. A variety of clothes were folded underneath. Digging into the pile, Magnolia found a white feathered boa. There could be several disguises made from the clothes.

At the bottom of the suitcase, there was a large purple scrapbook. Magnolia picked it up. Placing it on her lap, she opened it.

"Baby Ophelia pictures?" snorted Reuben.

Magnolia looked at the scrapbook's contents. "No. Articles about Raphael Capone."

Turning each page, Magnolia scanned the articles. She stopped at a page with actual photos. "Here's pictures of the paintings she stole from him."

Reuben moved the suitcase. He sat next to her on the bed.

Magnolia adjusted the scrapbook so they both could see. She stared each picture.

The first painting showed a woman in a white raincoat holding a red umbrella above her head. A caption had been written under the picture: *Alice. Recaptured on November 21, 2010.*

The second painting showed a lighthouse on the shore overlooking a stormy sea. The caption read: *A Light in the Darkness. Recaptured on March 3, 2012.*

Turning the page, Magnolia cringed at the next picture. She gritted her teeth.

The third painting showed a butchered man's corpse. The caption read: *Dark Reality. Recaptured on September 12, 2013.*

Reuben said, "I would call that one gross."

The fourth painting showed wildflowers with butterflies flitting around. The caption read: *Field of Tranquility. Recaptured on June 10, 2014.*

Magnolia looked across the page. She could see two more pictures.

The fifth painting showed dinosaurs running from an active volcano. The caption read: *End of an Age. Recaptured on January 24.*

"No year," Reuben mumbled.

"It must have been last year's Art Expo because look."

The last painting showed slaves rejoicing as they went to freedom.

Magnolia said, "That's Sweet Freedom."

"The one she stole from us," Reuben said ominously.

Magnolia turned the pages back and forth looking at each of the paintings again.

Reuben stood up and continued to search the small cabin.

Magnolia reexamined each of the paintings. She found herself puzzled by the theme of the pieces of artwork. *A woman with an umbrella, a lighthouse on a stormy sea, a corpse, wildflowers with butterflies, dinosaurs near a volcano, slaves going to freedom, and salon girls straddling cowboys.*

"Notice something?" Reuben asked from the bathroom door.

Magnolia patted the scrapbook. "They're all so different. Most artists stick to a theme."

"Like your landscapes."

"Right."

Reuben returned to the bed. He took the scrapbook. Turning the pages, he examined the pictures again. "It's like they're painted by different people."

Magnolia recalled what had happened to Ophelia's mother. "That's because they are."

"Think so?"

Magnolia nodded, "Yes. That's why Ophelia wrote recaptured. If she stole his work, then she would probably have written captured. I think Raphael stole these paintings from different people probably women."

Reuben rubbed a hand over his face. "If that's true, we have a lot more suspects. Any one of these artists could have found out Raphael was here like Ophelia did and got a ticket for the cruise."

Magnolia realized he was right. "There's no way to find out who they are either because we don't know who the original artists are. I doubt even Ophelia knows."

Magnolia took the scrapbook from Reuben. She closed it with a sigh. "Do you think I could borrow this?"

"Sure. You're Ophelia's friend after all."

Magnolia wanted to refute his words. However, she was starting to believe Ophelia was telling the truth. *I won't trust her fully yet. This could still be a trick to get away with murder.*

Charlotte Knight strolled around the pool looking for Doretta. She assumed the older woman enjoyed sitting near the pool since she had been spotted by their group there two days in a row. Her hunch had turned out to be on spot.

Doretta sat in a blue lounge chair. She read her Bible while her bodyguard sat in a nearby chair.

Charlotte walked toward her. "Hello, Mrs. Brewster. May I join you?"

Doretta looked up at her. She used a hand to shield her eyes from the sun. "And you are?"

"My name is Charlotte Knight. I heard about how you found that body. You poor thing. Are you okay?"

Closing her Bible, Doretta set it on her lap. She gestured at the chair next to her. "Yes, Charlotte. Please join me."

Charlotte sat down thanking her.

Doretta said, "It was horrible to find him in that condition. However, I am not surprised he was murdered. Sin is never without consequences."

"Of course. I understand you did not like his painting. I found it quite vulgar," Charlotte replied.

"True. It was degrading to women. He should have been ashamed, and I told him so."

Charlotte sat up straighter. "Good for you. Someone needed to stand up for the decency for women."

Doretta smiled warmly with a nod.

Glancing over at the bodyguard, Charlotte raised a hand to her heart. "Is he with you? Or are we being stalked?"

Doretta turned to look at him. She laughed, "He's my bodyguard. Jimmy Caplin."

Charlotte examined the man. He could be Doretta's son. He looked like the picture London had sent. However, his name was not the same. Could he have changed it after his issues with the law?

Charlotte looked at Doretta. It was time to end the niceties and intensify the conversation. "Had you or your son ever met Mr. Capone before the cruise?"

Doretta's smile faded into a frown. "My son?"

Charlotte glanced over at the bodyguard then returned her attention to Doretta. She raised her eyebrows.

Doretta snapped, "I don't think we have anything more to say, Mrs. Knight."

Charlotte smiled sweetly at the mention of her married name. Maybe she needed to hint about her husband's occupation. People tended to try to avoid talking to the police. "My police detective husband was curious, but I thought you might rather talk to another woman."

Fanning herself with her hand, Doretta said, "It is hot out here and I am parched. Will you accompany me inside to the bar? I don't drink, but we can get something other than liquor."

Agreeing, Charlotte stood then waited for the older woman to be ready. The bodyguard helped Doretta to her feet. He took her Bible and towel. Leaning down to put them in her straw bag, his sunglasses slipped from his face.

Charlotte stared at his face. Without the sunglasses, she could get a good glimpse of him. *I can't believe it.*

CHAPTER 11

LOADED LABORS

Leo Knight walked into the gym looking for his target. He had a hunch Patton would be back in the gym keeping in shape. In his experience, athletes continued to train even if they were retired. It was a hard habit to give up.

Patton stood near the back where there was a boxing ring and a few hanging punching bags. He slammed his gloved fist into one of the bags.

Leo watched him for a moment recalling his violent temper. Maybe he should have brought back-up. However, he had dealt with tough suspects in the past.

Shaking away his doubts, Leo strutted over to the boxing area. He picked up a pair of boxing gloves from a rack. Putting them on, he stood in front of Patton's punching bag.

Glaring at him, Patton grunted, "There are other bags ready to use."

"I'm looking for a sparring partner," Leo said.

Patton moved around the bag. He looked at him. "I think you need someone else, man."

Leo placed his gloved hands on his hips. "Oh. So, you can't handle me? Okay."

Patton slammed a fist into the punching bag. "I can more than handle you, small fry."

"Let's see."

Patton marched over to the boxing ring. Climbing in easily, he stood in the middle. He gestured for Leo to join him.

Leo glanced around the gym. He was glad no one he knew was there. They would have a fit at his plan to get information from the muscular suspect. Climbing into the boxing ring, he faced Patton. "Ready when you are, big boy."

Patton hit his gloved fists together. He began to move quickly side to side. His footwork showed he was a professional.

Moving around, Leo looked for an opening to strike.

Patton slammed a fist toward him.

Leo dodged to the side. He swung his right glove to hit Patton on the side. His fist made contact.

Chuckling, Patton bounced backwards. "That's as hard as you can hit? It's more of a tickle."

Leo ignored his taunts. He needed to remain focused.

Patton danced around using his fancy footwork. He advanced a fist toward him.

Leo blocked the blow with his own glove. He staggered back at the force of the punch.

Patton said, "That's how you handle an opponent."

"Like you handled Raphael Capone?"

Pointing a gloved hand at him, Patton hissed, "He slept with my wife. He deserved that punch."

Leo circled around looking for another opening. "I'm talking about his death."

Halting, Patton snarled, "I didn't kill that punk."

"Prove it. Do you have an alibi?"

Waving his gloved hand at him, Patton turned toward the ropes of the ring. "I don't have to answer you. You can't make me."

Leo rushed forward. He punched him in the back.

As Patton spun around, Leo hit him in the face as hard as he could.

Patton fell to the floor. He shook his head dazed. Touching his face with his gloved hand, he blinked his eyes several times.

Leo snapped, "If you can't prove you didn't kill him, then I'm going to ship security. Chief Jackson will be interested to know you hit and threatened Raphael before he disappeared."

Patton struggled to get up. He fell back to the floor with a thud.

Leo could not believe he had hurt the boxer that much. Maybe his police training had helped him more than he thought.

Patton muttered, "I was here working out. Rob the attendant can vouch for me. He came back here to listen to boxing stories."

"I'll check it out," Leo said turning to get out of the boxing ring.

"Hey, small fry."

Leo turned back with his gloved hands raised in defense. He relaxed at no threat.

Patton still sat on the floor. "That was quite a punch."

Leo climbed out of the ring. Taking his gloves off, he halted at a chuckle.

"Forget D'Angelo."

Leo turned at the voice.

Ellison stood near the edge of the boxing area. "I'd put my money on my son to take that big boy."

Leo walked over to him. "What are you doing here, Dad?"

"Charlie sent me. She thought you might need some back-up. I can honestly tell her you didn't need me at all."

Leo set the gloves back on the rack. He muttered, "Let's keep my methods to myself."

"Okay. But how will you explain your hand?"

Looking down, Leo winced at his swollen hand. He knew it would be bruised. He hoped it was not broken. Glancing back at the ring, he saw Patton still struggling to his feet. "I guess the truth is always best." *She might even be proud of me for defeating that big boy.*

⚓

Charlotte Knight sat at a table in the indoor bar. She waited for Doretta to talk. She focused on what she had discovered about the bodyguard. How could it be possible?

A young woman walked over to the table. "Welcome. My name is Sasha. What can I get you?"

Doretta said, "Something without alcohol. Do you have anything that fits that category?"

Charlotte pursed her lips at the woman's rudeness.

Sasha's smile remained in place. She opened the drink menu. Pointing to one of the pages, she said, "These are all non-alcoholic."

Charlotte studied her own menu deciding on a drink. She waited for the other woman to order hers first.

Doretta said, "I'll have a non-alcoholic Bahama Mama, but hold the grapefruit juice. Most disgusting juice in the world."

Sasha wrote the order on her pad. She looked at Charlotte. "And you, ma'am?"

"I'll have a Fuzzless Navel."

"As is?" Sasha asked.

"Yes. I love the idea of peach nectar and orange juice."

As Sasha walked over to the counter to get the drinks, Doretta turned toward Charlotte. "Now, what do you want to know?"

Charlotte's mind whirled with several questions. She tried to figure out what she wanted to know first. "Is he Raphael's son?"

Doretta jerked back at the question. She placed a hand on her heart. "Why would you ask that?"

"He looks like him."

Doretta turned her head to regard him. She motioned for him to sit down at the table. "I am not a tramp, Charlotte."

Charlotte opened her mouth to assert she had never thought that.

Doretta held up her hand. "However, I did have an affair twenty years ago. I was in my early forties. My husband, James, was a nice man, but he was often in other countries for his business. I met a man. His name was Ralph Caplin. He was handsome and charming. We had…our time together. Then he was gone…It wasn't until a few days later that I found out he had stolen my bank account information. I lost several thousand dollars before the bank stopped all the withdrawals. The police could not find him though they tried admirably."

Sasha returned with their drinks. She set them down then walked away.

Doretta added, "A few months later, I found out I was pregnant. James and I had never been able to have children. He was sterile. I was going to tell him about the affair. However, he claimed the pregnancy was a miracle. I never told him the truth. He was a wonderful father."

Charlotte glanced over at the bodyguard.

Jimmy silently bobbed his head in agreement.

Doretta said, "It wasn't until I saw a picture of Raphael Capone in a magazine that I realized why the police had never been able to find him. I read about this cruise, so I booked us passage."

"So, you could confront him?" asked Charlotte.

Doretta took a sip of her drink. Her nose wrinkled. "Yes, but he didn't even recognize me. I insulted his rudeness and his heinous work because I didn't want people to know what he really did to me."

"Did you encounter him anymore?"

"No. Not until I was looking for my jewelry and pulled back that sheet," Doretta said with a shudder.

Taking a sip from her drink, Charlotte reflected on the explanation. Her mind flicked to what she saw on the miniature golf course. Looking at Jimmy, she asked, "What about you?"

Shaking her head, Doretta said, "No, he didn't."

Jimmy cleared his throat. He focused on his mother. "Actually, I did."

Doretta raised her hand to her mouth. "Please tell me you didn't kill him."

Jimmy scowled, "How can you even think that?"

"Well, the cart was outside your cabin."

"That doesn't mean I killed him," Jimmy snapped.

Charlotte remained silent. She looked back and forth between the two adults. She had learned over the years to listen without participating to get the best clues.

Doretta hissed, "Then what?"

Jimmy leaned back in his chair. "I argued with him on the golf course. I told him my name. He shoved me. I thought I could live with not confronting him further, but I couldn't…I went to the exhibit room to talk to him. I wanted to confront him about being my father. He wasn't there. I walked the deck hoping to see him. He was nowhere. I headed back to my cabin. He was in the hallway. I…"

Jimmy grew silent.

Doretta leaned forward. She reached a hand to grab her son's arm. "You what? What did you do, James?"

"I told him who you were and who I was. He laughed in my face. He said he wasn't my father. He said you…you must have been sleeping with other men and I was one of theirs. I hit him. He fell to the floor. I went into my cabin. That's the last I saw of him."

Charlotte finished her drink. She pulled out money and set it on the table. "Thanks for talking with me."

Doretta pushed the money back to her. "My treat, Charlotte."

"Thanks."

Charlotte shouldered her purse. She stood then headed toward the exit.

"Charlotte?"

Charlotte turned back.

Doretta wrung her hands on her lap. She stuttered, "I don't suppose...you would be willing to...keep our conversation private."

Charlotte said, "What conversation?" *I'm only going to tell the ones on the case.*

Magnolia Ruby carried the scrapbook into the main dining room. With Reuben's help, she had located Shirley Kimble. She spotted the woman sitting at a table with her husband eating an early dinner.

Magnolia recalled how Shirley chattered on about art on their first night. Maybe she would be able to help her identify the jilted artists.

Magnolia walked over to their table. "Hello, Mr. and Mrs. Kimble."

Shirley smiled brightly, "Hello, Mrs. Ruby. Please join me. Nelson is getting ready to hit the golf course one more time before it gets dark. I will need some company."

Thanking her, Magnolia sat down in an empty chair. She set the scrapbook on the table.

A server walked over to take her order.

Certain she would have dinner with Gloria later, Magnolia only ordered a glass of sweet iced tea.

Standing, Nelson left without saying anything.

Shirley asked, "Now, what can I do for you, Mrs. Ruby?"

"Please call me Magnolia. May I call you Shirley?"

"Of course."

Magnolia motioned to the scrapbook. She pushed it toward her. "I have a scrapbook of artwork I would like you to look at."

Shirley reached for the scrapbook. "Are these some of your masterpieces?"

"No. Raphael Capone."

Shirley's smile faded. She opened the scrapbook. Turning the pages, she did not stay on any of them for more than a few seconds. She closed the scrapbook then pushed it back to her. "He was talented."

Magnolia pushed it back to her. "I was hoping you could look at them more closely and tell me if you have ever seen any works by other artists that use the same theme, techniques, or whatever."

Shirley mumbled, "I'm not sure I can be much help for you, Magnolia. I don't know much about art."

Tilting her head, Magnolia stared at the woman. Folding her hands on the table, she said, "Shirley, I believe you told me art is your hobby on our first night. You must know some things."

Shirley took a sip of her water. She set the glass on the table. "I let my mouth run away with itself. I'm no art expert. Sorry."

Magnolia pursed her lips. She recalled Shirley's change in demeanor when she mentioned the artwork belonged to Raphael Capone. Why would she react this way? "Did you know Raphael Capone?"

Shirley pushed the scrapbook toward her again. She averted her gaze. "No. I don't know anything about him."

Magnolia opened her mouth with more questions.

Standing, Shirley dropped her napkin on her plate. "I'm sorry, Magnolia, but I need to leave you now. Enjoy the rest of the cruise."

Shirley grabbed her purse. She strolled out of the main dining room.

Magnolia watched her leave the room. She assumed the woman was hiding something. Yet, it could be her detective radar making her suspicious.

Glancing around the room, Magnolia froze. Her eyes narrowed.

Norman Chalker sat at a nearby table. He stared at her. Turning a page in his notebook, he started to write quickly.

Unnerved by his constant appearance, Magnolia picked up the scrapbook. She decided to head back to her cabin. Maybe she could find more about the paintings if she spent more time looking at them.

⚓

Gloria Fairbanks stepped off the elevator. She carried shopping bags full of items she found on her shopping spree with Aunt

Lucretia. She could not wait to get home and give D'Quan the science fiction T-shirt she had bought him.

Jonas exited a cabin with a handful of used towels. He dropped them into a laundry cart.

Gloria said, "Hi, Jonas."

Jonas jumped startled dropping one of the towels on the floor.

Bending over to get the towel, Gloria said, "Sorry. I didn't mean to startle you."

Jonas reached down at the same time. He grabbed the towel with a grunt.

Gloria looked at his wrists not seeing the scars. Could she have imagined them before? Maybe it had been something with the lighting.

Jonas pushed his cart around her.

"Jonas?"

"Get lost, kid. No one wants to talk to you."

As he rolled the cart down the hallway, Gloria watched him go. She blinked away tears at his harsh reply. Why was he treating her like that? Could she have done something to change his behavior toward her? Maybe he was lectured about getting too friendly with the guests.

Gloria entered the cabin. She dropped her shopping bags on the floor in front of her bunk. Grabbing the remote control, she sat down on the couch and turned on the television. *Why is he being so mean to me?*

⚓

Yawning, Magnolia entered the cabin. She set the scrapbook on a table near the door.

Gloria sat on the couch with shopping bags at her feet. She clicked through the channels on the television.

Smiling, Magnolia said, "Hi, Gloria. How was your shopping day?"

"Fine."

Magnolia paused at the dull response. She looked around the room for any sign of why her daughter was moody. Gloria usually came back excited to show off her purchases. Could something have happened with Lucretia?

"Did you find anything nice?"

Gloria shrugged. She stared at the television.

Magnolia moved to block the television from her. "What's wrong?"

Gloria dropped the remote on her lap. She said, "I don't know what I did. I tried to be nice and he treats me like trash."

"Who?"

"Jonas."

Walking over, Magnolia sat down on the couch bending her head to keep from hitting it on the bunk above her. She put her arm around her daughter. "What happened?"

Gloria leaned against her. She whispered, "He's changed. He acts like he never read that book. He doesn't want to talk to me. He isn't even nice when he does talk to me."

Magnolia patted her shoulder. "Maybe he is under stress. We don't know his journey."

"It's like he changed. He doesn't even have scars on his wrists anymore," Gloria added.

Magnolia tensed at the news. Closing her eyes, she pictured the scars on Jonas' wrist. She recalled how he had instantly helped her into Ophelia's cabin. Something was not right with the man. "That is odd…Well, don't worry about it, honey. Why don't you figure out what we can do for dinner?"

Magnolia stood up carefully protecting her head from the metal bunk rail. She reached into her purse. Pulling out her cell phone, she headed to the balcony.

Magnolia stepped out into the warm breeze. Sitting down in a chair at the table, she clicked on a contact. She waited for an answer.

"Hello, Magnolia. Long time no see."

Magnolia smiled warmly. Her heart fluttered at the voice. She put aside her feelings to focus on the task at hand. "Reuben, I need your help."

Weldon Hitchcock sat at the bar counter scanning the drink menu. He did not want to get drunk. He only wanted a small drink to give him courage to ask Nolia to go to dinner with him.

Weldon had dwelled on his conversation with Nolia all day. He wanted to talk about their relationship again. Maybe he could convince her to give them a real chance.

Ordering a shot of whiskey, Weldon picked up some peanuts from a bowl on the counter.

"Hello, Magnolia. Long time no see."

Weldon tensed at the voice. He glanced over at a table.

Talking on his cell phone, Reuben said, "I am at your disposal, my lady. What do you need?"

Weldon clenched a fist. He focused on the counter listening for more information.

"I think I can handle that. See you soon."

Weldon glowered at the shot of whiskey set in front of him by the bartender. He returned his attention to the table.

Reuben had left the bar.

Weldon gritted his teeth angry at how Nolia must have invited the other man to dinner. Who knows where that would lead?

Drinking the shot of whiskey, Weldon slammed the glass on the counter. "Keep them coming."

The bartender picked up the whiskey bottle. "You got enough money?"

Weldon pulled out a handful of money.

The bartender poured a new shot of whiskey.

Glaring at the liquor, Weldon brooded on how his luck had changed. *Why would Nolia do this to me?*

Magnolia Ruby sat at a table in the Top Slice Pizzeria. She looked at the menu. There were endless options to choose from. Her stomach growled as she read the pizza specials. *Meat Explosion. Aloha Surprise. Vegetarian. Caribbean Paradise with bacon and BBQ chicken. Mexican Taco Pizza.*

"The Caribbean Paradise sounds amazing," Gloria said.

Magnolia nodded. She had to admit it sounded different than their usual pizza.

"Hi!"

Turning her head, Magnolia waved.

Lydia bounced across the restaurant to their table.

Magnolia looked past her expecting to see Ellison.

Genevieve approached the table.

Remembering to smile, Magnolia said, "Hi, Lydia. Hello, Genevieve."

"Hello, Magnolia."

Lydia held out her hand. Her fingernails were painted blue with diamond jewels on them.

Magnolia said, "Lovely."

"Wow. Cute nails," added Gloria.

Lydia squealed, "Genny let me do it."

Genevieve sat down in a chair. She kept her purse on her lap. "I hope her father doesn't mind. I've never had a girl to spoil."

"I'm sure Ellison will love it," Magnolia said.

Lydia pointed to the other side of the pizza parlor. Her eyes widened. She opened her mouth with a loud squeal.

Magnolia looked to see what was so exciting.

A chef stood behind a glass window. He tossed a flat piece of dough into the air.

"Why don't you girls go watch? I'll order for us," Magnolia suggested.

Gloria and Lydia walked over to the window. They sat in stools to watch the pizza being made.

A young man approached the table. "Welcome to Top Slice Pizzeria. My name is Joel and I'll be your server today. May I start you with drinks?"

"I'll have a sweet tea. I also need a cola and a lemon lime soda. Genevieve?" Magnolia said.

"Water no lemon."

Joel left to get their drinks.

Magnolia examined the menu again. She did not know what to say to Genevieve. The two women had tolerated and remained civil with each other. She did not want to mess things up.

Joel returned with the drinks. "I need to check on something. I will be right back."

Magnolia opened her mouth to call the girls back over.

"I want to apologize, Magnolia."

Jerking her head to look at her, Magnolia waited for the punchline. She could not believe her ears. Genevieve had hated her since her brother's death. Why would that have changed? Nothing had happened to explain the apology.

Genevieve said, "I've been bitter and mean-spirited. It wasn't your fault your meddling led to Vincent's death. Winter Dupree would have killed him anyway. I see that now…I'm sorry. There are no hard feelings. I don't expect us to become friends, but we can stop being enemies."

Magnolia placed a hand on her heart. She blinked away tears of joy. "Thank you, Genevieve. What brought on this change of heart?"

"I had a talk with Lydia. She's an insightful young lady."

"Yes. She is."

Genevieve took a sip of her water. She set the glass down then stood. "I should go."

Magnolia sat up straighter. She did not want the woman to leave now that they had made amends. "Won't you eat with us?"

Genevieve wrinkled her nose. She looked around her. Leaning forward, she said, "Not if you want to sleep in our cabin tonight. Pizza has a…strong effect on my digestive system. Enjoy your time with the girls, Magnolia."

"See you at the cabin, Genevieve."

Genevieve walked slowly out of the pizza parlor.

Magnolia thanked God for the wonderful moment. Who would have ever thought she would get an apology and peace treaty from Genevieve Sterling?

Gloria Fairbanks took a bite of her Meat Explosion pizza. She marveled at the pop of flavors. She was glad her mother had chosen to let them indulge on their vacation. At home, she would have had a supreme pizza to get some vegetables in her. *Veggies don't belong on pizza.*

"This is good," Lydia said.

Gloria pointed at the barbecue sauce all over her face. She could tell Lydia was enjoying the Caribbean Paradise pizza. Taking a sip of her cola, she glanced around at the other people enjoying the food and atmosphere.

A man sat at the next table. He stared at her while jotting something in his notebook.

Gloria returned her attention to her own table. She lowered her voice. "Mom, that guy's up to something. He keeps watching us and writing."

Magnolia looked over at him. "That's Norman Chalker. He ate at our table in the dining room our first night, remember?"

"I remember. I thought he was weird then."

Magnolia gave her lecture look. "Don't judge people, Gloria. We don't know anything about his life."

Gloria agreed. She had heard the speech before. Yet, the man was creeping her out. "But why is he writing about us?"

"I don't know. Maybe he's not. Eat your pizza, girls. We'll head over to the Sweet Tooth Sanctuary for a sweet treat."

Lydia grabbed another piece of pizza with a squeal. She began to gobble it down.

Gloria flicked her gaze at the man again.

Norman Chalker stared right at her.

Lydia elbowed her harder than necessary. "Come on, silly. I want a treat."

⚓

Magnolia Ruby sipped her refill of sweet tea. She looked over at Norman Chalker. Though she had reassured Gloria he was harmless, she could not get rid of her suspicions. She did not like how he kept showing up where she visited. Could he be following her?

Focusing on the girls, Magnolia watched Lydia wipe barbecue sauce off her mouth. She recalled what Genevieve had said about talking to the girl. What had Lydia said that led to an apology?

"Lydia, what did you and Genny talk about?"

"I told her I don't hate my mother anymore," replied Lydia grabbing her glass of lemon lime soda.

Magnolia waited for more of an explanation. She had never heard how Lydia felt about her mother. Nadine Knight had treated her daughter disgracefully. It had landed her in prison. How could Lydia forgive her? Maybe she did not remember what her mother did to her.

"Why not?" Gloria asked.

Lydia shrugged, "Because hate hurts my heart more than my mother's heart. I don't want my heart to hurt anymore."

Magnolia smiled at the girl's insight. "That's nice. What did Genny say?"

Lydia took a big bite of pizza. She chewed it carefully then swallowed. "She said she needs to stop hating someone too."

"Who?" Gloria asked.

"Not my business, silly."

Magnolia thanked God for helping her make amends with Genevieve. Her cell phone buzzed. Pulling it out of her pocket, she clicked on a text from Charlie. *Raphael Capone is Ralph Caplin.*

Magnolia returned her phone to her pocket. She needed to find more information about Ralph Caplin. Maybe it would help her to figure out who else had a reason to hate him. "Gloria, will you text D'Quan and see if he can do some research for me?"

Gloria leaned back against her chair. "I thought you didn't want me texting him while we're on the ship because it is more expensive."

"That was to keep you from texting back and forth too much. I need information. Ask him to see what he can find about Ralph Caplin. He can email me what he finds."

Gloria pulled out her cell phone and started to type her text.

Magnolia checked her phone again. Nothing from Reuben. *What is taking him so long?*

Reuben Malone sat in a blue chair outside of the infirmary. He tapped his foot impatiently. Glancing at his watch, he leaned back and crossed his arms. *This is taking forever.*

When Magnolia had called with a favor, Reuben had hoped it would be a simple task that they could discuss over dinner. However, he had not imagined she would want him to examine Capone's body. He had practically begged Chief Jackson to let him do it. In the end, he had asked the chief how many murder cases he had handled. Since the answer was none, Chief Jackson had agreed to give Reuben more of a role in the investigation.

The door opened. A middle-aged woman stepped into the hallway. "Detective Malone. I'm Dr. Patricia Leonard. Please come in."

Standing, Reuben followed the doctor into the infirmary. He scanned the medical area. There were a couple of examination beds. On a far wall was one metal door resembling the body drawer of a morgue.

Dr. Leonard walked over to the door. She opened it then pulled out a tray. A white cloth covered a bulge. "I don't suppose the head has been found?"

"Not yet. Did you find any scars?"

"Tons. They are all over his body."

Dr. Leonard pulled the cloth off the body.

Reuben thanked his police experience. Seeing horrible things in the past helped him not vomit at the disgusting appearance of the body. He gritted his teeth at multiple scars on the man's body. "What else did you find?"

"His blood type was AB negative. He was diabetic. He is missing part of his left foot."

Reuben pulled out his cell phone. He headed toward the exit. "Thanks, Doc."

Clicking on a contact, Reuben sank back into the blue chair in the hallway. He needed confirmation before he could report his findings to Magnolia.

"Jackson."

"Malone. Chief, do you have an employee file on Jonas Archer?"

"Of course. Just a moment."

Reuben rubbed a hand through his gray hair.

"Got it. What do you want to know?"

"Blood type."

"AB negative."

Reuben asked, "Diabetic?"

"Uh. Yes."

"Any other medical issues?"

"Not really. Marty knew him well. He said Jonas was in the military and lost part of his left foot in a bombing…Marty says he was a prisoner of war for a few weeks. He had lots of scars. Why?"

Reuben closed his eyes. His heart pounded at the news. He mumbled, "Because the body is not Raphael Capone. It's Jonas Archer." *What in the blazes happened?*

CHAPTER 12

MIXED MATTER

Magnolia Ruby studied the inside of the Sweet Tooth Sanctuary in all its beauty. Bright colors splashed everywhere. A white wooden tree stood in the middle of the shop. Lollipops of every shape, size, and color filled in the tree as the leaves. Big rubber gummi bears and gumdrops hung from the ceiling. The walls were lined with huge plastic containers full of candy. *I've never seen so many different kinds of candy in my life.*

Lydia squealed.

Understanding her excitement, Magnolia said, "Okay, girls. Get a bag and fill it with candy. We'll go back to the cabin and eat while we watch a movie."

Lydia and Gloria stepped forward eager to choose their candy.

Magnolia walked along the wall of candy. She read the labels of the different treats. She did not usually indulge in candy herself. Yet, they were on vacation.

Her cell phone buzzed continously. Pulling it out of her pocket, Magnolia accept the call. "Hello?"

"Magnolia, it's Reuben. You won't believe this."

Magnolia walked farther away from the girls. She lowered her voice. "What did you find out?"

"The body isn't Raphael Capone."

Closing her eyes, Magnolia whispered, "It's Jonas, isn't it?"

"Yes."

Magnolia opened her eyes. She turned to the opposite side of the shop. Her gaze fixed on Gloria. How would her daughter take the loss?

"Magnolia?"

Refocusing on the case, Magnolia said, "Then the steward on our hallway has to be Capone pretending to be Jonas."

"Do you think he killed Jonas?"

Placing a hand on her forehead, Magnolia replied, "Yes, but I have no idea why."

"I'll take ship's security with me to arrest him," Reuben said.

Magnolia said, "Be careful."

"I will. Talk to you soon."

Ending the call, Magnolia walked over to Gloria. *Dear Lord, help me tell her about Jonas.*

Gloria turned around with a bright smile. "They have all my favorites."

Magnolia forced a smile on her face. She did not relish the pain that would come from her news.

"What's wrong, Mom?"

Magnolia opened her mouth to tell her. Seeing the joy on her daughter's face, she changed her mind. She did not want to upset her in a public place. "We'll talk about it later. Let's see if Lydia is ready." *I need more time to prepare my words anyway. Maybe we will get more answers before I have to tell her.*

Charlotte Knight returned to her suite. She pulled out the keycard unlocking the door. Entering the cabin, she halted. Her heart soared.

Leo lay on the bed taking a nap.

Charlotte set her purse down. Taking off her shoes, she lay next to him. "Oh, Sleeping Beauty, time to wake up."

Leo mumbled, "You must kiss me."

Charlotte leaned over him kissing him gently on the lips. Ducking away from his arms, she climbed off the bed. "Sorry, Leo, but we have work to do."

Sitting up, Leo groaned as he straightened his shirt. "Okay. The mood's spoiled anyway. What work?"

Charlotte pulled her cell phone out of her purse as she sat on the sofa. "I'm calling Mags. We need to get together and talk about what we found out today."

"Can't we do that tomorrow?"

"No. Murder cases take top priority. You knew that when you married me."

Leo chuckled, "True. Okay. Call her."

Charlotte clicked on Mags' number. She waited for her friend to answer.

Leo climbed off the bed. He walked over to sit by her on the sofa.

"Hello?"

"Hi, Mags. Do you want to come to our suite and talk about the case?"

Silence. Charlotte exchanged a glance with Leo. "Mags?"

"Sure, Charlie. I'll head that way."

Charlotte swallowed hard. She could tell something had happened. Her heart pounded at the possibilities. "Mags, what's wrong?"

"A terrible twist in the case. See you soon."

Mags ended the call.

Charlotte set her cell phone on the table beside the sofa.

"What's up?" Leo asked.

"I'm not sure, but it's not good."

Leo reached over her. He grabbed the portable cabin phone. His hand was swollen and bruised.

"What happened to your hand?" Charlotte asked.

Leo raised his hand to look at it. "I had to be…creative to get Patton to talk to me."

Charlotte leaned away from him. Scowling, she muttered, "Explain creative."

"I sparred with him."

"In the ring?"

Nodding, Leo averted his gaze from her no doubt expecting a lecture.

Charlotte bit her lip. She wanted to scold him for putting himself in danger. However, she had put herself in danger many times. Maybe this was how Leo felt when she did something reckless.

Charlotte smirked, "Did you win?"

"What?"

"Well, if you're going to be a fool, then you need to at least win. That's what D'Angelo says."

Leo chuckled, "Yes. I knocked him down with a hard punch in the face."

"My hero."

Dialing the cabin phone, Leo said, "I'll call room service. I think it's going to be a long night."

Frankie Lemmons entered her apartment. She considered her list of things she needed to get to make her night successful. She waved at Jolie sitting on the couch watching T.V. "Hey, kid."

"Hey. How was your day?"

Frankie mumbled, "It's not over yet. How about you?"

"Good. I love school breaks. Are you heading back out?" Jolie asked staring at the comedy movie.

"Yeah. Soon. I just came home to change."

Jolie said, "I made dinner if you're hungry."

Heading for her bedroom, Frankie said, "Thanks. I don't have time to eat."

"Okay. Maybe when you get back."

Entering her bedroom, Frankie searched through her clothes for her darkest outfit. She needed to be able to blend into the shadows. *I never wanted to be a vigilante. Now, I have no choice.*

Frankie changed into black clothes. She grabbed a ski mask and tucked it into the waist of her pants. Satisfied with her disguise, she left the bedroom.

Looking at Jolie, Frankie said, "Why don't you see if you can hang out with Big Mama tonight?"

"Why?"

"I may be late. You could spend the night with her."

Narrowing her eyes, Jolie examined her foster mother from head to toe. "You're acting funny. What's with the funeral clothes?"

Frankie headed toward the door ignoring the question. She hated to worry the teenager with the news that her act of vengeance would probably end with her foster mother being arrested. What would happen to Jolie if she got caught?

Frankie shook her head. She needed to get going if she was going to accomplish her mission. "Don't worry about me. I'm going undercover."   .

Remembering her keys on the coffee table, Frankie reached for them. The ski mask fell to the floor.

Jolie grabbed the ski mask. She examined it then looked at her.

Thanking her, Frankie took the ski mask from her. She marched toward the door.

"What are you doing, Frankie?"

Refusing to look at her, Frankie opened the door. "My job. Catch you later, kid." *I hope.*

Jolie Price stared at the apartment door long after Frankie had left. She had been worried by the dark clothes, but the ski mask scared her. What could her foster mother be up to tonight?

Jolie pulled out her cell phone. She clicked around on her contacts until she found the one she wanted. She waited for Big Mama to answer.

"Hello?"

"Big Mama, it's Jolie. Frankie is going to do something terrible. I know it."

"Calm down, honey. Now, tell me what happened."

Taking a deep breath, Jolie said, "She came home acting weird. She changed into black clothes and took a ski mask. She said she was working undercover. I don't know what she is up to, but it can't be good."

Silence. Jolie listened hard. She could hear muffled talking on the other end though she could not understand what was being said.

"Jolie, D'Angelo is going to handle Frankie. He's going to drop me by the apartment. I'll spend the night with you."

"Thank you, Big Mama."

"You bet, honey."

Jolie ended the call. She lay down on the couch. Closing her eyes, she tried to calm down. What if Frankie got mad at her and did not want to be her foster mother anymore? Her heart ached at being homeless or put in a group home for orphans. *Did I mess this up already?*

Magnolia Ruby strolled out of the elevator. She knew Leo and Charlie's suite was down the hallway and around the corner. She could not wait to talk to Leo and Charlie.

Magnolia had called Ellison to see if he could watch a movie with the girls. She had whispered to him about what had happened.

Ellison had agreed if the girls shared their candy with him. He had started a negotiation with them in the cabin as Magnolia left.

Magnolia turned the corner.

Weldon stumbled down the hallway toward her. Noticing her, he pointed a shaky finger. "Where are you going?"

Magnolia pursed her lips at his slurred speech. She could tell he had been drinking. "Weldon, what are you doing here?"

"Coming to see my daughter."

"Charlie doesn't need to see you like this."

Staggering closer to her, Weldon snapped, "You're doing this to me. I came here to spend more time with you, but you only have time for your new boyfriend."

"What are you talking about?"

Weldon hissed, "That other cop. I saw you talking to him after breakfast. You couldn't wait to get rid of me and rebound to him. Then he got a call from you this afternoon. I guess you're spending lots of time together...I don't know what you see in that chump."

Magnolia opened her mouth to protest.

Weldon added, "Looks like you'll share you love with anyone who shows you any attention."

Magnolia narrowed her eyes at his rude remarks. She pointed a stern finger at him. "You better sober up, Weldon Hitchcock, before you say something you're going to regret."

"All I regret is not punching that chump in the face the first night. I should have staked my claim then."

Glowering, Magnolia placed her hands on her hips. "You have no claim on me. I told you we're through."

The door opened. Leo and Charlie stepped out into the hallway.

Magnolia focused back on Weldon. She hissed, "Go away before you make an even bigger fool of yourself."

"You're the fool. That cop is using you for his career. I know his kind."

"And I know your kind. You lie and manipulate to get what you want. How can I trust anything you say?"

Weldon waved a hand at her. Losing his balance, he fell against the wall.

Leo rushed forward to help him.

Weldon shoved him off. He snarled, "I don't need your help. I don't need any of you."

Heading in the direction of the elevator, Weldon stumbled down the hallway.

Magnolia glanced at Charlie regretting the tears shining in her eyes.

Leo rejoined them. He put his arm around Charlie's shoulders. Looking at Magnolia, he mumbled, "What was that about?"

Magnolia assumed they heard most of the argument. Taking a deep breath to cool her temper, she said, "Never mind. We have a murder to solve."

⚓

Charlotte Knight grabbed three bottles of water from the mini fridge. She walked over to the sitting area.

Mags sat in a red velvet armchair perpendicular to the sofa.

Leo stationed himself on the far end of the sofa leaving the part closest to Mags open for his wife. He raised his eyebrows at Charlotte. Clearly, he expected her to take charge of the conversation.

Accepting her role, Charlotte handed a bottle of water to each of them before sitting down. What could she say? She wanted to talk to Mags about what had happened with Pop. However, she wanted to respect her friend's privacy and wishes.

Deciding to focus on the murder, Charlotte said, "Elise Quincy has an alibi. She was in a bar seducing another man. I checked with the bartenders. She's telling the truth."

Mags opened her purse. She pulled out her notepad and pen. She wrote the information on their suspect list.

Charlotte glanced at Leo. She jerked her head to encourage him to speak.

"I fought a round in the ring with Patton Quincy," Leo said.

Mags gaped at him. "You what?"

"Don't worry. He won," Charlotte said.

"With only a minor injury," Leo added holding up his bruised hand.

Mags asked, "Did you find out anything relevant to the case?"

"Patton was in the gym. The attendant vouches for him," Leo replied.

Charlotte opened her bottle of water. Taking a drink, she noticed the pause in the conversation. Returning the lid, she said, "I had a talk with Doretta Brewster. She and Capone had an affair twenty years ago. Her bodyguard, Jimmy Caplin, is her son, James Brewster. He hit Capone in the same hallway where he was later found dead. Doretta and Jimmy don't really have a strong alibi so they could be in it together."

Mags rubbed a hand over her face. Sighing, she mumbled, "They didn't kill Raphael Capone."

Charlotte recalled how the artist had changed his name after his affair with Doretta. "Right. Ralph Caplin."

Mags shook her head. She set her water bottle on the coffee table. "No. The body is not Raphael Capone or Ralph Caplin."

"Then who is it?" asked Leo.

Mags said, "It's Jonas Archer."

Charlotte did not recognize the name. "Who?"

"The steward from my hallway."

Leo grunted, "Who would kill a steward?"

"Raphael Capone," shrugged Mags.

Charlotte swallowed hard. She thought about all the investigating they had done. Had it been worthless? It sounded like they had their killer. "Why?"

Mags shook her head. She picked her water bottle back up. Opening the lid, she said, "I have no idea. Reuben has gone to find the fake Jonas. Maybe we will have some answers soon."

Reuben Malone stepped off the elevator with two ship security guards behind him. He scanned the hallway of the employee cabins. Seeing no one in sight, he pulled his Glock pistol from its holster. Walking toward the cabin used by Jonas Archer, he held his weapon ready.

Stopping at the right door, Reuben stood directly in front of it. He motioned for the security guards to move to the sides of the door. Knocking on the door, he waited for the imposter to answer.

Silence. Knocking again, Reuben said, "Archer, police. Open up."

Listening for any sounds, Reuben motioned to the security guards.

One of the men slid a keycard into the lock. He pushed the door open.

Reuben bounded into the cabin with his gun pointing at the small space. He lowered his weapon with a groan.

Pulling out his cell phone, Reuben clicked on a contact. Holding the phone to his ear, he waited.

"Hello?"

"Magnolia."

"Reuben, did you find him?"

Reuben looked back at the bed. "Yes, but he's dead."

CHAPTER 13

NEEDY NONSENSE

Frankie Lemmons sat in her car in a shadowy part of the community center parking lot. She could not remain patient much longer. It was time to get her mission completed. *Justice will be served.*

The community center door opened. Several teenagers and adults streamed out of the building. They scattered in different directions.

Frankie observed the people. Jontray Scott was not with them. Based on her surveillance and questioning visitors of the community center, she had discovered the man stayed after closing hours to clean up and prepare for the next day. *Alone.*

The door opened again. Jontray Scott walked out of the building carrying a bag of trash. He headed to an alleyway on the side of the building.

Climbing steathily out of her car, Frankie shut the door softly. She crept across the parking lot scanning often to see if there were any witnesses. Reaching the building, she pulled out the Glock pistol she had bought off a gun dealer.

Frankie took a deep breath. She peeked around the building into the alley. Her heart pounded at the silence of the night.

Jontray set the bag of trash on the ground. He lifted the lid of a dumpster.

Stepping into the alley, Frankie pointed the gun at him. She waited for the killer to see her.

Jontray threw the bag of trash into the dumpster. He closed the lid. Turning around, he slapped his hands together.

Frankie hissed, "Don't move."

Jontray squinted to see better. His eyes widened at a click from her pistol. He raised his hands into the air. "I don't have any money."

Taking a step closer, Frankie said, "I'm not here to rob you."

Jontray mumbled, "Then what do you want?"

"I'm going to kill you."

Stepping off the elevator, Magnolia Ruby tensed at a ship security guard. Her interference might cause trouble with Chief Jackson.

"I'll take you to the detective, Mrs. Ruby," the guard said pointing down the hallway.

Magnolia relaxed. She followed the guard down the employee hallway. Taking a deep breath, she entered Jonas Archer's cabin. She breathed in relief at how the body had already been removed. Blood stained the bed. Clothes and other items were scattered on the floor. Could it have been a robbery? If it weren't Raphael Capone, she could have believed that. It would be too much of a coincidence for their murder suspect to be murdered in a robbery.

"Magnolia."

Magnolia focused on Reuben. She stepped farther into the cabin.

Walking over to her side, Reuben said, "Dr. Leonard believes he was stabbed an hour ago. She is going to examine the body for other clues...Of course, she isn't equipped to do a full autopsy on the ship. That will have to wait."

"Did you find the murder weapon?" asked Magnolia.

"Not yet."

Magnolia walked around the room. She turned back toward the door. "How was he laying on the bed?"

"On his back."

"Straight on the bed?"

Reuben gestured sideways on the bed. "Like he was facing the door then fell backwards."

Magnolia moved back toward the door looking at the large space between the door and the bed. "If he was stabbed when he opened the door, he would have fallen onto the floor."

"Right. He must have known the person well enough to invite them inside."

Magnolia strolled through the rest of the cabin. What could the person have wanted? If there was something to steal, then the killer must have taken it.

"You won't find anything of value," Reuben said.

Magnolia nodded. Who would have a motive to kill Raphael Capone? She recalled the suspects they had been questioning earlier in the day. "Someone must have found out he was alive. Maybe they decided to kill him for real."

"I agree, but who?" asked Reuben.

Magnolia shrugged, "All I know is it isn't Ophelia Hart. She's still in the brig."

Silence. Magnolia looked at Reuben. She did not like how he averted his gaze from her. "What?"

"Chief Jackson released her with orders to stay in her cabin until we reach port."

Magnolia covered her face with her hands. She hated that Ophelia could have decided to kill Raphael Capone after all. Dropping her hands, she groaned, "Why would he do that?"

"Because he has no idea what he's doing."

Magnolia agreed. She could not understand why the chief hadn't kept Ophelia in the brig on the theft charges. "What are we going to do?"

Reuben motioned toward the door. "We're going to go see if she followed his orders."

D'Angelo parked his car in the police precinct parking lot. He needed to see London Bridges. Maybe she knew what Frankie was planning. Climbing out of the car, he headed across the parking lot.

Bridges stepped out of the precinct. She tapped around on her cell phone as she crossed the parking lot.

"Bridges!"

Bridges turned toward him. She smirked, "Hey, Big Boy. Want to take me to dinner?"

Shaking his head, D'Angelo lumbered over to her. "I can't. I'm looking for Lemmons."

Bridges' smile faded. "You like her?"

D'Angelo averted his gaze. Though he liked Lemmons more than a friend, he did not want to make it public until he knew if she felt the same way. Shaking his head, he said, "I'm trying to help her. I think she's going after that fool."

"Jontray Scott?"

Returning his attention to her, D'Angelo nodded.

Bridges pointed to her car. "Hop in, Big Boy. I'm driving."

D'Angelo stomped toward the passenger side of her car. He waited for her to unlock it. "Do you know where to find Lemmons?"

Bridges jogged to the driver's side. Opening her door, she said, "No. I know where to find Jontray Scott."

⚓

Ellison Knight chuckled at a funny part of the movie. He reached his hand into Lydia's candy bag.

"No, Daddy. I'll pick for you," Lydia said pulling on his hand.

Ellison retrieved his hand from the bag. He waited for his daughter to choose his treat. Taking a red candy she handed him, he said, "Thanks."

Lydia said, "It's too spicy so you get it."

Laughing, Ellison popped the cinnamon candy into his mouth. He chewed on it then coughed at the spiciness of it. His tongue burned. Tears swelled in his eyes. Picking up his water, he took a sip. "Those are spicy."

"And you get all of them," Lydia said.

Ellison put an arm around her pulling her closer. "You are too good to me, sweetie."

A loud knock banged on the door. Ellison peered out at the balcony.

Genevieve sat in a chair at the table looking out at the ocean.

Another loud knock resounded on the door. Gloria and Lydia looked at him with wide eyes.

Smiling to reassure them, Ellison said, "I'll get it."

Ellison struggled from his place on the floor. He ignored the ache in his legs. Though he was not young, he did not consider himself old yet. Opening the door, his good mood sank.

Weldon struggled to stay on his feet. His hair was disheveled. He smelled like whiskey.

Ellison looked back at the girls. He stepped into the hallway. "Weldon, what are you doing?"

"I need to talk to Genevieve," Weldon stammered.

"I don't think she would want to talk to you in this condition. Maybe you should go back to our room and sleep it off."

Shaking his head, Weldon snarled, "Everyone wants to boss me around. It's none of your business. Genevieve!"

Ellison tensed at the loud shout. He opened the door. "Girls, let's get ice cream to go with the candy."

Lydia stood with a squeal. She put her flipflops on then hurried to the door.

Gloria used the remote to pause the movie. She slipped on her sandals. Grabbing her purse, she walked to the door.

Weldon leaned on the hallway wall. He mumbled softly to himself.

Lydia and Gloria strolled down the hallway toward the elevator.

Ellison turned his head toward the balcony. He called out, "Genevieve, Weldon is here to see you."

Genevieve motioned with a hand through the balcony window, giving her permission.

Ellison left the cabin. He held the door open.

Weldon stumbled through the doorway.

Ellison allowed the door to close. Pulling out his cell phone, he clicked on his contact list.

"Who are you calling, silly?"

Ellison smiled at his daughter. "Your brother. I'll meet you at the elevator."

Gloria led Lydia down the hallway. She kept looking back at him.

Ellison clicked on his son's number. Leaning toward the cabin door, he listened for any sounds for help.

"Hi, Dad."

"Leo, you and Charlie might want to visit Aunt Genevieve."

"Why would we want to do that?"

"Weldon is here to talk to her. He's clearly drunk."

Silence. Ellison listened to muffled sounds on the other end of the phone.

Leo said, "We're on our way."

Weldon Hitchcock staggered through the cabin. He dodged bags of candy and cans of soda. He glared at the happy movie paused on the screen. Stumbling out onto the balcony, he said, "Enjoying yourself?"

With pursed lips, Genevieve peered at him. Her eyes examined him. "Not as much as you I see."

Weldon shuffled his feet to stand at the small railing. He snorted, "I guess you played your part well, Gen."

"What are you talking about?"

Turning back toward her, Weldon said, "You hate Magnolia Ruby and now she hates me. You get your way. Well played, Auntie."

"I don't hate Magnolia. We've made amends. If she hates you, then it is your own doing…I don't blame her if she saw you like this," Genevieve said.

Weldon placed his hands behind him on the railing. He growled, "She's been duped by that other cop."

Shaking her head, Genevieve scoffed, "Don't be ridiculous. No one can dupe Magnolia. Her mind is as sharp as a dagger. She finally saw through your façade and discovered the real you. I always hoped she would."

Weldon pointed a finger at her. His arm shook. Holding onto the railing, he balanced himself. "You orchestrated all of this. You're the reason I can't be happy."

"Now, you listen to me, Weldon Hitchcock. I will not sit here and be accused of stealing your happiness when your own insecurities, lies, and manipulation did that. You're unhappy because you choose to be."

Weldon turned away from her. Placing both hands on the railing, he lowered his head.

"Now, you will get out of my cabin, or I will call security. Good night," Genevieve added.

Weldon stared out at the ocean. His shoulders slumped. He closed his eyes. *Maybe she's right. Maybe I will never be happy.*

⚓

Gloria Fairbanks walked along the deck toward an outdoor ice cream shop. She assumed they had abandoned the movie for ice cream because Mr. Weldon had stopped by the cabin not looking well. What was wrong with him?

"Gloria!"

Gloria spun toward the voice. She waved with a bright smile. "Hi, Aunt Lucretia."

Lucretia marched toward her. She wrapped her arms around her in a strong hug. "I just heard. Are you okay, honey?"

Gloria tilted her head. She did not know what her aunt could have heard. Why would Aunt Lucretia be worried? "Heard what?"

"I heard that they identified the headless body. It sickens me to think you were so close to him."

"I don't understand. I mean the body was found in our hallway, but that's all."

Lucretia placed a hand on her heart. She sighed, "Well, you are braver than me. I would be appalled if my steward were murdered and decapitated."

Gloria tried to process what her aunt was saying. Could Aunt Lucretia be talking about Jonas? She admitted that something was odd about the man's behavior, but it couldn't be that Jonas was dead. Could it?

Lucretia added, "I think his name was Jonas or Jonah something."

A gentle hand touched her shoulder. Gloria turned to look at Ellison. She could see his mouth moving, but his words blurred in her hearing.

Waving a hand at him, Gloria walked over to the railing. Tears sprang into her eyes. Who would want to kill Jonas? He had not hurt anyone.

"Gloria?"

Gloria closed her eyes. She let the tears stream down her face. Lowering her head, she whispered, "Is it true?"

"Yes. Mags was going to tell you when she got back," Ellison said.

Gloria wished she had not learned about his death this way. Opening her eyes, she wiped the tears from her face. She swallowed the bile rising in her throat. She focused on the darkness unable to see the ocean anymore. Her hands clutched the railing tighter. "Do they know who killed him?"

"The case isn't solved yet, but Mags will figure it out."

Gloria hoped her mother would find the killer and make him pay. *Jonas deserves justice.*

Weldon Hitchcock leaned farther over the railing. He ignored Genevieve's demand for him to leave her cabin. His vision blurred at the ocean disappearing into the darkness.

"Step back from the rail, Pop."

Weldon spun around. He closed his eyes briefly at his vision swimming at the sudden movement and the amount of booze in his system. His eyes opened.

Charlie and Leo stood on the balcony next to the table.

Genevieve sat straighter in her chair with a hand on her heart.

Weldon grunted, "I was just looking, Charlie. That's all."

Taking a step closer, Charlie said, "Why don't we go to your room? You can rest."

Weldon stepped forward. He stumbled.

Leo reached for him. He took one of his arms helping him find his balance. "We'll escort you."

Surrendering to them, Weldon looked at Genevieve.

His aunt turned her head from him.

Weldon staggered out of the cabin. He tried to think about what could do once he was sober. Maybe he still had a chance to find happiness. It would start with winning Nolia back.

Chatter from down the hallway attracted his attention. Weldon turned his head to see who was walking down the hallway away from them.

Nolia walked down the hallway with Reuben Malone.

Charlie muttered, "Come on, Pop."

Weldon shook Charlie and Leo off him. He stumbled down the hallway. His vision blurred.

Hurried footsteps came behind him. Charlie yelled, "Mags!"

Magnolia Ruby exited the elevator with Reuben. She could not wait to get down the long curvy hallway to Ophelia's cabin. Had the thief stayed in her cabin? She found herself hoping Ophelia would not be guilty of the murder. She had started to believe everything she had said. It would be painful to be proven wrong again.

Passing her own cabin, Magnolia hesitated. She wanted to check on the girls, but she knew they were safe with Ellison. Deciding she would return to her cabin after talking to Ophelia, she walked on down the hallway.

Reuben said, "Hart better be there."

"She should be. I can't imagine her getting her freedom and then killing someone to get back into the brig."

"After all your time with criminals, you think they are rational people?" chuckled Reuben.

"Neither criminals nor police detectives."

Reuben opened his mouth no doubt with a witty retort.

"Mags!"

Magnolia spun around at Charlie's shout. Her eyes bulged.

Weldon stumbled into Reuben knocking him to the floor.

Magnolia raised her hand to her mouth. She stood to the side unable to get close enough to break the men apart without getting hurt herself.

As Charlie moved to Magnolia's side, Leo rushed forward reaching for the men. Struggling to get them apart, he pulled at the two men.

Fearing Reuben was fighting back in his anger, Magnolia said, "Reuben, don't fight back. Get away from him."

Leo grabbed Weldon's arm with both hands.

Shoving at Weldon, Reuben crawled away then struggled to his feet.

Standing, Leo positioned himself between both men. He faced Weldon with hands raised. "That's enough."

Weldon raised a fist.

"Pop, please," Charlie begged.

Looking over at her, Weldon lowered his fist. He reached into his pocket. Pulling out his keycard, he stomped toward his own cabin. He slid the card into the lock. Pushing the door, he entered his cabin then slammed it behind him.

Magnolia shook her head. What was wrong with him? She understood how he wanted to be with her, but his obsession was becoming too much.

Peering at Reuben, Magnolia asked, "Are you okay?"

"Yes."

Reuben adjusted his clothes. Fixing his disheveled hair, he looked at Leo. "Thanks for your help. That man is strong."

"You're welcome," Leo said.

Reuben turned toward the end of the hallway. "I need to check on Ophelia."

"I'm coming," Magnolia said.

Magnolia followed Reuben down the hallway. Her heart ached at how hard Weldon was taking their break-up. However, she needed to focus on the case. There was a murderer to find. *I can deal with Weldon later.*

⚓

Leo Knight watched Mags and Reuben head down the hallway. He was glad no one was hurt, but he hated the fight he had to breakup. His curiosity was peaked by why Ophelia needed to be checked on. Could she be involved in the murders?

Leo shook the question away. He did not want to investigate the case anymore tonight. "We should head back to our suite."

At his wife's silence, Leo looked over at her.

Standing at her father's cabin door, Charlie knocked on it. "Pop? Please let me in, Pop."

Leo walked toward her. He did not like the desperation in her voice.

The door remined closed. Charlie knocked harder. She leaned closer to the door. "Pop, open the door. Please."

Silence. Charlie turned toward him. "He's not answering."

"He probably passed out."

"No. Something worse is wrong. I can feel it."

Leo opened his mouth to argue with her. He believed Weldon was already sleeping off his booze binge. He recalled how the drunk man had been leaning over the balcony railing in Genevieve's cabin. Could he be suicidal in his drunken state?

Charlie knocked again. "Please, Pop. Just answer me and I'll leave you alone."

Realizing the possibility of Weldon committing suicide, Leo looked both ways down the hallway. "We have to find a steward. We need his keycard."

Charlie pounded on the door. "Pop! Answer me!"

Leo marched down the hallway. Maybe Reuben had a master keycard. *If not, he could at least call security for us.*

"What's wrong?"

Leo spun around at the voice.

Doretta's bodyguard stepped into the hallway from his cabin.

Charlie turned toward him. "Jimmy, my father's not answering. I need to get in there."

Jimmy rushed back into his cabin. He left the door open.

Leo tilted his head at the odd behavior.

Returning from his cabin, Jimmy jogged down the hallway with a keycard in his hand.

Leo did not see how Jimmy's keycard could help them. Each cabin had their own card. It would not work on another cabin.

Sliding the keycard into the lock, Jimmy pushed the door open.

Charlie rushed into the cabin. "Pop!"

Leo longed to follow her. However, his cop mode activated. There was only one way the keycard would work on both cabins. He stared at Jimmy. "Where did you get a master keycard?"

Magnolia Ruby knocked on Ophelia Hart's door. She listened to movement inside the cabin.

The door swung open. Ophelia stood in the doorway. Her appearance resembled how she had looked at the Amateur Art Expo when she first asked for help.

Magnolia reflected on how the younger woman had deceived her with her suspicions and fake attack. Was Ophelia deceiving her again?

Ophelia said, "I knew it was you, Magnolia."

Looking over at Reuben, Ophelia's nose wrinkled. "Detective."

Magnolia examined Ophelia seeing the nails on her right hand were chipped. Could she have damaged them in a fight with Raphael Capone?

"What can I do for you?" Ophelia asked in a sweet voice.

Magnolia motioned toward the cabin. "May we come in?"

"It depends."

"On?"

"Why are you here?"

Magnolia looked at Reuben. She waited for him to take over the questioning. It was his job after all. She only wanted to help.

"Have you left this cabin since you were escorted here by ship security?" asked Reuben.

Ophelia replied, "No. I ordered room service for dinner. I've been stuck here bored to death."

Magnolia winced at the reference to death. She opened her mouth to speak.

"Stop! Police!"

Magnolia and Reuben exchanged a startled glance. They turned toward the way they had come.

Magnolia gasped, "That's Leo."

Reuben pulled his Glock pistol from its holster. He rushed down the hallway.

Magnolia reached for her purse. She pulled her hand back. Her Glock had been left at home. She had assumed she would not need it on a cruise. *Maybe I was wrong.*

Leo Knight peered at Jimmy Caplin. He could not believe he had a master keycard. Could he be Raphael Capone's killer? "Where did you get a master keycard?"

Jimmy snapped his attention to him. "What?"

"Where did you get a master keycard, Mr. Caplin?" Leo repeated with a glare.

Jimmy looked down at the keycard in his hand. He took a step back. "I found it."

"How convenient. Where?"

Jimmy took another step backwards. He dropped the master keycard. Turning, he ran down the hallway toward the elevator.

Leo chased after him. He pumped his arms to gain more speed. As he came closer to him, he tackled the man to the floor.

"I didn't do anything," Jimmy yelled.

Leo reached into his back pocket. He pulled out his handcuffs. Fearing he would have to use them on Weldon, he had brought them to Genevieve's cabin. Now, he was glad to have them.

Leo cuffed the man. He heard fast footsteps behind him.

Reuben tromped down the hallway toward him. He had his Glock pistol ready in his hands. "What happened?"

Leo pointed back at the master keycard stationed on the floor. "He had a master keycard. It probably belonged to the steward."

Reuben raised his eyebrows. "Then to Capone…You have a lot to explain, Mr. Caplin."

Leo and Reuben pulled Jimmy to his feet.

"Jimmy?" Mags asked.

Leo looked down the hallway.

Mags leaned on the wall across the hall from Weldon's cabin. She focused on the floor. Her forehead wrinkled.

Leo had seen this expression on her face many times. It usually meant she did not believe the suspect as the killer. He opened his mouth to assure Mags that it made sense. Why else would Jimmy have a master keycard? He took a step toward her ready to explain his theory.

A gunshot popped from down the hall.

Leo jerked at the familiar sound. Where had it come from?

Staring at Weldon's cabin, Mags stood straighter with her mouth open. She placed a hand on her heart.

"Charlie!" Leo screamed running toward the cabin door.

Another gunshot popped.

Leo pounded on the door. No answer. Remembering the master keycard, he searched the floor. Leaning down, he picked it up where Jimmy had dropped it. "Charlie!"

CHAPTER 14

OBSCURE OPINIONS

Frankie Lemmons stepped closer. She clutched her Glock pistol tightly. Finding Jontray Scott alone and unarmed, it would be easy to get justice for Dillon now.

"Who are you?" Jontray asked in a shaky voice.

Glaring at him, Frankie hissed, "Someone who is tired of you getting away with your crimes."

"What crimes?"

"Santiago Montoya."

"I did my time for that."

Frankie took another step closer. She snapped, "What about Dillon Pickler?"

Jontray lowered his hands slightly. "I didn't kill him."

Frankie clung tighter to the gun. She shook her arm at him. "I saw you point that gun at us."

Jontray took a step forward. His hands lowered. "Are you that girl?"

"Don't come any closer," Frankie barked.

Jontray took a step backwards. "I won't. I'm sorry. I didn't kill that boy. I killed Montoya, but no one else. I wouldn't hurt kids."

Frankie snorted, "Yeah, because you're such a great guy."

"Look, lady. I killed Montoya because he and his boys beat a friend of mine to death. He got away with it so I did a little street justice."

"How ironic."

"Okay. Like you want to do to me, but I didn't kill that kid. Our gangs started shooting around. A stray bullet must have hit him. I'm sorry he died, but you can't blame me for it."

Taking a step forward, Frankie placed her finger on the trigger. She longed to pull it and end Jontray's lies. "Oh? Can't I?"

Jontray shook his head. His hands shook in the air.

Frankie said, "Okay. If you didn't kill him, then why did you threaten the cop on the case?"

"I didn't."

"He was my grandpa. I was his witness. His notes said he was dropping the case because I was in danger."

"It wasn't me."

Frankie scowled at how he had an explanation for everything. "Enough excuses. You killed Dillon and threatened my life causing my grandpa to stress out and have a heart attack. The penalty is death."

Charlotte Knight stepped into her father's cabin. She hoped he had not done anything foolish. Her father had been leaning over the railing like he wanted to jump when they had found him on the balcony in the other cabin. Would he really do something to hurt himself?

Charlotte looked around the cabin. She did not see her father on either of the beds. Could he have jumped already? "Pop!"

"Go away."

Charlotte turned toward the bathroom. She could see light streaming out of the ajar door. Peering inside, she sighed in relief.

Weldon sat on the bathroom floor beside the toilet. Clearly, he had been vomiting.

Opening the door, Charlotte said, "It's going to be okay, Pop."

Weldon snapped, "I told you to go away."

Charlotte sat on the edge of the tub. "I can't leave you like this, Pop. We're family."

Weldon grunted, "Well, Nolia ain't your family. You should be loyal to your father not your friend."

Charlotte gritted her teeth. She wanted to tell him how Mags was more like a mother than a friend. Her trust in Mags was stronger since she had never failed her. She did not have the same trust in her father yet. However, she did not want to make things worse since he was drunk. "I'm here, aren't I?"

Weldon grabbed a towel. He wiped his mouth. "Everyone would be happier if I died."

"That's not true, Pop. No one wants you dead."

Weldon struggled to his feet.

Charlotte grabbed an arm to help him. She tensed at how he jerked his arm from her.

Weldon staggered out of the bathroom. He picked up his suitcase from the floor. Dropping it on the bed, he opened it with a grunt. He rummaged through his clothes.

Charlotte watched him hoping he would pull out his pajamas and get ready for bed. What else could she say to make her father feel better? She accepted he might be more reasonable tomorrow when he was sober. Maybe she should stay with him tonight or at least until Ellison returned.

"Goodbye, Charlie."

Weldon pulled his Glock pistol out of the suitcase.

Charlotte sprung forward. Her heart raced at what he planned to do. Reaching him, she grabbed his arm.

A loud gunshot popped into the air toward the ceiling. Weldon struggled against her.

Charlotte tried to pry his fingers off the gun.

"Let me go, Charlie!"

Charlotte swept her leg under his legs to trip him.

Weldon fell to the carpet with a thud.

A second gunshot popped.

Charlotte froze. Her heart pounded at the struggle. She rushed forward and grabbed the gun. Backing up, she put it behind her back.

Weldon sat on the floor. He leaned against the wall. His gaze fell to his lap.

"Charlie!"

The door swung open. Charlotte turned her head. "It's okay, Leo. I got the gun."

Leo stomped across the room. He reached out taking the weapon from her. "I heard two shots."

Charlotte looked up at the ceiling. She winced at a bullet hole.

"Where's the other one?" Leo asked.

Charlotte took a deep breath. She mumbled, "Stay calm, Leo."

"Why?"

Charlotte peered at her left shoulder. She turned her body toward her husband. "I think it's inside my shoulder."

Magnolia Ruby leaned against the wall. Her body relaxed slightly at Charlie's voice. However, not hearing Weldon kept her tense. What had happened?

"Were those gunshots?"

Magnolia flicked her eyes to the side.

Down the hallway, Genevieve stood in the open doorway of their cabin. She tightened the belt of her bathrobe. "What in the world?"

Magnolia shrugged. She could not get her mouth to work. Her heart pounded at no news.

Loud footsteps hurried down the hallway. Magnolia watched two ship security guards arriving. Had someone called them about the gunshots? Maybe Reuben had called them while she was focused on Leo.

One guard ran into Weldon's cabin. He had a baton in his hand.

Reuben surrendered Jimmy Caplin to the other guard. He said something to him. Walking over to join her, he said, "It's not ethical for me to get involved with this one. Not since Weldon and I fought."

Magnolia moved her mouth trying to speak. No words would come.

Reuben took her free hand into his own. He squeezed it tenderly. "Just breathe, Magnolia."

Magnolia nodded. She liked how he always seemed to make her feel better. She took a deep breath to show she was listening to his advice.

The first guard raced out of the cabin. He spoke quickly into a walkie talkie.

Magnolia stood straighter. She did not catch what he said. Following him with her eyes, she froze.

Ellison walked down the hallway with Gloria and Lydia.

Magnolia examined Gloria's sorrowful face. Releasing Reuben's hand, she approached her daughter. "Gloria, what's wrong?"

Gloria wrapped her arms around her mother and buried her face into her chest. Her sobs rose muffled.

Magnolia clung to her tightly. She had not seen Gloria so heartbroken since her father Wally died.

"Lucretia told her about Jonas," Ellison said putting an arm around Lydia.

Magnolia's eyes widened. She rubbed a hand up and down Gloria's back. Why didn't Lucretia think before she ran her mouth?

Magnolia mentally kicked herself for not taking time to tell Gloria about Jonas. She would have done it in a more delicate manner. "I'm sorry, honey."

The security guard stomped past them pushing a wheelchair. He rolled it into Weldon's cabin.

Magnolia turned her body keeping her gaze on the open doorway relaxing. *Weldon is only hurt. If he was dead, they wouldn't have used a wheelchair.*

Magnolia turned away. She could not stand to look at Weldon after his irrational, drunken behavior. Her temper flared at how foolishly he had acted.

Genevieve gasped, "Dear Lord, help us. It's Charlie."

Magnolia and Gloria pulled apart. They turned toward Weldon's cabin.

Magnolia opened her mouth then closed it unable to speak again. She saw Charlie sitting in the wheelchair. Her heart ached at blood on her friend's shirt near her shoulder.

Leo pushed the wheelchair with a firm scowl on his face. He stared straight ahead as if he could not focus on anything but getting his wife to the infirmary.

As she rolled by, Charlie said, "I'm fine. It's not bad."

Magnolia followed the chair with her eyes. She did not know if she believed her. Charlie would say she was fine no matter how bad she was hurt. *Lord, please help her to be okay.*

"I didn't mean to!"

Magnolia snapped her gaze at the scream.

The security guard escorted a handcuffed Weldon down the hallway.

Weldon struggled like a madman. Clearly, he had not sobered up even after shooting his daughter. His gaze fell on her. "Nolia, please. It was an accident. You've got to believe me."

Averting her eyes from him, Magnolia shook her head. She did not care whether or not it was an accident. Charlie was hurt and Weldon had caused it.

Genevieve gestured toward her. She said, "Let's get out of the hallway...This night is intolerable. I'll order us some tea."

⚓

Frankie Lemmons pointed the gun at Jontray Scott. She took delight in the fear on his face.

Jontray knelt on the concrete. He folded his hands in front of him. His eyes closed.

Frankie thought he was going to beg for his life. "What are you doing?"

"I'm praying for you."

"Praying for me not to kill you?"

"No. I'm praying you will find peace after you kill me."

Frankie hesitated at the response. She was going to kill him, so why would he pray for her? Maybe he had changed.

Frankie ignored the possibility. It did not matter how Jontray Scott had changed. He had murdered Dillon. She put her finger on the trigger. *This is for you, Dill Pickle.*

⚓

Reuben Malone stepped into the brig cell. He examined his murder suspect.

Jimmy Caplin sat on the bed. He scowled at the detective. "I didn't do anything."

Reuben placed his hands on his hips. "Then maybe you can explain how you got a master keycard."

Lowering his head, Jimmy stared at the floor without a word.

"We have already identified the keycard as the one belonging to Jonas Archer. Raphael Capone took it when he took Jonas' place."

"So what?"

Reuben said, "So, Capone had the keycard. Now, he's dead and you have it."

Jerking up his head, Jimmy glowered at him. "I didn't kill him. He was my father."

"Your biological father who jilted your mother and stole from her. He also rejected you when you confronted him. I believe you hit him too."

Jimmy held up his hands. "Okay. I hit him, but I didn't kill him."

"Then tell me how you got the keycard."

Jimmy lowered his head again.

"I left it in his cabin."

Reuben turned around at the voice. Stepping to the side, he gestured with a nod. "Mrs. Brewster, please join us."

Doretta marched past him. She entered the brig cell.

Jimmy stood with a weak smile.

Doretta hugged him. Releasing him, she turned back to Reuben. "I had the master keycard, Detective. I left it in his cabin when I visited him this evening. Jimmy has nothing to do with this."

"And where did you get the keycard?" asked Reuben.

Doretta looked at her son. She gave him a stern look. Flicking her gaze back to Reuben, she said, "I took it when I killed Raphael Capone."

Sipping her tea, Magnolia Ruby watched the movie on the television not able to fully focus on it. Her mind reflected on the events of the last few days. Would Charlie have been shot if she hadn't broken up with Weldon? The end of their possible relationship had clearly unhinged the man enough to drink too much and shoot his daughter.

Magnolia refused to take the blame for Weldon's actions. *I have the right to date who I want to date. Weldon could have handled it like an adult.*

Her cell phone buzzed. Magnolia picked it up from the nightstand beside her bed. Seeing it was Reuben, she excused herself and stepped out onto the balcony. She closed the door then accepted the call. "Hi, Reuben."

"I have great news, Magnolia."

"I could use some. What is it?"

Reuben said, "We've arrested Capone's killer."

"Jimmy Caplin?"

"No. It was his mother. Doretta Brewster confessed."

Magnolia sat down in a chair at the table. She took a deep breath of the salty sea air. She rubbed a hand over her face. With Weldon's behavior and Charlie's injury, she had forgotten briefly about the case. She did not even care about Raphael Capone's killer.

Sighing, Magnolia said, "I'm glad, Reuben. Congratulations."

"One less thing for you to worry about, Magnolia. Get some rest."

Agreeing, Magnolia ended the call. She spotted a notification at the top of the phone screen. She clicked on it. *An email from D'Quan.*

Magnolia recalled how Gloria had asked D'Quan to email any research he found about Ralph Caplin. She snorted at how that seemed like a lifetime ago even though it had only been a few hours.

Magnolia debated with herself about what to do. Her first reaction was to close the email. After all, Reuben had found the killer. It was not needed anymore.

Magnolia peered out at the darkness. Her curiosity peaked. What if the email contained information to confirm Doretta as the killer? Maybe it would shine a light on another suspect.

Changing her mind, Magnolia set her phone on the table. *Doretta confessed. The case is over. Let it go, Magnolia.*

⚓

Leo Knight sat in the waiting area outside of the infirmary. He tapped his foot anxiously. What was taking Dr. Leonard so long? He needed an update on Charlie's condition. The waiting was beginning to weigh on him.

Movement drew his attention. Leo looked over at his father.

Ellison paced back and forth across the waiting area. He had always been a patient man. Yet, he appeared to be as anxious as his son.

"Dad, you're making me more nervous."

Ellison halted with a glimpse at his son. He walked over and sat in the blue chair next to him. "Sorry. She's going to be fine."

"She'll be in better shape than Weldon when I get done with him."

Ellison patted his shoulder. "Let the police handle it, Leo."

"I am the police."

"You know what I'm saying."

Standing, Leo began to pace. "I'd break his neck myself if I could. I'll make sure he's charged with attempted murder."

Ellison moved to stand in front of him. He placed his hands on his shoulders. "Don't be hasty, Leopha. Charlie may not want that."

"He shot her. Of course, she's going to want him thrown in prison."

Ellison replied, "I've known Charlie for a while now, son. She doesn't seem the type to want revenge."

"It's not revenge. It's justice."

Ellison pierced him with a hard look. He dropped his hands from his shoulders.

Leo looked away. Why did he always feel like a little kid when dealing with his father? He sank back into the chair.

Ellison joined him. "Do you even know what happened?"

Leo opened his mouth with a retort.

Ellison held up a hand. "Do you know what really happened? Or just what you have dreamed up while waiting here?"

Leo closed his mouth. He shook his head.

Ellison said, "Then let's pray for Charlie. We can decide other things once we know she's okay."

Surrendering, Leo leaned forward. Bowing his head, he closed his eyes. *If she's okay.*

Climbing out of London's car, D'Angelo Walker scanned the community center parking lot. He saw Lemmons' car parked at the end of the lot in a dark spot. He leaned down to look inside at Bridges. "I see her car."

Bridges said, "I'm going to patrol. Maybe I can spot her."

D'Angelo stepped back from the car. He turned around to face the community center. Lumbering forward, he headed for the front door. Maybe he would find Jontray Scott inside. Then he could get the fool away before Lemmons did something foolish.

A gunshot popped in the air. D'Angelo stopped walking. His heart pounded. He looked around. Where had the shot come from?

A dark figure emerged from the alley beside the community center. The person reached up and pulled off the ski mask.

D'Angelo sucked in a breath. His eyes widened. Rushing across the parking lot, he yelled, "Lemmons!"

Lemmons looked over at him. She holstered her weapon.

Reaching her, D'Angelo asked, "What did you do?"

"I found closure."

D'Angelo glanced toward the alley. "Please tell me you did not kill Jontray Scott."

Lemmons walked past him toward her car. She opened the door then tossed the ski mask into the passenger seat. "Dillon's killer is dead."

With wide eyes, D'Angelo grabbed her shoulders. He turned her around to face him. He panted, "Then I have to hide you."

Lemmons raised her eyebrows at him. She opened her mouth no doubt with a retort.

D'Angelo held up a hand. He stuttered, "You'll have to lose your car. It's too noticeable. We'll take mine. Maybe we can get to another state before they find his body."

"Look, Big Boy…"

D'Angelo interrupted, "No, Lemmons. I'll do anything to keep you safe. Cops don't do well in prison."

"I'm not going to prison."

"I know because I won't let you."

Lemmons said, "You're not listening to me."

"That's because you don't make sense. You have to run, or they'll catch you. Maybe we can…"

Lemmons grabbed his face with both of her hands. She stood on her tiptoes then kissed him hard on the mouth.

Frankie Lemmons kissed D'Angelo thrilled at how he was willing to abandon his family to get her out of town and safe from the police. She released him then stood a step back.

D'Angelo stared at her with wide eyes.

Frankie smirked, "Now, that I have your attention. There's no need to run because I didn't do anything."

D'Angelo opened his mouth.

Frankie placed an index finger on his lips. "I shot in the air. Jontray Scott is fine."

"But you said Dillon's killer is dead."

Frankie stepped backwards. She leaned on her car hood. Crossing her arms, she said, "And he is as far as I'm concerned. We'll never know who killed Dillon. I think I will let my friend rest in peace…I could use some peace too."

D'Angelo's frown transformed into a smile. He glanced toward the alley.

Frankie followed his gaze.

Jontray Scott walked out of the shadows. He looked their way then raised a hand to wave.

Frankie suppressed a snort at how he waved at a woman who had planned to kill him. She nodded toward him thankful he would not be pressing charges.

Jontray Scott walked back into the community center.

Frankie returned her attention to D'Angelo. "And how did you know what I was doing, Big Boy?"

"Jolie was worried. Bridges knew where to find Jontray Scott," D'Angelo shrugged.

"I figured."

"Jolie cares about you, Lemmons…We all do."

Frankie said, "If we're going to date, you should probably start calling me Frankie."

D'Angelo raised his eyebrows. "We're going to date?"

"Unless you don't want to."

Stepping closer, D'Angelo leaned forward. "I'd be a fool if I didn't want to date you."

"Good answer."

Frankie stood up. She brought her lips a few inches from D'Angelo's mouth.

"Hey, lovebirds!"

Frankie and D'Angelo pulled back from each other.

Frankie turned her head toward the loud voice.

Leaning out of her driver's side window, London added, "Are you going to stand there flirting all night? It's getting late."

Frankie said, "Yes. Don't worry about Big Boy. I'll drive him home."

London raised her hand in a thumbs-up. She drove her car out of the parking lot.

D'Angelo mumbled, "I have a car."

Frankie scanned the empty parking lot. She could only see one car which had to belong to Jontray Scott. "Where?"

"At your precinct."

Frankie gave a wave of dismissal. "That's too far away. I need to show Jolie I'm okay." *And that we're okay.*

⚓

Ophelia Hart opened her cabin door. She peered into the hallway. Her mind raced with all that had happened. She had been talking to Magnolia and Detective Malone when they heard someone shouting. Shortly after they left, she had heard two gunshots. Though she wanted to know what was going on, she did not want to be spotted out of her cabin. She refused to be put back in the brig.

Now, it was quiet. Ophelia longed to sneak out and get a drink at the bar. She looked down at her newest disguise. Her smile grew at how she looked like one of the wealthy passengers. She adjusted her green knee-length dress and flipped her white feather boa around her neck.

Wobbling slightly in her black high-heeled shoes, Ophelia stepped into the hallway. Thrilled to be alone, she strutted down the hallway toward the elevator. She pushed the button. Tapping her foot, she hummed at her cleverness.

A strong hand covered her mouth. Ophelia tried to scream but it came out muffled. She struggled against her attacker.

An arm wrapped tightly around her waist. The elevator doors opened with a ding. Her attacker forced her into the elevator. As the doors closed, Ophelia heard a male voice. "It's no use, Ms. Greene. I'm too strong for you."

CHAPTER 15

PANICKY PLEAS

Still sitting on the balcony, Magnolia Ruby listened to the quiet night. She had said good night to Genevieve and the girls before they settled down for the night. Though she was exhausted, she refused to go to bed yet. She would have vivid nightmares until she knew Charlie was okay.

Magnolia checked her phone for the hundredth time. *What is taking so long?*

Magnolia began to put her phone on the table when she had an idea. If she read D'Quan's email, it would give her something to think about while she waited for news about Charlie's condition. Clicking on the email, she read the information.

D'Quan had typed the facts into bulleted points to make it easier for her to read. She looked at the first fact. *His full name is Ralph Grant Caplin.*

Magnolia repeated his middle name. She closed her eyes trying to recall who she had talked to about a son named Grant. Her eyes snapped open. *Reuben had a son named Grant. He died in the army. Or did he?*

Magnolia shook away the idea. There were lots of men named Grant. She accepted it as a coincidence. She read the second fact. *He was born in Savannah, Georgia in 1975.*

Magnolia pursed her lips. She remembered talking about Savannah, Georgia on the cruise. Who had she been talking to? *Reuben visited his grandparents in Savannah every summer.*

Her suspicions escalated at the possibility of this being a coincidence. Could she have fallen for another deceitful liar? Maybe Reuben killed Ralph to hide they knew each other.

Standing, Magnolia tiptoed into the room. She rustled through her purse to find her notebook and pen.

"People are trying to sleep, Magnolia."

Magnolia whispered, "Sorry, Genevieve."

Taking the notebook and pen, Magnolia returned to the balcony and sat down. She opened the notebook to the page with her list of suspects. Scanning the list, she added Reuben Malone to the end of it. Next to his name, she wrote he shared a connection through Savannah, Georgia and Ralph's middle name as the same as Reuben's son.

Magnolia returned to the email. She read the next fact. *He attended school in Savannah, but graduated from Missouri State University with a bachelor of fine arts degree in acting within theater and dance.*

Magnolia knew the university was in Springfield, Missouri. It was another connection. *Reuben is a police detective in Springfield.*

Magnolia wrote the connection on her list next to Reuben's name. She did not like where the clues were beginning to point. She scrolled down to the next set of facts. *Ralph married Adeline Quincy. They were married for twelve years. Adeline died. Coroner said natural causes. Adeline's family did not accept cause of death.*

Magnolia's eyes widened at the woman's last name. *Quincy. Patton and Elise Quincy?*

Returning to her notes, Magnolia wrote how Ralph's wife could have been related to Patton Quincy. Patton would have had a motive if he recognized Raphael. Magnolia focused on the order of her investigation. *First, I need to know if Patton and Adeline were related. The last name could be another coincidence.*

Magnolia returned her attention to the email. She read the last fact. *Ralph had a painting praised by the art community. It was entitled Alice.*

Magnolia remembered the picture of the Alice painting in Ophelia's scrapbook. Could Adeline have been the original artist? Maybe Ralph had painted it himself. It could be the only one of his paintings that belonged to him.

Clicking off the email, Magnolia looked at her notebook. She could not disturb Patton and Elise at night. She would have to wait until morning.

Magnolia looked at her notes about Reuben. She doubted she would sleep with the uncertainty hanging over her. Clicking on his cell phone number, she waited for him to answer.

"Hi, Magnolia."

"Reuben, we need to talk. Can we meet somewhere?"

"Is this business or pleasure?"

Magnolia asked, "Does it matter?"

"Not really. I know better than to turn you down. I don't want you busting into my cabin for our meeting."

Determined to remain objective, Magnolia forced her smile away. She needed a busy place for them to meet in case of trouble. "Meet me at the Paradise Bar in twenty minutes."

"Your wish is my command."

As the call ended, Magnolia gathered her stuff. She reentered the cabin and grabbed her purse making sure her keycard was in it. Tiptoeing toward the door, she froze at a voice.

"Is it Charlie?"

Magnolia turned back to the bed. She squinted into the darkness seeing a shadowy figure sitting up in bed. "No word yet, Genevieve."

"Where are you going?"

"I need a drink."

Laying back down, Genevieve said, "Don't we all."

Magnolia exited the cabin closing the door softly behind her. Walking down the hallway toward the elevator, she prayed she was wrong about Reuben. She did not like the idea of losing him now that she was starting to like him. She had been wrong about Weldon. *It won't be the first time I was deceived.*

Pushing the elevator button, Magnolia noticed the buttons were not lit up. She listened for sounds of the elevator moving to her floor. However, there was no noise. Tapping her foot, she tried to be patient. *Why isn't it working?*

Giving up, Magnolia headed for the stairs. She did not want to wait any longer. She needed to get to the bar. *I need some answers.*

Inside the elevator, Ophelia Hart hoped for a chance to escape from her attacker before he harmed her. The elevator stopped, but the doors did not open. She looked at the control panel and realized the man had stopped the elevator trapping her inside. What was he going to do with her?

The man released her stepping around to stand in front of her. He held up his empty hands.

Ophelia did not recognize him though she felt like she had seen him somewhere earlier. "Who are you? What do you want?"

"My name is Jimmy Caplin. I want you to help me prove my mother's innocence."

Opening her eyes, Charlotte Knight winced at pain in her shoulder. She flashbacked to earlier when she was shot while trying to stop Weldon from harming himself. Where was her father?

Charlotte tried to sit up. She groaned in pain.

"Don't move, Charlie. You'll hurt yourself."

Charlotte rested her head back on the pillow. She turned her head to the right to find her husband.

Leo picked up her hand. He kissed it tenderly. "How do you feel?"

"Like I got shot."

"That's not funny."

"Sorry. I'm fine. My shoulder hurts a little, but not as bad as I expected."

Leo said, "Good. They can give you more pain medicine in about an hour."

Charlotte thanked the Lord for pain medicine. Sighing, she asked, "Where's Pop?"

"Where he belongs."

Charlotte tensed at his harsh tone. She reached up and touched his face. "It was an accident, Leo."

Leo adjusted her blanket to keep her warm and cozy. "We don't need to talk about it right now. You need to rest."

Charlotte opened her mouth to explain what had happened.

Standing, Leo leaned over and kissed her on the forehead. He turned to leave the room.

"Leo?"

Opening the door, Leo said, "I'll be back soon. Get some sleep."

Charlotte watched him leave. What was his problem? She understood he was angry at Weldon, but he did not know the whole story. She was sure he would change his attitude once he heard what had really happened.

Charlotte looked around the room. Her cell phone was set on the table next to her bed. Reaching out, she picked it up. Who could she call? She longed to call Mags, but her friend did not need to be disturbed any further about Weldon. Maybe she could call Ellison. Her father-in-law would be full of advice, but what could he do other than that?

Charlotte's frown transformed into a bright smile. She clicked around on her contacts until she found the one she needed. Choosing it, she waited for an answer.

"Hello?"

"Aunt Genevieve, I need your help."

Ophelia Hart entered the Paradise Bar with Jimmy Caplin. She had no idea who his mother was or what her crime could be. However, she agreed to hear the man out and refrain from reporting him to ship security if they could get a drink.

Ophelia followed him over to a table away from the lively party-goers dancing and socializing around the bar. She sat down fluffing her feather boa.

Jimmy sat down in the seat next to her.

A server walked over with a bright smile. "Hi. My name is Adam. What can I get you?"

Ophelia picked up the drink menu looking at her options.

Without looking at the menu, Jimmy said, "Whiskey sour on the rocks."

"Of course, And you, ma'am?" Adam asked.

"Paloma on the rocks."

Adam walked away to get their drinks.

Ophelia leaned back in her chair. "Now, Jimmy, who is your mother and what is she accused of?"

Jimmy looked around the bar. He leaned forward. "Doretta Brewster. She's been accused of murdering Raphael Capone."

Ophelia raised an eyebrow at the news. "Oh? Why would she kill him?"

"She had an affair with him years ago. I was the result. Detective Malone thought I killed him for rejecting me and jilting my mother. She spoke up and confessed to killing him, but there is no way she would kill him. I know it."

Ophelia remained silent as Adam returned with the drinks. Waiting until it was only the two of them, she asked, "Why would she confess?"

"To protect me. She thinks I did it, but I didn't."

Ophelia took a sip of her Paloma. Her nose wrinkled at the strong flavor of lime and grapefruit juice. She could barely taste the tequila. She stalled by looking around at the other people in the bar. She had no idea how she was supposed to prove the woman's innocence. How could she help when she did not know who really killed Raphael Capone?

Ophelia studied a table on the other side of the room. Her lips curled up into a smirk. *Perfect.*

Magnolia Ruby waited at her table as patiently as she could. She had reached the Paradise Bar before Reuben. How could she start the conversation? She wanted to know the truth. However, she was afraid what that truth would be.

"Hello, ma'am. My name is Tina. I'll be your server tonight. May I get you a drink?"

Magnolia opened her mouth to decline. She would wait until Reuben arrived. Turning her head to the entrance, she spotted the man approaching her table.

As he sat down, Reuben smiled warmly at her.

Magnolia looked at Tina. "I'll have a Virgin Pina Colada."

"Moscow Mule," Reuben said.

Tina thanked them then left to get their drinks.

Reuben said, "This was a good idea."

Magnolia returned her attention to him. She pulled her hands away as he reached for them.

Reuben said, "Uh oh. What did I do?"

"I was doing research about Ralph Caplin. There are similarities to things you told me on our date."

"Oh? Like what?"

"His middle name was Grant. Your son's name was Grant."

Reuben stared at her like she must be joking. "There are tons of men named Grant."

"He grew up in Savannah, Georgia."

Leaning back, Reuben crossed his arms. "So?"

"That's where you spent summers with your grandparents."

Reuben shook his head with another chuckle. "Magnolia, the guy was over twenty years younger than me. We didn't spend time together if that's what you're implying. Besides, there are over one hundred forty thousand people in Savannah. Do you think I know them all?"

Magnolia tried to discern if he was being honest. "He graduated college in Springfield."

Reuben rubbed a hand over his face. "Darling, I think you're stressed out about Charlie and worn out from the investigation. There are more people in Springfield than Savannah. I promise you I did not know Ralph Caplin."

Magnolia focused on Tina placing their drinks on the table. She thanked her. Picking up the glass, she took a sip of her Virgin Pina Colada. Was Reuben blowing her off to keep her from suspecting him?

Sighing, Magnolia said, "Why do you think it was Doretta Brewster?"

"She confessed. She said she followed him to his cabin. He let her inside. She stabbed him then left."

"And the murder weapon?" Magnolia asked.

"She said she threw it overboard. We'll never find it."

Magnolia hated to admit it, but it sounded like Doretta was the killer. "Okay. I just wanted to check. I'm sorry."

Reuben reached for her hand again.

Magnolia surrendered it to him.

"That's what I like about you," Reuben said.

Reuben picked up his Moscow Mule mug. "To us."

Magnolia picked up her glass. She tapped it lightly against Reuben's drink. Taking a sip, she examined him. Could he be telling the truth? It did seem unlikely Reuben would know Ralph Caplin in two huge cities. Maybe she was being paranoid because of how Weldon had acted.

Her cell phone buzzed. Magnolia picked it up from the table. She read a text from Leo. "Charlie is going to be okay. Dr. Leonard removed the bullet and patched her up. She's staying in the infirmary overnight and maybe tomorrow depending on how she is doing."

"Praise the Lord."

Magnolia raised an eyebrow.

Reuben shrugged, "What? I give God credit."

"You better."

"I know. You don't want to date a heathen."

Nodding, Magnolia sipped her drink. *Or a liar. Please, Lord, give me discernment.*

Frankie Lemmons opened the door to her apartment. She entered her living room with D'Angelo following her.

Jolie jumped up from the couch. She hugged her.

Frankie returned the embrace. "Nosy kid."

"I'm sorry. I just don't want to lose another mother," Jolie stammered.

"I get it. I'm not going anywhere. You're stuck with me."

"Good," Jolie said releasing her.

Big Mama struggled to stand from her spot on the couch. She groaned at aches in her legs. "You didn't do anything stupid, did you?"

Frankie replied, "No. It's over and I didn't cross the line."

"That's good, honey, but I was talking to D'Angelo," Big Mama said pointing at her eldest grandson.

Laughing, Frankie turned to look at the man.

D'Angelo grunted, "Always picking on me. Mean old woman."

Big Mama placed her hands on her hips.

Frankie snorted, "Yeah. Be nice to him, Big Mama. He's having a rough time."

"What do you mean?" Big Mama asked.

"He's dating me now."

Big Mama clapped her hands with a whoop of joy. She stepped forward to hug Frankie. "I knew it! I've been waiting for you both to stop being foolish."

Frankie hugged her back.

D'Angelo said, "You don't have to tell her everything, Frankie."

Big Mama released Frankie. She walked over to her grandson. Slapping him on the shoulder, she said, "It's about time you stopped being a fool."

D'Angelo opened his mouth with a retort.

Frankie interrupted, "Why don't we celebrate? Jolie made dinner. Do you all want to sample her cooking with me?"

Big Mama said, "Absolutely."

"I could eat," D'Angelo shrugged.

Frankie headed to the table. Grabbing some plates, she sat down in her usual chair. Her heart soared at her loving friends who had become more like family.

Waiting for the food to be passed around, Frankie reflected on her visit to see her mother. Dominique had been standoffish the whole time she was there. Why couldn't they have a loving relationship too? She admitted to herself it was mostly her own fault. She was the one who had stopped calling and visiting. She allowed the relationship to crumble over the years.

Frankie pictured how her mother had answered the door in the middle of the day dressed in a bathrobe. Dominique had gone to take a nap while Frankie was in the attic. She had also mentioned the shop closing.

Frankie slapped a hand onto her forehead.

"What's wrong, Frankie?" asked Big Mama.

"Nothing. For a cop, I sure miss a lot of clues."

Weldon Hitchcock groaned at his splitting headache. He opened his eyes carefully, annoyed with the lights. Sitting up, he moaned at his aching body. He was in a small room with a bed. *Where am I?*

Weldon rubbed his head. He struggled to remember what had happened. He recalled having several whiskey shots at the bar. His memory of grumping at Genevieve and attacking Reuben filled his mind.

Weldon closed his eyes. *Then what happened? I went in my cabin and Charlie…*

Weldon struggled to his feet. Hobbling over to the door, he pounded his fists on the metal. "Open up! Hey! I want to talk to someone! Now!"

Weldon stepped back at the sound of the lock unlocking. He peered at the door. As the door opened, he sat down on the bed. His head swam in dizziness.

A muscular man in a navy-blue polo shirt stood in the doorway. He towered over him. His glare pierced through him. "I'm Chief Jackson. What do you want?"

"Is my daughter okay?"

"Who's your daughter?"

"Charlie."

"You shot your own daughter? I had no idea that's who she was. That's low, man."

Weldon swallowed the bile in his throat. He could vaguely remember two gunshots. His heart wrenched at how Charlie was shot. "Is she alive?"

"Yes. Dr. Leonard called with an update. She's resting, but she should recover."

Weldon released the breath he had been holding. He lowered his head. His heart soared with thankfulness.

Chief Jackson added, "I guess it will be attempted murder instead of murder. Lucky you."

Weldon winced at the charge. He would never try to kill his daughter. He had wanted to kill himself while he was in a drunken pity party. Now, he realized he did not want to die. *I'm an idiot.*

"Anything else?" Chief Jackson asked.

"Yes. I need to speak to my aunt."

Tilting his head, Chief Jackson placed his hands on his hips. "Is she a scary-looking old lady with a sharp tongue that pierces right through you like a knife?"

Weldon narrowed his eyes at the description. He had to admit it fit Genevieve well. "Yes."

"What a coincidence. She's at the front desk berating us to let her see you…I guess she can have a few minutes with you. I doubt she'll leave if I don't let her."

Weldon nodded without a word. He knew all too well how Genevieve would not give up until she was given what she wanted.

Chief Jackson stepped out of the room. He closed the door.

Weldon closed his eyes. He tried to think through what he could say to explain himself.

The door opened. Weldon took a deep breath. He opened his eyes and raised his head.

Genevieve stood in the doorway with her hands on her hips.

"Thank you for coming," Weldon mumbled.

Genevieve hissed, "I wasn't planning on it."

"Then why did you come?"

"For two reasons. First, Charlie asked me to check on you."

Weldon cherished his daughter's concern for him. "And the other reason?"

Pointing a stern finger at him, Genevieve snapped, "I came to straighten you out, Weldon Hitchcock."

⚓

Magnolia Ruby sat at the table long after Reuben had left to check in with Chief Jackson about Doretta Brewster. Her mind flip-flopped with whether to trust Reuben. She wanted to believe everything he told her. However, there were doubts plaguing her.

"May I sit down?"

Magnolia looked up at the sweet voice.

A young woman dressed in a green dress with a white feathery boa around her shoulders smiled down at her.

Magnolia nodded. Could she know the elegant woman? Maybe they had met on the ship somewhere.

The woman sat down setting her own drink on the table.

Magnolia examined her trying to place how she knew her. Her gaze returned to the boa. There had been one in Ophelia Hart's suitcase. Her eyes widened in realization.

The woman held up a hand. "Stay calm, Magnolia. We need to talk."

"What are you doing out of your cabin, Ophelia?"

"I needed a drink."

Magnolia opened her mouth with a retort.

Ophelia added, "And I have something interesting to tell you."

Magnolia leaned back against her chair. "What?"

Ophelia took a sip of her drink. She looked over her shoulder.

Magnolia followed her gaze. She sat up straighter. "Is that Jimmy Caplin?"

"Yes. He needs your help."

Magnolia sighed, "I know I'm going to regret this. Why does Jimmy need my help?"

Leaning forward, Ophelia smirked, "Because your cop boyfriend has arrested the wrong killer."

CHAPTER 16

QUOTABLE QUIRKS

Weldon Hitchcock winced at his aunt's stern glare. He prepared himself for a scolding remembering past lectures from her.

Genevieve sneered, "Do you remember the last time you were drunk?"

Weldon bit his lip. He remembered well a time many years ago when his wife had died and he had been left behind with his infant daughter. His own recklessness had led to the car accident that took his wife so guilt consumed him. "Yes."

"When?"

"When Estelle died."

Weldon blinked tears at the reminder. He had taken her death so hard. Instead of clinging to friends and family, he had chosen to drink his sorrow away. It had led to many missed calls from his aunt. Genevieve had ended up visiting him. He had been passed out on the floor with Charlie crying in her crib, wearing a filthy diaper, and sick with hunger.

"And what did I tell you then?" asked Genevieve.

Weldon replied, "You said if I didn't straighten up, you would leave me to my fate."

Weldon's fate would have been to have Charlie taken away while he was arrested for child neglect and endangerment. His police career would have been ruined. He would have been shunned by his family and friends. His life would have been destroyed.

"I'm saying the same thing to you tonight, Weldon. If you don't straighten up immediately, I will leave you to your fate. I won't pay a cent for you to have a lawyer and I will encourage Charlie to press the greatest charges she can against you. Do you understand me?"

Weldon nodded not looking at her. He would never be able to afford a good lawyer without her help. He feared the attempted murder charge.

"You can be a good man, Weldon, but not if you let alcohol rule your life and make decisions for you."

Weldon bobbed his head again.

"I don't understand head nods, Weldon."

Weldon said, "Yes, ma'am. I understand. I'm not touching the stuff ever again. I can do that for Charlie."

"Good...Now, let's talk about Magnolia Ruby."

Weldon had allowed Reuben and Magnolia's interest in each other to cause him to become discouraged and drink until this mess happened. He did not want to talk about her now. "What about her?"

Genevieve folded her hands in front of her. Her facial expression softened. "I know you have feelings for her, but she does not reciprocate them. She has clearly moved on which she has the right to do. You have the right to be upset by her decision, but you can't continue to obsess over her or try to force her to change her mind about you."

Weldon did not want to admit defeat. He longed to renew their romance. However, his heart told him it was too late. He acknowledged they could never have the relationship they once enjoyed. Nolia did not want to be with him. How could he survive the rejection? Maybe he could focus on his relationship with Charlie instead.

"What are you going to do, Weldon?"

Taking a deep breath, Weldon released it in a loud huff. "I'm going to let Nolia go."

Leo Knight listened to Chief Jackson's information about protocol. He had learned that since the ship was registered with the U.S. and had not reached any ports yet, the FBI would control the investigation and processing of the criminal.

Leo would get the ball rolling by calling the FBI to report the crime and press charges. He wanted Weldon charged with attempted murder.

Footsteps drew his attention to the hallway leading to the brig cells. Leo looked over to see who was coming.

Genevieve walked toward him. Her face was cemented in a frown. "Hello, Leopha."

"Genevieve. Charlie is going to be okay."

"I know. She called me."

"Why?"

Glancing around, Genevieve motioned toward the door. "Let's take a walk."

Leo wanted to protest. He did not want to talk to her. There was too much to do.

Genevieve strolled past him like he had no choice.

Leo followed her out onto the deck. His uneasiness increased as they walked in silence for several minutes.

Moving to the railing, Genevieve leaned her back against it. "Charlie wanted me to check on her father."

Leo waited for her to continue to speak.

"He's sobering up. He understands what he did."

Leo took a deep breath to cool his temper. He did not care how Weldon was feeling.

Genevieve added, "He's giving up drinking and accepting the end of his relationship with Magnolia."

"That's great, but it has nothing to do with anything."

Leo moved to the railing. He stared out at the dark ocean.

"You're wrong, Leo. It has everything to do with it. Weldon would never have done any of this if he had been sober."

Shaking his head, Leo turned to leave her on the deck. "But he did do it. You better get him a good lawyer because he's going to need one."

Leo marched away from her.

"Leopha Knight!"

Leo halted at the harsh shout. He refused to turn around to face her.

Genevieve said, "Before you try to destroy Weldon, you may want to talk to your wife."

Turning around, Leo asked, "Why?"

"Because she's the only one who can press charges against him. No one was a witness to the crime."

"Charlie will press charges."

Genevieve turned toward the ocean. She placed her hands on the railing. "Like I said. You may want to talk to your wife."

Waving his hand in dismissal, Leo walked away. He was tempted to talk to Charlie tonight. However, he knew she had been through a lot and needed her rest. It could wait until morning. *I'll convince her to go to the maximum on the charges.*

⚓

Magnolia Ruby entered the main dining room for breakfast alone. She wanted to have a private conversation about Ralph Caplin. Luckily, Ellison had invited the girls to have breakfast at Rock 'Til You Drop Diner. He had also invited Genevieve, but the older woman had declined due to lack of adequate sleep last night.

Seeing her targets, Magnolia strolled toward the table. "Good morning, Elise. This must be your charming husband."

Patton stabbed a piece of pancake with his fork without speaking.

Elise wrinkled her nose at her husband. "This is Patton. You are?"

"Magnolia Ruby. We met the other day."

Elise motioned toward the chair across from them.

Sitting down, Magnolia picked up a menu at the sight of the server hurrying over to take her order.

"Good morning, ma'am. My name is Timothy. What can I get you?"

"I'll have a cup of hot tea and the parfait with vanilla yogurt, blueberries, and granola crumble."

Timothy headed off to fulfill the order.

Magnolia waited for Elise or Patton to say something to her. However, neither of them seemed to remember she was sitting there. She decided to be bold and blurt out about Adeline. "Do you know Adeline Quincy?"

Patton glowered at her.

Elise placed a hand on her husband's arm. "Now, Patton…"

Patton snarled, "Do you know her?"

Magnolia replied, "No. I never had the pleasure. I saw her name somewhere."

"I can't imagine where," Elise sneered.

"Are you related to her?"

Patton said, "She was my baby sister."

Magnolia had hoped it would be a more distant family connection. "I'm sorry for your loss."

Patton grunted, "I knew Ralph was trouble when I first met him. He was no good for her, but you could never tell Adeline anything. She always believed the best in people."

"She even liked me though I never deserved it," Elise added.

Patton put his arm around his wife.

"How did she die?" asked Magnolia.

Retrieving his arm, Patton stared at his plate.

Elise said, "Ralph murdered her. The coroner said it was natural causes, but we never believed that. Adeline had always been healthy."

"He killed my sister and got away with it," Patton added.

Timothy returned with Magnolia's tea and parfait.

Magnolia thanked him.

Elise took a sip of her orange juice then set it down. "Now, why did you want to know about Adeline?"

"Her name appeared on some facts about Raphael Capone."

Patton looked up at her. "You mean that artist chump?"

"Yes."

Elise said, "There's no way Adeline knew that creep. She was too wholesome of a girl to have anything to do with him."

Magnolia focused on both adults wanting to witness their reactions to her next statement. "Raphael Capone was Ralph Caplin."

⚓

Leo Knight walked into the infirmary pleased to see his wife sitting up in bed. Giving her a kiss, he turned his attention to Dr. Leonard. "How is she?"

Dr. Leonard replied, "She's doing very well. In fact, she can return to her suite if she doesn't overdo things."

"Deal," said Charlie.

Leo handed the bag to her. He had packed her an outfit along with her toiletries, not sure of what the doctor would say. "I'm glad we can leave. We can stop by the security area on the way to the suite."

"Great idea. I want to check on Pop," Charlie said pulling out the clothes.

"We're going there to finalize the charges against him."

Charlie focused on the contents of her bag. "I'm not pressing charges. It was an accident, Leo. Let me tell you what happened."

Leo snapped, "It doesn't matter what happened. Weldon shot you and he's going to pay."

"I'm not pressing charges."

Leo gritted his teeth. What could he say to get her to change her mind?

Charlie pointed a finger at him. "And if you won't listen to me, then you should go stay with your father in his cabin. I want to be alone in the suite."

Leo opened his mouth with a retort. He threw his hands up in exasperation. Storming out of the infirmary, he grumbled under his breath. *Why does she have to be so stubborn?*

Charlotte Knight buttoned the last button on her green blouse. She moved her stiff shoulder as she reached for her hairbrush. Her heart ached more than her shoulder. She hated having a fight with Leo. However, she would not be bullied into pressing charges against her father. *Why does he have to be so stubborn?*

Dr. Leonard walked out of her office. She handed Charlotte a bottle with pain medicine. "You'll need to change the bandage at least twice a day. You can come here, and I will do it if…if you don't have anyone to help."

Charlotte tensed at the doctor's attention on her clipboard. She assumed she had overheard their argument from her office. "I have friends on board who will help me."

Thanking the doctor, Charlotte shouldered her bag on her good shoulder then left the infirmary. She sat down in a blue chair in the hallway. Pulling out her cell phone, she clicked on her aunt's phone number.

"Hello?"

"Hi, Aunt Gen."

"Charlie, my word. I've been hoping to hear from you. How are you, dear?"

Charlotte did not want to tell her about the fight with Leo. There was no reason for her to know. "I'm fine. The doctor said I can go back to my suite. What happened with Pop?"

Silence. Charlotte closed her eyes. She prayed her father hadn't done anything else foolish. "Aunt Gen?"

"He's sober and remorseful. In fact, I haven't seen him that broken in a long time."

"I would like to visit him, but Leo wouldn't like it."

"Oh?"

Charlotte explained, "Yes. Leo wants me to press charges. I told him I wouldn't. He got angry and left. It wasn't good."

"Charlie, I was married for an extremely long time to one of the most stubborn men in the world. Now, I am going to share some advice with you that I hope you will use often. It is how I managed to survive my marriage."

Charlotte braced herself for some lovely advice to make her feel better.

Genevieve said, "Don't let fear of a fight with your husband keep you from living your life."

Surprised by the odd advice, Charlotte said, "Okay, Aunt Gen."

"You have a right to visit your father wherever he is," Genevieve added.

"Thanks, Aunt Gen. I'll talk to you later."

Ending the call, Charlotte stood. She decided she would go to the brig and talk to her father. As she walked down the hallway, she prayed God would mend her relationship with Leo.

Magnolia Ruby waited for the Quincy couple's reaction to her statement about Raphael Capone and Ralph Caplin being the same person.

Elise stared at her. Her eyes bulged as she realized who she had spent the night with. She raised her napkin to her mouth. Wiping it repeatedly on her lips, she attempted to get the memory of his kisses off her mouth.

Patton slammed a fist on the table. "That lousy son of a…"

"Patton, please. She's a lady," Elise scolded.

Patton pursed his lips together. His forehead wrinkled in fury.

Magnolia stared at the couple. Both acted like the truth about Raphael Capone was new to them. Could they be excellent actors? Maybe they truly did not know about him. At the end of D'Quan's email, Magnolia had seen a picture of Ralph around the time he was married to Adeline. He had weighed at least thirty pounds less. His hair had been brown instead of black. He had worn glasses which Raphael probably switched to contacts. Maybe they were colored contacts to change his eye color from brown to blue. Even Ralph's clothes were a different style than Raphael's. The artist she had met did not look anything like Ralph Caplin.

Magnolia pulled her cell phone out of her pocket. She texted Reuben for a time of death for Raphael Capone. She wanted to see if the couple had an alibi when he was murdered. Her mouth rose in a smile at his quick response. *Good morning, Magnolia. Dr. Leonard said he died at 7:30. Why?*

Magnolia texted back. *I like details. Talk to you later.*

Elise rubbed a hand over her face. "I feel sick."

Patton said, "You should. You slept with your brother-in-law who killed your sister-in-law."

"Just drop it, Patton. We don't need to air our dirty laundry in public," Elise snapped.

"I didn't think you cared about what you did in public."

Elise opened her mouth.

Magnolia tapped the table with her fist. "Please. Do you have an alibi for 7:30 last night?"

Elise and Patton exchanged a glance. "Why?"

"Well, I'm afraid you're suspects since you hated him for what he did to Adeline."

Patton growled.

Elise slapped a hand on his arm. "Quiet, Patton...Magnolia, we didn't know he was Ralph. If we did, we would have killed him, but I swear we didn't. We thought he was that artist. That's all."

"And your alibi?"

Elise looked at her husband. Her face blushed. "I was entertaining."

"Who were you sleeping with?" asked Patton.

"None of your business."

"I bet he wasn't as amazing as that brunette woman I slept with."

Elise's eyes bulged. She leaned back from her husband. "What?"

"I got tired of you having all the fun. I met her at the gym. She's...extremely healthy."

Elise opened and closed her mouth several times.

Magnolia blurted, "Before this gets worse, please tell me the names of your companions so I can check your alibi. Then I will leave you alone."

Elise smirked, "I was with a smoking hot Latino man I met at the nightclub. His name is Ramon Diaz. Cabin C12."

"That sexy flexible brunette was Tara Moore. I don't know her cabin number because we were in ours," boasted Patton.

Rising to her feet, Elise hissed, "You used our cabin?"

"You weren't needing it."

Magnolia picked up her teacup and parfait. She mumbled her thanks then walked away from the table. She looked for a safe place to eat.

Norman Chalker sat at a table across the room. He wrote frantically in his notebook.

Magnolia strolled over to his table. "Hello, Mr. Chalker. May I join you?"

Norman looked up at her. "Of course, Mrs. Ruby."

Magnolia set her breakfast on the table before she sat down. "May I ask you a question, Mr. Chalker?"

"Please. It's Norman. What do you want to know?"

Magnolia looked him straight in the face. "Why are you stalking me?"

Reuben Malone unlocked the door to Jonas' cabin. He needed to examine the crime scene of Raphael Capone's death more carefully. Though Doretta Brewster had confessed, he was beginning to agree with Magnolia that some things did not line up. Could someone else be the killer?

Walking around the employee cabin, Reuben looked everywhere for a clue to what had happened to the murder weapon. Though the security guards had already looked, he wanted a chance to search for it himself. *Dr. Leonard believes it was a knife of some kind.*

Reuben knelt beside the bed. He leaned down to look on the floor and the bottom of the mattress. No luck. Maybe the killer had taken the knife. It could have even been thrown overboard like Doretta said.

"Detective?"

Reuben turned his head toward the door. He nodded at Marty. Struggling to his feet, he grunted at the ache in his legs. He turned to face the security guard.

"What are you doing, Detective?"

"I'm looking one more time for the murder weapon. If I had that, then I would know who the killer was."

"Oh. Well, good luck."

As Marty left the room, Reuben tilted his head. He did not understand why the security guard had come to the cabin without a purpose. Moving to the open doorway, he said, "Marty."

Marty stopped walking. He turned around with a smile. "Yes, sir?"

"Why were you here at the cabin?"

"Oh. I knew Jonas. I saw the door was open. I didn't want anyone stealing his stuff."

Nodding, Reuben locked the door again. "Don't worry, Marty. No one is going to steal Jonas' belongings. I'll make sure of that."

Entering the security area, Charlotte Pearl sighed in relief at Leo not being present. She hated the disagreement they had experienced.

"May I help you, ma'am?"

Charlotte smiled at the security guard sitting at the reception desk. "I would like to see my father. Weldon Hitchcock."

Footsteps came from the side. Charlotte turned to see a tall muscular man.

"I'm Chief Jackson, ma'am. Are you the lady who was shot?"

"Yes. It was an accident. I want to see my father."

"I don't think that's a good idea. It might mess up your case."

Charlotte explained, "I understand, but you don't. My father did not mean to shoot me. He was drunk and distraught. I'm not pressing charges."

Chief Jackson walked over to her. "Are you sure?"

"Yes."

"Well, I still have him on drunk and disorderly behavior."

Charlotte rubbed her hand over her face. She had forgotten there could be other charges that did not involve her.

"He'll be released in a couple of hours since there are no more charges," Chief Jackson added.

Charlotte peeked at a clock on the wall. She debated with waiting somewhere nearby or returning to her suite until he was released.

Chief Jackson said, "I supposed I can let you see him, but I'm keeping a guard nearby in case he tries something."

"Thank you, Chief. I would appreciate time with him."

"Scott, take her to the cell, but stand outside with the door open in case she needs something."

Following Scott, Charlotte gritted her teeth. She hoped her visit would be welcomed by her father. How would Weldon react to her coming to see him so soon after his drunken night?

Opening the door, Scott motioned for her to enter the brig cell.

Thanking him, Charlotte walked into the cell.

Weldon stood then forced himself to sit back down. He wrung his hands on his lap. Clearing his throat, he said, "Are you okay, Charlie?"

"Yes. I've been released to rest in my suite, but I wanted to see you first."

Weldon stammered, "I'm sorry, Charlie. I didn't know what I was doing. I would never hurt you. Please believe me. And I didn't want to kill myself for real. I was drunk and having a pity party. Please forgive me."

Charlotte walked over to her father. "I do forgive you, Pop. I know you didn't try to hurt me."

Weldon raised his head. Tears shone in his eyes. Standing, he hugged her.

Charlotte returned the embrace. She ignored the slight ache in her shoulder.

Weldon muttered, "I try to be happy, but nothing works."

Closing her eyes, Charlotte hugged him tighter. She understood how it felt to look for happiness and find disappointment instead. Maybe she could share how she found happiness. "That's because you're looking for happiness in the wrong places. Can we sit down and talk?"

Weldon stepped back. He motioned to the bed. Sitting down, he returned to wringing his hands on his lap.

Charlotte sat down next to him. She took a deep breath. Hoping her father would not be offended, she said, "I have struggled a lot looking to be happy. After the Pearls were killed and I bounced from foster home to foster home, I thought I could never be loved or happy. Even after meeting Mags and Leo, my life has been one disappointment after another…I've lost friends. I was framed for murder. I've been hunted by insane people…But all that has been easier to handle since I chose Jesus."

Charlotte paused to decide whether to continue or not. She did not want to force her father to listen.

Weldon shrugged, "Aunt Genevieve forced me to go to church when I was younger. Your mother…Your mother always liked us to go together. I know about Jesus, but I can't choose Him."

"Why not?"

"Because I've done too many horrible things."

Charlotte reached for one of his hands.

Weldon took her hand eagerly.

Charlotte said, "That's what I thought too. I believed no one could ever love me. But Mags helped me to see the truth."

"She's good about making sure people know the truth," snorted Weldon.

Charlotte patted his hand. She said, "Mags told me that God loves us and wants us to know He is always with us. He loves us so much He send His only Son Jesus to die on the cross. He died for all our sins, Pop. Nothing you have done is too bad for Him to forgive."

"I've done things you couldn't imagine," Weldon said.

"Nothing is too bad for God to forgive. He loves you and wants you to be with Him forever. If you were the only person in the world, Jesus would have chosen to die for you."

Weldon nodded without a word.

Charlotte said, "Choosing Jesus and becoming a Christian doesn't mean your life will be easy, but the struggles are easier to bear when you know God is with you."

"How do I do it?"

Charlotte's smile grew. She recalled how she had become a Christian. "All you need to do is talk to God. There's no magic prayer. Just speak from the heart. You can admit to God that you are a sinner and that you need a Savior because you can't save yourself. Then you can tell Him what you believe about Him and Jesus. Finally, you tell Him you want to confess Him as your Savior and Lord letting Him be in control of your life."

Weldon closed his eyes. His lips moved yet no words came out.

Charlotte bowed her own head. Her heart soared at her father choosing to follow Jesus. She thanked God for giving her the words and courage to witness to him.

"Amen."

Charlotte leaned over to hug her father. Her smile grew at his strong embrace.

"Now, what do I do?" Weldon mumbled.

"Stick close to God and me. We'll help you figure it all out."

Magnolia Ruby looked across the table at Norman Chalker. She took a bite of her parfait savoring the fruity sweetness. Her eyes narrowed at how Norman scribbled in his notebook. "I've noticed you have been everywhere I have gone."

Norman stammered, "I haven't…I have just been enjoying the cruise…It's a coincidence I have shown up where you are."

Magnolia leaned back against her chair. "I'm not buying it, Norman."

Norman set his pen on the table. Closing his notebook, he said, "I didn't mean to stalk you. Once I realized who you were, I had to keep track of you."

"How did you know who I was?"

"I have followed some of your cases. I'm intrigued by how you defeated Winter Dupree, Peter Cavanaugh, and Rose Woods. What evil business."

Magnolia relaxed. Her name had appeared in the news a few times with the cases she had helped solve. "I see. But why have you been following me?"

"I'm a mystery writer, but I can't get any books published because the publishing companies say my detective isn't realistic enough. I thought if I could follow you, I would be able to use your methods to make my book more realistic," Norman explained.

Magnolia said, "That explains it."

Norman leaned forward. "I think I can help you with your current case too."

Magnolia could not see how he could help her.

"I have quotes from people all over the ship. Maybe I have something that will help," Norman said opening his notebook.

Magnolia shook her head. She did not think his nosy notes would help. Opening her mouth to tell him, she stopped at an idea. "Norman, can you tell me what all was said on our first night when we had dinner together?"

Norman flipped through the pages to one near the beginning of his notebook. "Anything specific?"

"Yes. Tell me everything Shirley Kimble said."

⚓

Leo Knight settled on Weldon's bed in his father's cabin. He had returned to the couple's suite after his fight with Charlie to get his belongings. After packing a suitcase with some essentials, he had gone to his father's cabin.

Leo sighed at how Ellison had decided to take the girls out for breakfast. He did not want to endure anymore lectures about marriage and compromise.

Charlie was acting irrationally. Leo hoped she would spend some time alone and miss him. Then she might change her mind.

Sitting up, Leo reached into his pocket for his cell phone. Maybe she had already contacted him. He checked his phone. No message or missed call. He tried to ignore his disappointment.

Leo gritted his teeth at his low battery. He needed to charge his phone. Grabbing his suitcase, he searched for his phone charger. Nothing.

Groaning, Leo realized he must have left it in the outlet by the bed in the suite when he went back to get his suitcase. He wanted to keep his phone charged for emergencies. Deciding he had to go back to get his charger, he climbed off the bed. Maybe he would be able to make amends with Charlie while he was there.

⚓

Reuben Malone took a bite of his waffles. He wiped the syrup off his lips with a napkin. His mind whirled with all the confusing facts of the case. He felt no closer to finding the killer of Raphael Capone.

His cell phone buzzed on the table. Picking it up, Reuben recognized the number. He had exchanged numbers with some of the security guards to make it easier to get ahold of him than using walkie talkies. "Malone."

"Detective, it's Marty. I think I found the murder weapon."

"Where?"

Marty exclaimed, "A cook at the Southern Bliss restaurant found a bloody knife behind the oven. She freaked out. Luckily, I was having breakfast there because I love their chicken and waffles breakfast platter…"

Reuben could tell the man was becoming frantic in the excitement. "Take a breath, Marty. No need to lose our heads."

Silence. Reuben cursed under his breath. He had chosen the wrong words. His mind filled with the image of Jonas Archer's headless body. "Sorry. Bad choice of words…I want you to remain calm. Where is the knife now?"

"I put it in a plastic bag."

Reuben paused, "You did use a glove to pick it up, right?"

"Uh…I picked it up without thinking. My prints are probably on it now. I'm sorry, Detective…I'm not used to murder cases."

Reuben gritted his teeth. He wanted to bark about common sense and protocol. "It's okay, Marty. We might be able to get other prints off it." *I hope. We could use a break in this case.*

Magnolia Ruby listened to Norman's recitation of everything Shirley Kimble said. There were a lot of facts about art. Why had Shirley acted like she did not know about art when she showed her the scrapbook? Clearly, Shirley was hiding something.

Magnolia said, "Thank you, Norman. I assume you wrote about the conversation I had with Shirley yesterday. I had a scrapbook with me."

"Sure. She acted like she didn't like art or know anything about it…I did overhear something before you arrived at their table."

"What?"

Norman flipped the pages of his notebook. He pointed to a page. "Here it is. Shirley arrived after Nelson. She sat down upset."

Magnolia hoped to hear something that would help her with the case.

"Shirley said, 'We have another chance, Nel. He's still alive.' Nelson asked, 'What do you mean?' Shirley said, 'I saw him dressed as a steward. We must try again.' Nelson replied, 'I'm not good at this. It doesn't sound safe.' Shirley patted his arm. She said, 'We'll go together. We can follow him to his room.' Nelson nodded, 'I will get a weapon first.' Shirley said, 'Get a weapon. I'll meet you at our room soon. Then we will end this.' Then you showed up, Magnolia."

Magnolia raised her hand to her mouth. She could not believe how much it sounded like Shirley and Nelson were going to kill Raphael Capone. How could the harmless couple do such a thing?

Her cell phone buzzed. Magnolia glanced at the screen. She answered it. "Hello, Reuben."

"Magnolia, we found the murder weapon. It's an antique knife of some kind. It was found behind an oven at the Southern Bliss restaurant."

Magnolia looked at Norman. Her mind flickered back to facts from the first night. However, she wanted to confirm what she recalled. She placed a hand over the phone. "Norman, what was Nelson's hobby?"

Norman flipped through his pages again. "He collects antique knives."

Magnolia dropped her hand from the phone. "Reuben, we need to talk to the Kimbles."

CHAPTER 17

RAMPANT REVEAL

Frankie Lemmons walked toward her mother's house. She needed to find out the truth about Dominique. Stepping up on the porch, she knocked on the door.

No answer. Frankie knocked again. She leaned closer to the door listening for sounds. Not hearing any, she looked at the flower bed overgrown with weeds. She had never seen her mother's flowers so neglected. Even in the winter, Dominique kept them cleaned out and ready for spring.

Hopping into the weeded mess, Frankie searched for a frog statue. She lifted it up and grabbed the spare key her mother kept for emergencies.

Using the key, Frankie opened the door. She stepped into the living room. "Mom!"

Silence. Frankie wrinkled her nose at a burnt smell. She hurried into the kitchen. Smoke wafted through the air. Coughing, she rushed to the stove. Turning it off, she removed a skillet of burnt bacon. "Mom!"

Frankie headed upstairs to her mother's bedroom. She opened the door. The bed had not been made. Her mother had always taught that making the bed was the most important thing to do in the morning. The lesson had always annoyed her daughter.

Frankie heard a groan. She turned toward her mother's bathroom. Seeing Dominique laying on the floor, she rushed over to kneel next to her.

"Mom!"

Frankie pulled out her cell phone. She dialed 911 eager to get an ambulance to come to the house to transport her mother to the hospital. "Hang on, Mom. I've got you."

Magnolia Ruby stepped off the elevator and walked down the hallway that was a floor below her own cabin. Waving a hand at Reuben, she hurried to join him outside of the Kimble's cabin.

Reuben held out a plastic bag.

Magnolia examined the antique knife covered in blood. She leaned closer taking in every detail she could of it. It had a black handle with an ivory square at the bottom. The blade had a straight edge with no jaggedness. She recognized the weapon. "It's a George Woodhead Bowie Knife from the early nineteenth century."

Reuben gave her a skeptical look.

Magnolia shrugged, "I do a lot of research on weapons."

"Of course," Reuben said.

Turning toward the door, Magnolia hoped they would finally get some answers about the case.

Reuben knocked on the cabin door.

The door opened. Shirley peeked out at them. Her eyes widened. She pasted on a weak smile. "Yes?"

Reuben pulled out his badge. "Detective Reuben Malone. You know Magnolia Ruby. May we come in?"

Shirley opened the door wider. She motioned for them to enter the cabin.

Following Reuben, Magnolia walked into the cabin.

Nelson paced back and forth muttering under his breath. His hands wrung together as if he was nervous.

Shirley said, "Nelson, we have company…Nelson!"

Jerking at her shout, Nelson halted. He turned to look at their guests. His nose wrinkled in disgust.

Gesturing to the couch, Shirley said, "Sit down, Nelson."

Nelson sank down on the couch. He wrung his hands on his lap. His foot tapped anxiously.

Shirley sat down next to him. She whispered in her husband's ear then patted his hands. "What can we do for you, Detective?"

Reuben held the plastic bag behind his back. "Do you know Raphael Capone?"

Shirley and Nelson looked at each other. They shook their heads almost with perfect timing.

Exchanging a glance with Magnolia, Reuben moved the bag in front of him. He held it out so the couple could see the murder weapon. "Have you ever seen this knife before?"

"Yes. It's a George Woodhead Bowie knife from 1850," Nelson said.

Shirley blurted, "He only knows because he collects antiques."

Tired of all the tiptoeing around the truth, Magnolia asked, "Is this knife part of your collection, Mr. Kimble?"

Nelson stood to his feet.

Magnolia took a step backwards in case of trouble.

Reuben touched the butt of his holstered Glock pistol.

Walking over to a dresser next to the bed, Nelson picked up a wooden case with a glass cover. He held it out to them. Eight knives of different styles set in the box. There was an empty space.

Nelson looked at the bloody knife in the bag. "When you're done with that, I would like it back. I'll get the blood off myself. It is a delicate process."

Magnolia asked, "Do you know how your knife could have ended up with blood on it?"

Nelson hugged the case against his chest. He looked over at Shirley. Pointing a finger, he said, "It's all her fault."

⚓

Leo Knight used his keycard to enter the suite. At the click, he opened the door. Hearing voices, he halted. He peeked around the door.

Charlie sat on the sofa with Weldon.

With wide eyes, Leo walked farther into view. His temper flared at the scene. He asked, "What in the world?"

Charlie and Weldon jerked their heads toward him.

Glaring at him, Charlie said, "What are you doing here?"

"I forgot my charger. What is he doing here?"

Standing, Charlie walked over to him. "He's staying here since you are staying with your father."

"So, you kicked me out so you could give refuge to your father who shot you? Real smart, Charlie."

Charlie pointed a finger at him. "Be careful what you say, Leopha Knight."

Leo winced at his full name. "I don't know why I came back here to try to make amends with you. You're the most stubborn woman in the world."

"And you're the most pigheaded man in the universe," Charlie snapped back.

Leo glowered at her. His mind raced with what else he could say to her. He wanted to win the argument this time.

"Leo. Charlie. Please."

Leo and Charlie turned their heads toward the sofa.

Rising to his feet, Weldon held his hands up. "Please don't fight. I have messed up every relationship I have ever had. I don't want to be the reason you mess up your relationship too. You two remind me of my own marriage. You're both so in love. I was madly in love with Estelle, but I never appreciated her like I should have. Then she was gone... You don't want to follow in my footsteps."

Leo lowered his head. He remembered when he thought Charlie had died. It had torn him up. His life had never been that low. He had not wanted to live without her.

Leo raised his head. He looked at his wife.

Charlie averted her gaze. She placed her hands on her hips.

Putting his arms around her waist, Leo hugged her closely to him. "I'm sorry, Charlie. I don't want to fight anymore."

Charlie hugged him back tightly. She whispered, "Me neither. This is our honeymoon after all."

Leo pulled back a few inches from her face. "Will you forgive the most pigheaded man in the universe?"

Charlie said, "Only if you'll forgive the most stubborn woman in the world."

"Deal."

Leo kissed her tenderly. His heart swelled with love for her. He had only been away from her for a few hours, but it had been too long.

Weldon cleared his throat.

Leo and Charlie pulled apart.

"I think I'll return to my own cabin. You can get your luggage later, Leo," Weldon said heading for the door.

As his father-in-law left, Leo refocused on his wife. "Now, will you tell me what happened last night? I think I'm ready to listen."

⚓

Tapping her foot nervously, Frankie Lemmons waited in the hospital waiting room. She could not believe her mother's weak state when she had found her. What could be wrong with her?

"Frankie."

Standing, Frankie walked over to D'Angelo and hugged him. She found comfort in his strong arms. Smiling at Big Mama and Jolie, she released D'Angelo.

Frankie hugged her foster daughter and the older woman at the same time. "Thanks for coming."

"Of course, honey. How's your mama?" Big Mama asked.

Releasing them, Frankie shrugged, "I don't know. The doctor hasn't come out yet."

Walking back over to the chairs, Frankie sat down.

D'Angelo sat beside her. He took her hand into his own.

Frankie patted his hand with her other. She thanked God for her family. Now, she needed Him to take care of her mother.

A doctor walked into the waiting room. "Lemmons' family?"

Standing, Frankie said, "I'm Dominique's daughter. How is she?"

"I'm Dr. Barnes. Your mother is resting peacefully now. She passed out from exhaustion caused by the chemotherapy."

Frankie asked, "Why is she taking chemo?"

"Ms. Lemmons, I'm afraid I'm not at liberty to say. I doubt your mother would want me to tell you if she hasn't explained it to you. Maybe you should talk to her."

Frankie could not believe her mother had not told her about taking chemotherapy. What else had she refrained from telling her?

"We'll wait here, honey. You visit with your mama," Big Mama said from her chair.

Frankie said, "What do I say to her? We have a worse relationship than I thought."

Big Mama reached into her little black purse. She pulled out a couple of dollar bills. Looking at her grandson, she said, "D'Angelo, take Jolie to get us some drinks and snacks."

"Yes, ma'am."

As D'Angelo and Jolie walked to the other side of the waiting room, Big Mama patted the chair next to her.

Sighing, Frankie trudged over to the chair. She sat down then crossed her arms over her stomach. She could feel a lecture coming.

"Frankie honey, I haven't seen my daughter since D'Quan was a baby. When I think about how she had three boys and abandoned each of them for me to raise, I could strangle her. Yet, if she showed up right now, I would be so happy."

Frankie sat up straighter. She had never asked about D'Angelo's mother. Her heart hurt for the family that had been rejected and abandoned.

"Your mama loves you, Frankie. It doesn't matter what you have done or what she has done. You two are family. That's all that matters…God put you together. He will help you fix your broken relationship."

Frankie turned toward her. "I don't know why your daughter left, but she's clearly a fool."

Big Mama reached out to hug her. She clung to her tightly. Whispering, she said, "And your mama is a fool if she doesn't treasure you, baby."

Thanking her, Frankie released her. Her eyes swelled with tears. Standing, she said, "Well, there's no time like now. I'll be back."

"Take your time, honey. We'll be here," Big Mama said reaching for a magazine from the table in front of her.

Frankie walked toward her mother's hospital room. She hoped she could talk to her mother without the two of them getting annoyed and angry. *It would be the first time.*

Magnolia Ruby sat in one of the chairs on the balcony of the Kimble's cabin. She had suggested they sit together and discuss what had happened.

Shirley said, "Several years ago, I had an affair with Raphael Capone. When he left me, he stole a painting I had created. I called it Alice."

Magnolia recalled the scrapbook with the stolen paintings. "It had a woman in a white raincoat with a red umbrella in the rain."

Shirley flicked her eyes to her. "How do you know?"

"I saw a picture of it in a scrapbook. It's lovely."

Shirley placed a hand on her heart. "Alice was my sister. She loved the rain. When she was in college, she was murdered. I painted my painting in her memory."

Magnolia said, "I'm sorry."

"Thank you…Raphael stole my Alice painting. It broke my heart. When I saw him on the ship, I believed I had a chance to get the painting back. I tried to talk to Raphael, but he blew me off. Then he was a headless corpse."

Nelson mumbled, "No more than he deserved."

Shirley shushed him. "Then I saw Raphael dressed as a steward. I realized he must have killed the real steward and took his place. I can't imagine why. I told Nelson we needed to confront him together about my Alice painting. Nelson took the antique knife for protection."

"A George Woodhead Bowie knife would scare off anyone. It was used by the military," Nelson said.

Shirley scowled at him. "I threatened Raphael. I told him I would tell the police he had killed the steward if he didn't give me my painting. He laughed at me. Nelson showed him the knife. Raphael took it away from him easily…Then we left."

Reuben jotted notes in his notebook. He asked, "And the knife was left in his cabin?"

Nelson answered, "Yes. I went back for it, but he was dead, and the knife was gone. Tragic really. I'm glad you found it."

Magnolia rubbed a hand over her face. She wished Nelson would stop being so concerned about the knife over human life. "Did you see anyone when you left his cabin?"

Shirley said, "Just the security guard."

Reuben jerked up his head from his notetaking. "What security guard?"

"The one we told about Raphael killing the steward."

Reuben Malone gestured for Shirley and Nelson Kimble to enter the security area. He hoped they would be able to identify the security guard they had talked to about Raphael killing Jonas. Why had the guard kept the information to himself instead of reporting it to him?

Chief Jackson motioned to a line of security guards. "These are the ones on shift right now. The others will be here in an hour. That's when their shift starts."

Shirley and Nelson stepped forward. They walked down the line and looked carefully at each security guard. At the last man, they exchanged a glance then shook their heads.

Shirley turned back to Reuben. "He's not here, Detective."

As the Kimbles turned to leave the area, Reuben cleared his throat. "Mr. and Mrs. Kimble?"

The couple turned back to him.

Reuben said, "Until I can corroborate your story, you two are staying in the brig."

Chief Jackson ordered two of his guards to escort the couple to their separate cells. "It's getting crowded around here."

"Sheriff!"

Reuben turned toward the door at the shrill voice.

A wealthy woman dressed in a red dress with a diamond necklace on her neck stormed into the security area. She barked, "My name is Lucretia Cushings. I am a friend of Doretta Brewster. I've called my lawyer, and he tells me that unless you have evidence of her crime, then you need to let her go."

221

Reuben hated when wealthy citizens interfered with his cases. However, he decided to let the chief take care of it. *It's his jurisdiction after all.*

Chief Jackson replied, "First, it's Chief. Second, she confessed to the crime."

"Her confession would not hold up in court. She's a mother trying to protect her son. You have nothing."

Reuben interrupted, "She has a point, Chief. I think we could let Mrs. Brewster return to her cabin. We're on a ship. It's not like she can escape anywhere."

Chief Jackson said, "Fine. She can go, but I'm assigning a guard to keep an eye on her. Hendricks, release Mrs. Brewster. Stay with her until your shift ends."

Lucretia snorted, "Waste of manpower."

Reuben strolled over to the main desk. Sitting in the empty chair, he reflected on the case. Could a security guard be the killer? Maybe he was incompetent and forgot to report the information.

Looking at the desk, Reuben saw pictures of family members and friends with some of the guards. He smiled at each picture. Maybe he should take time soon to visit his daughter, Savannah, and his granddaughters.

Reuben picked up a photo of two men in military uniform. "I don't believe it."

"Believe what?" Chief Jackson said walking over to join him.

Reuben tightened his fingers on the photo frame. His stomach twisted at the truth. "I know who the real killer is."

CHAPTER 18

SAVVY SOLUTIONS

Entering the Southern Bliss restaurant, Magnolia Ruby looked for a light switch. She had convinced Reuben to let her look for clues in the kitchen. Though the restaurant was closed and locked up for the investigation, Reuben had lent her a key. Flipping the lights on, she called, "Hello?"

Silence. Magnolia placed the key in her pocket. She had expected at least a security guard to be present. However, the locked door must have been enough for security.

Not seeing anyone, Magnolia entered the kitchen and walked over to the big commercial oven. She inspected the size of it then looked behind it. The space behind the oven was too small for the large Bowie knife to fit behind it. How did the cook find it there? Maybe it had been wedged in the small space, but the paint on the wall would have been scraped or stained with blood flakes.

Magnolia pulled out her cell phone. She snapped a picture of the space. *Things are not making sense.*

"Hello, Mrs. Ruby."

Magnolia spun around at the voice. She placed a hand on her heart with a sigh of relief. "Oh, Marty. Thank goodness it's you."

"What are you doing here, Mrs. Ruby?"

"Detective Malone gave me permission to see where you found the murder weapon."

"The cook found it. Do you want to see what else we found in our investigation?"

Magnolia answered, "Yes, please."

Motioning at a door at the end of the kitchen, Marty said, "There were several odd things in the pantry."

Magnolia walked toward the door. She could not wait to see what else ship security had discovered. Opening the door, she peeked into the pantry.

Marty shoved her from behind.

Magnolia stumbled but kept her balance. Turning around, she stood with her back to the pantry wall.

Marty shut the door behind him.

"Why are you doing this, Marty?"

"Come on, Mrs. Ruby. Surely, you've figured it out."

Magnolia said, "You killed Raphael Capone. What I don't know is why?"

"It's simple. He killed Jonas."

"Jonas was your friend?"

Marty shook his head. He rubbed a hand over his face. "He was more than my friend. Jonas and I were like brothers. We were in the army together. We were captured at the same time. Jonas saved my life. I wouldn't be here if it wasn't for him…I got him a job on this ship because he had a rough time looking for work. PTSD hit him hard."

Magnolia was aware of how trauma could affect soldiers. Her heart hurt for Jonas. He had survived only to be murdered. "How did you find out Jonas was dead?"

"I didn't know until that couple bumped into me. They were in the hallway of the employee cabins. They told me that Raphael Capone had killed Jonas and he was in his cabin with their knife."

Magnolia could see where the story was going. "So, you killed him?"

Marty held up his hands. "I wasn't going to. I thought they were crazy. I went to see Jonas. Then I learned the truth. I asked him why he killed my friend. He said they looked alike."

Magnolia wrinkled her nose at the explanation. "That's it?"

Lowering his hands, Marty snorted, "That was my reaction. Why would you kill someone just for being the right height, weight, and appearance?"

Magnolia nodded in agreement. It seemed like a callous reason to murder someone. Could there be more to the story?

Marty clenched his fists at his sides. "Capone boasted all about it. He said he caught some maid trying to steal his painting. When he confronted her, she knocked him in the head with a baton. His head was bleeding, but he covered it with a hat and headed to his assistant's cabin. On the way, he bumped into Jonas."

"And he saw that they looked alike," Magnolia said.

"Right. Capone said it was his chance at a fresh start. He was going to jump off at the first port. He showed Jonas his head wound and asked for help. Jonas led him into a storage closet at the end of the hallway. As Jonas got the first aid kit, Capone saw an emergency axe hanging on the wall. He hit Jonas with the axe knocking him into a laundry cart."

Magnolia closed her eyes. Killing Jonas in the laundry cart explained why there had not been blood anywhere else. Her stomach twisted at the image of Jonas' headless body. "And he had to get rid of the head so no one would figure out the body wasn't him."

Marty lowered his gaze to the floor. "He threw it with the axe into the ocean. Sick freak...Anyway, I was going to arrest him, but he threatened me with the knife. I took it away from him and used it on him instead...I pretended to find the knife behind the oven then told Malone it was the cook. I even made the excuse of touching it by accident to give a reason for my fingerprints...That's my story."

Magnolia said, "And now, you have to kill me because I know the truth."

Marty shook his head. "No, ma'am. I'm not going to kill you. You're a nice lady. I'm going to lock you in here until I can escape at our first port. With the restaurant closed, it will take some time before you are found."

As he turned to leave, Magnolia looked at the nearest shelf. Her eyes fell on a medium sized can of peaches. Picking it up, she threw the can as hard as she could at his head.

With a yell, Marty grabbed his head. He fell to the floor with a groan.

Magnolia picked up another can. She prepared to throw it at him if he started to get up.

The door opened. Reuben stood in the doorway. He pointed his Glock pistol at Marty.

Sighing, Magnolia lowered the can. She set it back on the shelf.

Two security guards grabbed Marty by the arms. Lifting him to his feet, they escorted the killer out of the pantry.

Magnolia smiled warmly at Reuben. She stepped toward him. "How did you know it was him?"

"The Kimbles couldn't identify the security guard based on the ones on duty. I saw a picture of Marty and Jonas. I got to thinking he would want to kill the man who murdered his friend. When I showed the picture to the Kimbles, they identified Marty as the guard they talked to," Reuben explained.

Magnolia said, "He told me his whole story."

"Well, you do have a trusting face."

Blushing at the sentiment, Magnolia thanked him.

Reuben chuckled, "And apparently a killer throw."

Taking a deep breath, Frankie Lemmons opened the door to her mother's hospital room. Entering the room, she walked closer to the bed. Her mother looked weak and ashen.

Frankie stopped at her bedside. "Hi, Mom."

Dominique looked at her. She turned her head away. "Why are you here, Francesca?"

"I came to see how you're doing."

"I'm fine. You can go back to your life," her mother said.

"You're part of my life."

"Since when?"

Begging her temper to remain cool, Frankie pulled a chair closer to the bed. She sat down.

Dominique glanced at her then turned her head away again.

Letting her breath out in a huff, Frankie said, "I know I'm a failure, Mom. I'm never good enough for you."

Dominique jerked her head toward her. "Why would you say that, Francesca?"

"Because it's true. I'm not ladylike like you. I don't say the things you want me to say. I don't do what you want me to do."

Dominique opened her mouth no doubt with a protest.

Frankie held up a hand. "But I love you, Mom. If you want me to leave, then you'll have to have security remove me. Of course, they'll have their hands full with me."

Dominique said, "I love you too."

"Then tell me why you're taking chemo."

Dominique averted her gaze.

Frankie took her hand. She squeezed it gently. "Please tell me, Mom."

Sighing, her mother said, "I have Stage IV breast cancer. It's spread all over."

Frankie swallowed the bile in her throat. She hated to imagine cancer cells running rampant destroying her mother's body. "That sounds bad."

"It's not good."

"What's your prognosis?"

Dominique sneered, "I don't listen to such things. It's up to God how long I live."

"Mom…"

"Francesca, I refuse to die until I see you settled down with a husband and a child."

Frankie leaned back against her chair. "Well, I have the child part covered."

"You're pregnant?"

"No. I'm fostering a teenager…I do have a new boyfriend. Do you want to meet them?"

Smiling warmly, Dominique whispered, "Maybe later. I need to rest."

Frankie nodded.

Her mother closed her eyes.

Standing, Frankie said, "Okay. But before you take a nap, I want you to know something."

"What?"

Frankie leaned over. She kissed her mother on the forehead. "You're moving in with me."

Silence. Frankie stood straighter. She assumed her mother was asleep.

"We'll kill each other," mumbled Dominique.

Frankie smirked, "Probably, but I'm up for the challenge."

"Me too."

Leo Knight danced along to the bouncy music. He smiled warmly at Charlie. His heart soared at how they had made amends. As they danced, he said, "We need to have the talk."

Shaking her head, Charlie said, "We haven't even been married a month, Leo. I don't think we're ready to have children."

"Not that talk," Leo laughed.

"Then what?"

Leo spun her then pulled her close again. "Where are we going to live?"

"I guess we never did decide on that. So, your apartment or mine?"

Leo leaned closer to her. He said, "There is a third option. We could get a house."

Charlie pulled back. "Are you serious?"

"Yes. What do you think?"

Charlie glanced around at the busyness on the dance floor. She motioned toward their table. "We need to talk about it. I need to visit the restroom first."

Leo said, "Then I will order us some drinks."

As Charlie headed toward the ladies' bathroom, Leo trudged toward the table. He did not like how his wife did not seem thrilled with the idea of buying a house. He had assumed she would want to get a house in a nice neighborhood. Had he misjudged what she wanted? Maybe Charlie was happy in her apartment.

Leo motioned to a server. He glanced toward the ladies' bathroom. *Lord, don't let me mess this up.*

Charlotte Knight looked into the mirror in the bathroom. She washed her hands. Did she want to live in a house? She had lived in apartments all her adult life. It would be nice to have a house she could make her own. There was plenty of money left in their account from their fathers and Aunt Genevieve.

Closing her eyes, Charlotte pictured her dream house. She wanted one with three bedrooms, two bathrooms, and a fenced-in backyard. An image filled her mind. Her eyes snapped open. *I can't believe it.*

Drying her hands, Charlotte nodded with a bright smile. She knew exactly what she wanted. Her heart soared at a desire to get it. Returning to the table, she sat down.

Leo asked, "What are you so happy about?"

"I know where we're going to live."

"Where?"

Charlotte pulled her phone out of her purse. She clicked around on the Internet until she found the house. Her smile grew at how it was available. She turned her phone to show him.

Leo raised his eyebrows. "But that's…"

Charlotte nodded hoping Leo would agree.

Leaning closer to her, Leo said, "You want to live in your childhood home? It's where your family was…"

As Leo grew silent, Charlotte reflected on how to explain her feelings to him. She agreed it was a horrible time in her life. In years past, she would never have considered returning to that house. However, her memories before the murders had always been pleasant.

Charlotte said, "We're getting a fresh start, so I want the house to get one too."

Leo picked up his glass. "To fresh starts."

Charlotte lifted her own glass. She tapped it lightly against his glass. "To our happily ever after."

Ophelia Hart sat on the bed in her cabin. As the cruise ended, she pouted about having to miss the port visit to Nassau Bahamas. She had been confined in her cabin with a guard outside her door. Wishing she could have been allowed some fun and shopping before her life changed, she worried about her future. Her stomach twisted at how she would be going to prison for seven cases of art theft.

A knock tapped on her door. Ophelia stood from her bed. She wiped her sweaty hands on her pants. She took a deep breath.

Opening the door, Ophelia prepared to be escorted to the brig or off the ship in handcuffs. "Magnolia? What are you doing here?"

"I want to talk about your future."

Magnolia Ruby sat down in the wooden chair in Ophelia's closet of a cabin. She folded her hands on her lap. Waiting until Ophelia sat on the bed, she reflected on the significant risk she was taking. If things did not go her way, she would be responsible.

Magnolia said, "I have talked to a judge friend of my husband. Judge Patricks is willing to pull some strings and put you on probation with a few conditions."

"What conditions?"

"First, you will surrender all the stolen paintings. They will be returned to their original owners.

Ophelia shrugged, "I can return them, but finding their original owners won't be easy."

Magnolia nodded in agreement. "I know. That's the second condition. You will help me figure out who they are and locate them."

"Okay. What else?"

Magnolia reflected on her conversation with Judge Patricks. She had explained the situation and how she believed Ophelia needed a chance to change. The judge had been adamant about her being given some kind of punishment for her crimes. "You will have to do one hundred hours of community service per painting."

"Seven hundred hours? That sounds impossible," mumbled Ophelia.

"You'll be busy for awhile that's for sure, but it's better than prison."

Ophelia agreed. "Anything else?"

Magnolia wrung her hands at the last condition. She had tossed and turned all night thinking about it. When she had suggested it to the judge, she could tell what God wanted her to do. *This will be the hardest.*

"You will be required to stay under strict supervision until your probation period of one year is finished."

Ophelia covered her face with her hands. She took a deep breath then dropped them again. "Great. What Nazi will be my supervisor?"

"Me."

"You?"

Magnolia gave her a stern frown. She pointed a finger at her. "You will live in my house and follow my rules. You will not participate in any criminal activity...If you disagree with any of these conditions or break any of the rules, then you will be taken to prison for seven years per painting."

Ophelia lay back on the bed. She stared up at the ceiling. "So, it's forty-nine years of prison or a year under the supervision of Magnolia Ruby. How long do I have to decide?"

Magnolia gaped at her. She couldn't believe what she was hearing. How could she consider turning down the opportunity? It was a once in a lifetime second chance.

Ophelia shrugged, "I'm kidding. I accept the conditions."

Relaxing, Magnolia clapped her hands together. "Good. Then we'll get you settled at my house before we find the owners of the five paintings."

Ophelia sat up with a frown. "Five?"

"Well, one of them belonged to your mother. Peace in the Storm, I believe?"

"Yes."

"So, that one is rightfully yours...The one called Alice belongs to Shirley Kimble. She painted it in memory of her sister. That leaves five paintings." *Though I doubt it will be easy to find their owners.*

Rising to her feet, Magnolia headed for the door. She assumed there was nothing else to say.

"Magnolia?"

Magnolia turned back to her. She expected a snide remark or silly retort.

"Why are you doing this, Magnolia? You didn't have to help me like this."

Magnolia struggled with how to explain her charity. "God led me to do it...Sometimes, we have the privilege of second chances."

Ophelia nodded.

Magnolia placed her hands on her hips. "Just don't mess it up. I doubt there will be a third."

Weldon Hitchcock knocked on Nolia's cabin door. He wiped his sweaty hands on his pants. He had not talked to Nolia since before the shooting. He hoped she would let him say what he needed to say.

Lydia opened the door. "What do you want?"

"I would like to talk to Magnolia."

Tilting her head at him, Lydia asked, "Why?"

Weldon paused. He tried to figure out how to explain his visit.

Gloria peered around the door. She glanced at Lydia. "It's your turn on the computer game."

Lydia bounced out of sight.

Opening the door wider, Gloria said, "She's on the balcony."

Thanking her, Weldon entered the cabin. He headed for the balcony door.

Genevieve scowled at him. "Not here to cause trouble, are you, Weldon?"

"No, ma'am."

Stepping out onto the balcony, Weldon forced a smile on his face.

Nolia sat at the table with a book in her hands. She looked up with a smile that faded as she recognized him. "What are you doing here?"

Weldon tensed at her harsh voice. "I wanted to talk to you."

Nolia set the book down. "I have nothing to say to you."

"I know. I wanted to tell you three things. It will only take a moment."

Nolia crossed her arms. "Fine. Three things then you leave."

Weldon wrung his hands in front of him. He said, "First, Charlie helped me to see why my life is so messed up. I've asked Jesus to be my Savior and Lord. Charlie's helping me figure it all out."

Nolia's face softened. Her arms dropped from their aggressive position. "I'm happy for you."

Encouraged, Weldon said, "Second, I'm accepting that our relationship is over. I want you to know I won't pursue you anymore. I hope someday we can be friends, but I know that will take a while...I wish you nothing but the best."

"Thank you. I appreciate that. I wish you the best too."

Weldon said, "Thanks. Last, I want you to know I think Reuben is a nice guy. You should try to get to know him better."

"Do you think you're a good judge of character?"

Smiling at her sassiness, Weldon shrugged, "Not really, but you shouldn't give up a good thing when you've found it. I know what it's like to lose love."

Lowering her head, Nolia mumbled, "Me too."

Weldon reflected on her words. He assumed she was thinking about her deceased husband Edward. His heart swooned at how she might also be thinking a little bit about him.

Weldon said, "Well, that's all I wanted to say...I'm sorry, Nolia...Thanks for listening."

Weldon turned to leave the balcony.

"Weldon?"

Turning his head, Weldon glanced at Nolia. He smiled weakly at the pleasant look on her face. Maybe she had changed her mind about him.

"I accept your apology," Nolia said picking up her book.

Thanking her, Weldon left her on the balcony. He longed to get back to his cabin. How could he move on from her now? Maybe he could focus on his relationship with Charlie. *At least, she still wants to be around me. Thank You, Lord, for that.*

Magnolia Ruby stepped off the ramp of the ship. Reaching the deck of the harbor, she turned back to look at the beautiful cruise ship. The Wanderer of the Seas had been quite an experience. Though it was full of murder and turmoil, she reflected on the last few days of peace and fun.

Her group had enjoyed exploring Nassau Bahamas for two days. They had shopped in the Nassau Straw Market, visited the Bahamas National Art Gallery, and enjoyed a variety of activities at the Aquaventure Waterpark on Paradise Island.

Back on the cruise ship, the group had relaxed and tried many more of the ship's activities. Now, it was time to head home.

"You're not going to get a job on a cruise ship, are you?"

Magnolia turned at the voice. She smiled at Reuben. "And why shouldn't I?"

"Well, they do have an opening in ship's security. I guess I could keep an eye on you if we both worked here."

"I don't need anyone to keep an eye on me."

"Of course not. It's not like you put yourself in danger to solve a case."

"Only when the police need help," Magnolia retorted.

Reuben chuckled, "That's why I'm transferring to be closer to you. I will have good help nearby."

Magnolia tilted her head at the news. She could not imagine Reuben leaving Springfield. She had thought he loved his job there. "You're moving?"

Stepping closer, Reuben said, "Leo's precinct has need of more police detectives."

"I don't believe it. Why would you transfer from Springfield to St. Louis?"

Reuben moved even closer. He looked her straight in the eyes. "You don't know?"

Magnolia blushed. She averted her gaze. "Of course. Your daughter and her girls live there."

"How in the blazes do you know that?"

"The background of that picture you showed me had the St. Louis Arch."

"They could have been on a trip," Reuben muttered.

Magnolia agreed it made sense. "Maybe, but they weren't, were they?"

Reuben shook his head. He chuckled, "So, will I be seeing all my girls there?"

"Sure. I can help you with the cases you get stuck on."

Reuben took her hand into his own. He led her towards the row of taxicabs waiting to take the guests to the airport. "I wouldn't have it any other way."

"Hey!"

Magnolia and Reuben spun around at the shout.

Ophelia lugged her suitcases toward them. "Why don't you make yourself useful, Malone? These bags are heavy."

Rolling his eyes, Reuben looked at Magnolia. He lowered his voice. "Are you sure about babysitting her?"

Magnolia shrugged, "What's the worst that could happen?"

EPILOGUE

TACTFUL TOURIST

Norman Chalker stepped off the ramp of the cruise ship. He took in a deep breath of salty fresh air. He reflected on all he had seen and experienced on the Wanderer of the Seas. It had been nine days of research and work. He had to admit the trip had been worth his time.

Walking over to the carts, Norman nodded at a porter then handed him his cabin number.

The porter guided him to the correct cart.

Making sure it was the right one, Norman pulled his wallet out of his back pocket. Giving the porter a tip, he reached for his suitcases.

Turning to the street, Norman looked around for a free taxicab. His gaze fell on Magnolia Ruby. He stared at her taking in as many details as he could about her. His research on her had been eventful. He had witnessed her with her family as well as amid a murder.

Pulling out his cell phone, Norman clicked on a well-used number. He waited for an answer.

"Well?"

Norman glanced down at his notebook. He clutched it tighter. It was full of notes he had taken on the cruise. "I've learned a lot."

"Enough?"

Norman shook his head. He doubted he would ever have enough for his purposes. He flicked his gaze back to Magnolia Ruby watching her climb into a taxicab. "No, but I know how to get more."

"How?"

"I'm moving to Missouri."

ABOUT THE AUTHOR

Carrie Rachelle Johnson has always enjoyed reading a variety of fictional genres. She loves to curl up in her recliner with an enjoyable book. It is no surprise that Carrie decided to try her hand at storytelling in multiple genres as well.

Carrie spends much of her time worshiping and serving the Lord at her home church. She is incredibly involved in several children's ministries. Carrie also enjoys teaching at an elementary school in Missouri. She spends her free time with family, friends, and creating new stories for her fans.

Carrie is the author of many other books (see the next page). She has published her novels on Amazon in paperback and Kindle format. You will find her books by searching Carrie Rachelle Johnson books on Amazon.

Carrie would love to hear from her readers. Be sure to check out Carrie Rachelle Johnson on Facebook, email her at carrierachellejohnson@outlook.com, or check out her website www.carrierachellejohnson.wordpress.com!

OTHER BOOKS BY CARRIE RACHELLE JOHNSON

The Glory Chronicles
Journey to Glory
Return to Glory
Escape to Glory
Search for Glory
Lost from Glory
Reach for Glory
Misery or Glory
The Glory Chronicles Book Study

Magnolia Ruby Mysteries
Scorching Secrets
Cryptic Cuisine
Framed Fugitive
Wintry Wake
Locked Loss
Muddled Minds
Rampant Retirement
Jumbled Jury
Garbled Game
Shady Showdown
Violent Vacation
Hidden Horrors
Painted Puzzles
Woeful Wedding

Wild Eternity Series
Survival
Crossroads
Shattered
Forsaken
Recovered

Christian Romances
Lyric's List
Stranded Treasure
Bittersweet Souls

Nonfiction
Elementary, My Dear Teachers

Christmas Short Stories
Comforts of Christmas
Blessings of Christmas

SNEAK PREVIEW OF

MAGNOLIA RUBY MYSTERY #16

Sniffing, Charlotte Pearl wiped the tears off her face. She crawled out from under her bed. Her eyes darted around for any sign of the killer. Though he had left her bedroom, the six-year-old girl feared he could still be around. Averting her gaze from her father's dead body, she rose to her feet. She listened for any sounds of the killer or the rest of her family. Nothing.

Charlotte turned to her bed. She grabbed her stuffed penguin hugging him to her chest. Whispering, she said, "You'll protect me, Waddles."

Charlotte headed for the open doorway. Peeking out into the hallway, she looked for the killer. Nothing.

Charlotte stepped softly down the hallway to the stairs. Glancing down over the railing, she held back a scream. Her mother and her brother lay on the floor with blood everywhere. Looking away, she squeezed Waddles closer. She walked down the stairs keeping her eyes on the front door. Would she be able to make it out of the house and get help?

Reaching the door, Charlotte looked around for the killer. Not seeing anyone, she opened the front door swinging it open. Her eyes widened at the darkness of the night. She hated to be outside when it was dark. What if the monsters got her?

Realizing the real monster might be in the house, Charlotte forced herself to leave. She stepped down the porch steps. Looking around, she saw a light in a window next door. She ran across the yard toward the eerie gray house. Pounding her fists on the door, she sobbed. She stepped back as the door opened.

A plump woman smiled down at her.

"Who is it, Blair?" a harsh voice snapped from behind her.

"It's the Pearl girl."

"We should call the police on her parents. It's child neglect to let a child out this late at night."

"Yes. Call the police, Corinne. Something is terribly wrong."

Made in United States
Orlando, FL
19 May 2024